The Conquest of Don Pedro

The Conquest of Don Pedro

Harvey Fergusson

Introduction by John R. Milton

A Zia Book

UNIVERSITY OF NEW MEXICO PRESS

Albuquerque

Introduction

It seems fitting that this new edition of *The Conquest of Don Pedro* should be published in the twentieth anniversary year of the original publication. This novel was Harvey Fergusson's last, although he lived for another seventeen years. It was also, I think, his favorite among his own books. He once said that an earlier novel, *Wolf Song*, had more poetry in it, and he always felt good when he found the poetry in his novels; yet, *Don Pedro* had, he admitted, more craft, more of his own philosophy, more of the Gringo-Spanish relations that were so important in his home state of New Mexico, and a chief character who became very dear to him.

Because Fergusson's first novel of the Southwest was published in the early part of the century (*The Blood of the Conquerors*, 1921), and the next two, forming a kind of trilogy with the first one, followed not long after (*Wolf Song*, 1927 and *In Those Days*, 1929), it has been customary to think of Fergusson as an early writer of the West, not a contemporary with those of us who will now be reading and using in classes the new edition of *Don Pedro*. It is important to say that Fergusson's novels are not quaint; they have stood the test of time. But they have been out of print except for a short period when it was possible to get them in a single volume (*Followers of the Sun*, 1936) as a trilogy. Many libraries purchased this one-volume edition.

The fact remains that most contemporary readers are more familiar with Fergusson's last two novels (*Grant of Kingdom*, 1950 and *The Conquest of Don Pedro*, 1954). The first of these was available in a paperback edition for many years. The second could be found in most used book stores, in its cloth binding. Suddenly, neither book was easy to locate, and Fergusson could be read only in libraries. Now *Don Pedro* is back in print. What does this mean?

It means first that there is new and significant interest in the literature of the American West. When *Don Pedro* was first published, many academic people were just beginning to admit that American literature deserved a place almost equal to that of British literature. Twenty years later, the serious fiction of the West has at last taken its rightful place in the academic world. As for the general reading public, it was ready long ago for something better than the cowboy and Indian formula, but the good books were not given the proper attention by critics, reviewers, and booksellers and were therefore unavailable soon after publication. Fergusson's first eight novels, some of them set in the East, were published by Alfred A. Knopf in New York; his last two were published by William Morrow and Company, also in New York. Although Fergusson lived in the East for approximately twenty years, it is notable that his best novels are those of the land of his birth, New Mexico; it is these novels which are now attracting new interest, and deservedly so.

Perhaps Americans have been moved by the increasing emphasis on ecology to examine that literature which deals with the land, with wilderness areas, with philosophies grounded firmly in the soil, with nature-oriented themes, and with a spiritual quality (part of what Professor Max West-brook calls "sacrality") which can be found most readily outdoors, in contact with nature.

Or perhaps we are seeing the old and familiar pattern in literature of the revival of slumbering classics. And at this point we may wonder whether the reasons really matter. The important thing is that such writers as Harvey Fergusson,

Mary Austin, Paul Horgan, Walter Van Tilburg Clark, Vardis Fisher, and Frank Waters—to name but a few—are being recognized for their special contributions to American literature, even while many of their books are out of print.

Readers have their favorite authors and will argue the merits and relative importance of the major western novelists. However, all will agree that Harvey Fergusson stands very high in the ranks. Many will agree that his last two novels are superior to the preceding work, as Professor James K. Folsom suggested in the Steck-Vaughn Southwest Writers Series No. 20, a pamphlet on Fergusson. And some, at least, will maintain that *The Conquest of Don Pedro* is clearly the best piece of fiction written by Fergusson. Saul Cohen, a leading collector of Fergusson's works, has included *Don Pedro* in his list of the ten best novels of New Mexico and has further offered the opinion that it is the best of Fergusson's novels. Professor William T. Pilkington has called the book "the final, perfect fruition of Fergusson's genius."

The question then is whether Fergusson's genius holds up to that of other western writers of the twentieth century. I am convinced that it does. He was, however, different from some of them in that he refused to look at the past through rose-colored glasses. He believed that the West had changed and that trying to bring back what no longer existed was mere nostalgia and escapism. He admitted that the Old West (the nineteenth-century West) was good, somewhat innocent, fresh, and free. But it was not all that way. There was also violence and famine and prejudice, and the land itself was not always kind to the people who attempted to settle on it. Fergusson insisted that the simplicity of the past was an illusion created by men in the present who used the past as an escape from the complexities of modern life.

And so it seems that Fergusson was a critic of the American West. But, his point of view was that of the realist who could say that pioneering was good, and important, and yet it was not a way of life that could endure forever—not a way of life that he or anyone else could return to. It was, rather, a way of thinking. The people of the Old West had to push on, to discover, to find new places and new ideas. Or, if they managed to stay put, they were often forced to rebuild and to reconsider. This, Fergusson insisted, was what modern man should be doing—pushing on, pioneering in a different way, and not retreating in literature to a notion of the comfortable life or the romantic life or the illusory life of the past.

It is true that Fergusson wrote of the past, but he asked that his novels be considered historical only to the extent that they came from experience, from personal knowledge of the land, and not from research. A native New Mexican, he traveled widely, going to school in Virginia and in Washington, D.C. as well as in New Mexico, working as a newspaper reporter in Washington and New York and for a Chicago paper and then as a free-lance writer in New York, at one time covering stories in all of the Caribbean countries, but always he returned to New Mexico. He loved the wilderness and was at home in it. After 1932 he lived in California, first in Hollywood (where he wrote movie scripts, for money) and then in Berkeley. Each time he finished a book, he said, he felt very foul and needed to go hunting, to take a trip into the mountains, to get outdoors. Unlike many of his contemporaries, he had no desire to go to Paris, to Europe; he knew that he could not write there.

The Fergusson name is associated with Albuquerque—with New Mexico. Yet, like Leo Mendes, the peddler and storekeeper of *The Conquest of Don Pedro*, Harvey's people came from elsewhere. His father was born on a southern plantation. His maternal grandfather—whom he resembled in many ways—was a German Lutheran who renounced Christianity, arrived in Albuquerque by way of the Santa Fe trail in

1850, and became a successful merchant. Harvey's two sisters—Erna and Lina—engaged in writing and editing western books, but his brother Francis took up residence in the East and became a distinguished literary critic and professor. The Fergusson name is well known.

Although Harvey did not spend his entire life in New Mexico, his heart was always there. It was his native country in spite of the complexities of his ancestry and the many years he spent in the East and in California. He easily denounced writers who wrote books about the West without having the necessary experience to know the land well. He inherited from his grandfather, Franz Huning, a distrust of the supernatural, and, like Leo Mendes, he found a natural religion, a direct relationship between man and the earth under his feet and the sky and stars overhead. It is likely that he had more sympathy for Mendes than for any other major character in his novels. It is likely also that in *The Conquest of Don Pedro* he fulfilled a desire to put most of what he knew and believed into one big book—not big in the physical sense but in a wealth of information, attitudes, images, and conflicts of the Spanish-American West of the 1870s. It is a factual book but also a dramatic story. There are passages of exposition, or summary narrative, dealing with trading, with the Catholic Church, the Spanish *ricos*, the peasantry, horsebreaking, the military, Gringo-Mexican relationships, the special Texan-Mexican antagonism, class structures, guns, Spanish marriage customs and family relationships, and, of course, the land that supported it all. The area is that between Santa Fe and El Paso. The town of Don Pedro is Doña Ana, between Las Cruces and the Mexican border.

As rich as the novel is in facts, in truths of the time and place, the genius of the narrative lies in its rhythm, in the going back and forth between the facts of New Mexican culture and Leo Mendes's dramatic place in them, an alternation of exposition and action. This is, generally, the pattern of Fergusson's fiction: the establishment of images which are made up of dramatic acts set against an authentic background of desert, mountains, villages, and a bilingual culture. The Indians are there too, and the raw landscape, but these have been there for a long time and do not need the same attention. Fergusson is not a landscape writer, and yet every reader knows precisely where the action is taking place and, more importantly, he knows the spiritual as well as the physical values and qualities of the land. What is needed is always there, in the right place, however unobtrusive.

For Harvey Fergusson, the image was the primary building block of both prose and poetry—a moving image, always moving to a tune. In the procession of images some are crucial, such as the scene in Leo's store as Don Augustín flourishes the cane sword in Leo's face and the two men discover that they like each other after all, a liking acquired through respect. Through such images all the characters are linked; they form, in Fergusson's words, a "constellation in which the minor characters are some kind of variation on the major theme struck by the central character." Leo Mendes moves in the center of such a constellation, and the dramatic incidents between him and the minor characters are written so that they could well be put on a stage—a possibility which Fergusson contemplated over the years.

The succession of images in *The Conquest of Don Pedro* is rapid and never suffers interference from the wealth of factual information connecting the images. It is easy to see that Fergusson identified closely with Leo Mendes, and that the emphasis is not on Leo's rise to power and satisfaction with his new status but rather on his psychological and philosophical willingness to change, to move forward, to put the past into the past and walk bravely into the future. He deals wisely with both fortune and misfortune, blending into existing customs when it is necessary, challenging them when it is necessary, and always retaining a respect for the land.

The Padre is not entirely critical of Leo when he tells him, "I think you have no faith in anything but life itself." Leo, in turn, thinks that perhaps for himself God is "the God he had known when he lay naked beside the river and felt himself a part of the earth, when he danced and felt that music and rhythm made him part of the dancing whole." It is this land-based attitude that allows a man to move with change, because his spiritual rooting is deep and as eternal as the earth itself.

When Harvey Fergusson died in Berkeley in 1971, he was writing about his youthful years in New Mexico when his own attitudes toward life were being shaped. They differed little from those of Leo Mendes, the remarkable peddler.

John R. Milton
University of South Dakota
Vermillion

⚬. The town of Don Pedro stood on the eastern edge of the lower Rio Grande Valley, where it spreads out more than a mile wide and the silver river loops and wanders through the lush green of growing crops and the bosques of cottonwood, willow and overgrown mesquite. Although its history was more a matter of legend than of record, Don Pedro was known to be a very old town. When Leo Mendes came there shortly after the Civil War it must have been at least two hundred years old. It was nearly as old as El Paso, less than a day's ride to the south, and older than Mesilla and Las Cruces, the only other towns in the region important enough to have churches. Although it now belonged to the territory of New Mexico, Don Pedro was close to both Texas and Old Mexico, as the boundaries ran then. Its proximity to the Mexican border was one thing that made it interesting to Leo Mendes.

1

Don Pedro had nearby neighbors there in the lower valley, but it was separated by a long and sometimes dangerous journey from the capital at Santa Fe and from the principal New Mexico settlements in the valley just south of Santa Fe. Anyone coming from the north, as Leo Mendes did, had to leave the valley at the Hot Springs of Las Palomas, where the river enters a narrow and difficult canyon, and travel for about sixty-five miles over an arid upland known as the Jornada del Muerto. It was called the dead man's journey because a good many men had lost their lives there—some for lack of water and some by reason of Apache raids. It was not at all necessary to encounter such disasters, as Leo Mendes had demonstrated. A stage line now made a trip about once a month from Santa Fe to El Paso, carrying the United States mail, but Leo Mendes had driven his own burro the whole way, choosing a time when heavy rain had filled the water holes. He was not afraid of the Apaches because he had been doing business with them for several years.

New Mexico then had been a territory of the United States ever since General Kearney had run up the flag in Santa Fe after the Mexican War. There was now a Governor in Santa Fe, appointed by the President, and a duly elected legislature which deliberated in two languages, but otherwise little had changed anywhere in the territory. Most of the country was either desert or mountain or high arid plateau, so that it did not invite the plow like the fertile prairies farther east. Most of the good arable land was in the Rio Grande Valley and all of it had been privately owned and carefully cultivated for over two hundred years. For this strange country had the peculiar character of an arid wilderness with a fragment of an old civilization planted here in the heart of it, long isolated from the rest of Mexico, deriving most of its culture from the medieval Spain which had conquered it with men in armor. Here in the green valley were houses where seven generations had lived and died, and fields fertilized by the flooding river where grain had been harvested even longer. It was a place of old walls, old trees, old songs and stories, old feuds and hatreds, a place where human relations were ruled by old forms and customs too rigid for men to break.

The wilderness of mountain and desert was a hard one for pioneers to take and use, but this old and ingrown civilization was even more resistant to change and penetration. So the development and settlement of New Mexico had been slow, but pioneers had been coming in a trickle ever since the beginning of the wagon trade. Leo Mendes was one of these pioneers, but he was not one who would conquer deserts and mountains and wild Indians. Large empty spaces made him unhappy and he always crossed them in the dark if he could. He was not averse to mountains as delicate silhouettes on a distant horizon, but when he got close to them he always felt as though they were rearing to fall upon him. He regarded all forms of combat and contention as a gratuitous waste of human energy and peace of mind, and had never carried a weapon unless his walking stick could be considered one. So Leo Mendes would contribute nothing to the conquest of the wilderness, but for the business of penetrating a human society he had certain gifts which were not common among American pioneers.

---

2. He first saw Don Pedro from the bank of the river where he had to ford it. The town stood on slightly higher ground a few hundred yards to the east, showing only as a cluster of reddish adobe walls, with some treetops lifting above them. Beyond it the mesa, thinly grown with greasewood, was a dull and dusty olive green, reaching away toward a purple loom of mountains. It was a very hot, bright day in

early September. The heat waves shimmered and danced above the old walls, as though they had stood at the bottom of a troubled, limpid sea. No human figure was anywhere in sight, nor could he hear a human sound, for it was a little past noon and the whole town was doubtless sound asleep and would be for another two hours. To these people the siesta was as sacred as prayer, and Leo had long cultivated all of their customs. So now he unpacked his burro on the sandy flood plain beside the drought-smitten river, which was nothing more than a good sized trickle between clear pools.

Leo Mendes was a strong, stocky man of medium height with handsome heavy features, thick black eyebrows and thick curly hair. His complexion was naturally swarthy and darkened by long exposure to the sun. His blue cotton shirt and denim trousers, and his wide black hat did not distinguish him from most of the natives and neither did the Apache boot-moccasins with hard cowhide soles and turned-up toes which he found the most comfortable of walking shoes. He might easily have passed for a Mexican and often did so, for he spoke Spanish not only fluently but with an instinctive mastery of native idiom, gesture and inflection. He had a gift for taking on the color of his environment without effort and without conscious intention. So he was often taken for a native, but he never pretended to be one if he was asked. By remote origin he was a Portuguese Jew and by birth a New Yorker. He looked like a Mexican and sounded like a Mexican, and sometimes briefly he even felt like a Mexican—but only briefly. At heart he was always and everywhere a stranger, with the reticence, the detachment and skepticism of the man who can mingle in any society but feels he belongs to none.

When he had dropped the two rawhide panniers on the sand and taken the wooden pack saddle off his burro, he inspected its back carefully for incipient sores. Then he plucked a bunch of grass over beside the edge of the bosque, dipped it in the water and rubbed the sweating hide to a smooth coolness. The burro turned his head slightly, as he always did when he received this attention, as though to express an incurable surprise. Perhaps no other burro in the long history of New Mexico had ever been treated with such distinguished consideration. Burros were the pack and riding animals of the poorest Mexicans and they had always been objects of abuse, execration and neglect. A burro rider used neither saddle nor bridle. He sat well toward the rump of his mount, guided him by whacking him on the side of the neck with his burro stick, and propelled him forward by a steady pounding of his rear, and by calling him all the eloquent names known to Spanish profanity. When his day's work was done a burro was turned loose anywhere and picked up his living as best he could, eating weeds, brush and even cactus when no grass was available. Yet a burro was seldom thin and many observers had noted that a dead burro was a rare sight. Burros were not immortal but they did live to a great age, and they were peculiarly immune to accidental casualty and resistant to exploitation. In the service of mankind most burros seldom exceeded a slow walk, but let one of them smell a mountain lion and he would pass anything slower than a frightened jack rabbit.

Leo's attitude toward his burro, like many of his attitudes, was a delicate blend of expediency and compassion. This was a good burro and Leo needed a good burro in his business, but he also had a deep sympathy and respect for the entire race of burros, which was a persecuted race with a great gift for passive resistance, for endurance and survival.

While his burro went foraging along the edge of the bosque, Leo stripped off his clothes and bathed luxuriously in one of the clear pools where the current poured into it and the bottom was soft, clean sand. The water was too shallow for swimming, but he washed himself carefully all over and

wallowed in the cooling current with unctuous satisfaction.
After he had dried in the sun and put on his clothes, leaving
his feet bare, he dug into his pack and brought forth a stack
of tortillas, a small round cheese, a few peaches and a bottle
of native wine. Then he carefully surveyed the ground and
chose a spot in the shade of a small cottonwood where the
sand was smooth and a projecting root would make him a
pillow. His years on the road as a peddler had made him a
connoisseur of the face of the earth as a place of human repose.
He spread the top cloth of his pack in the shade and sat down
to his meal, slicing his white cheese to make a sandwich with
the tortillas, munching his peaches for dessert and drinking
exactly half his bottle of wine. It was frugal fare but his
road-whetted appetite gave it relish. When he had eaten he
deftly rolled a small yellow cigarette and stretched out on
his back, savoring the smoke with his nose, blowing rings into
the faint breeze which cooled his feet. Lying quiet he became
aware of the voice of the valley, which was mostly a hum of
bees, a droning of locusts and a soft chuckle of water over a
sandy bed. It was like a lullaby sent to soothe him. He was
full fed, supremely relaxed and comfortable. In moments
such as this he always felt at home on earth, even though he
was a homeless man, and at peace with himself, however
difficult his fellow beings might become. What more could a
man ask of life? But he knew he was now asking something
more, and something other than peace. Otherwise he would
not be here, camped on the edge of a settlement like an invader waiting the moment to strike.

His cigarette died between his fingers and he focused his
gaze upon a great black and yellow butterfly which fluttered
over him in the aimless fashion of its kind, then incredibly
settled upon the tip of his big toe and sat there slowly and
rhythmically opening and closing its gorgeous wings. He lay

very still so as not to frighten it. When it flew away he closed
his eyes and slept.

---

3. When he woke he knew at once by the
length of the shadows that he had slept nearly an hour. The
town probably would still be asleep but it would take him a
while to pack his burro and to find this man, Aurelio Beltrán,
if he could find him. He knew Beltrán, being a solitary and a
hunter, was much away from home, but he ought to be there
on a hot day at this time of the year. If not, he would have
to wait and try again. He needed an ally and all he had
learned led him to believe this man was the kind of an ally
he needed. What chance had he to persuade the man to
serve him? It seemed unlikely, but the conviction had grown
upon him that this was the test of his luck. If he could get the
kind of an arrangement he needed, then he would go ahead
with his plan, and if not, well, maybe not, or maybe some other
time and somewhere else. He believed a man's destiny is a
thing he discovers, a mystery that unfolds, and he pursued
his ends always in the spirit of inquiry rather than of heroic
determination.

He had been in the valley now more than a week, going
about among all the people who lived within ten miles of the
town, trading with them, getting acquainted with them, asking as many questions as he could without seeming too inquisitive. He had told all of them he had a fine rifle he wanted
to sell. Did they know of anyone who might be interested?
All of them mentioned Augustín Vierra, the richest man in
Don Pedro, the one who occupied there the position of feudal
baron, owning more land and cattle than anyone else and
having most of the others in debt to him. Here in the lower
valley there were not such powerful families as there were

farther north where the Pereas of Bernalillo were said to own
half a million sheep and rule several hundred peons, but even
here the order of society was a feudal order and each community was dominated by someone like Vierra. He was the
only one who would have money enough to buy a good gun
and he loved weapons of all kinds. Leo explained that he did
no business with the Ricos. A peddler or any other stranger
could seldom get his feet inside their doors. Was there anyone
else, a hunter perhaps, who would value a good gun?

He knew the man he needed would probably be a
hunter. Any of these peons would work for him, but most of
them would be deeply in debt to the Vierra family and he
knew from long experience the strength of their allegiance to
their overlords. They might hate Vierra, many of them probably did, but they would jump when he shouted, come when
he called and pass on their debts from father to son like sacred
heirlooms. But in every community, he knew, lived a few men
of rebellious spirit, who refused to become good peons.
Most of these were either bandits or thieves, specializing
in the stealing of sheep, cattle or goats, according to their
talents and opportunities. In fact, some form of larceny was for
the poor almost the only escape from bondage except that in
most communities would be found at least one professional
hunter, who lived by selling meat, fresh and dried, and also
hides and peltries. Most of the Mexicans, too poor to own
effective arms, were not hunters, and most of the good hunters
were more than half Navajo. A professional hunter would
generally be a proud, fierce, restless man, who cherished his
freedom and independence. Leo did not want to deal with a
thief or a bandit, but he was looking for a proud and independent man who could use weapons. Instinctively, he was
looking for a man who would complement himself. For if you
face the hazard of violence, you must be prepared to employ
violence, however little you like it.

He had inquired about this Beltrán at every house he visited, making whatever excuse he could for his curiosity, and gradually he had formed in his own mind the picture of an unusual man. Beltrán, for one thing, was unmarried, and it was very rare to find a Mexican who did not have a wife. It was said that he had married a beautiful girl when he was very young, she had died in childbirth, as so many Mexican women did, and he had lived ever since with a broken heart. That was his legend. But he had not, it appeared, taken any vow of chastity. On the contrary, he was a terror to husbands and fathers, the more so because of his great strength and truculent temper. Was he then an unreliable man? No, not at all, except that you never knew where he was. He disappeared into the mountains, sometimes for weeks at a time, had even gone as far east as the buffalo plains with his wagon, bringing it back loaded with meat and buffalo robes.

Beltrán might be hard to find, but he always kept his word. You could trust him with anything but a woman. The fact was admitted somewhat grudgingly, for Beltrán had few friends. One other thing Leo learned about him, which clinched his own conviction that this was the man he needed. Beltrán did not like the Vierras. He had a great contempt for Don Augustín and a grudge against the whole family, rooted deep in the past.

4.When Leo reached the plaza of Don Pedro there was still no sign of life except a few dogs asleep in the shade, and they did not even wake to bark at him. He sat down with his back to a wall, mopping sweat off his face with a red bandanna, surveying this place he proposed to invade. Like all Mexican towns, it was built around a public square, in this case nothing more than half an acre of sunbaked sand. The church marked its eastern limit, an old adobe church, its corners supported by heavy earthen buttresses, its bell hung in a wooden tower painted white. The Padre's residence was behind it and the two buildings were connected by high walls. The lift and droop of foliage above them suggested the Padre had created for himself a cool retreat. Not a single tree shaded the plaza, nothing grew there except a few yellow sunflowers over against the church and some gourd vines crawling over the crumbling red walls of a deserted building on the south side where Leo sat. Across the way was another tumbledown house, but evidently still in use, perhaps as a public hall where dances were held. The only sound building in sight besides the church was the long, low house on the opposite side of the plaza, with its porch supported by heavy hewn timbers, its whitewashed front wall and windows with heavy wooden bars and shutters. Treetops lifted above its roof, doubtless from the courtyard within, and the establishment reached far back toward the river in the form of a high-walled enclosure.

This, he knew, could only be the Vierra homestead, the castle which dominated this part of the valley. Somewhere behind those walls was a storeroom, where people got the few things they needed and could not produce for themselves, such as cotton cloth, needles and thread, knives and skillets. These goods were handed out to them on credit at whatever price the owner chose to ask. They all worked for him, more or less, but none of them ever worked themselves out of debt. Leo knew all about this business and he was acutely conscious of that primitive storeroom because he hoped to become its competitor, and he knew competition would not be welcomed.

At a glance the town did not look like a good place to found a business—a half-deserted place asleep in the sun and falling to pieces. But Leo was neither surprised nor discouraged. He knew that long ago this had been a much larger town, that it had been dwindling slowly for perhaps a hun-

dred years. Apaches had raided it once, smallpox had ravaged
it. When the Confederates had taken Arizona and made
Mesilla their capital, many of the people had gone there because the Army offered work for real money. So Don Pedro
had not thriven. But Leo was not thinking primarily of the
town. He had learned all about its decline before he came
south. He knew if he had any success he would draw trade
from all over the valley. He knew that only a few miles across
the Texas border was a famous salt lake, where people came
to gather salt from as much as a hundred miles away, from
Sonora and Chihuahua as well as New Mexico. Under the
Mexican law all usable salt deposits had been public property. Although this one now belonged to Texas, it was still
open to all comers, and many of them might be customers
for a good store that sold goods cheap and took almost anything in trade. Then, too, the Mexican border was nearby
and a great deal of movable property always crosses a border
—property of uncertain origin seeking a quick market. Best
of all, Fort Selden was only eleven miles up the river, with
a full company of United States cavalry. Leo had stopped
there briefly on his way south and had done a lively business
in playing cards, chewing tobacco, toothbrushes and other
light merchandise he had brought for that special purpose.
Probably soldiers would come to his store, but that was the
least of the benefits he might reap from the fort. Soldiers
ate beef and horses ate corn, and he hoped to have much
beef and corn to sell. Gringos in the southwest had found
army contracts for beef a lucrative business. Several substantial fortunes had already been founded upon them.

So Leo did not care how dead the town might be. Perhaps
he could inject a little life into it—if he was able to stay. In
the northern part of the valley gringos had opened stores
and some of them had succeeded and others had found it
expedient to move. He had heard the story of the Schoenfelt

brothers, who opened a large store in Santa Fe and received word mysteriously that if they did not move they would be quietly buried. They were men of commerce, not of battle. They had packed their goods upon three hundred burros and moved across the mountains to Las Vegas, where they still throve. So you could never tell what might happen. Leo knew of another peddler who had tried to open a store in a small town south of Albuquerque. He had been visited at night by mysterious strangers who beat him up and advised him to be gone by morning, which he was.

Leo knew he was not going to fight and win any battles, nor issue any heroic defiances. He knew that if a tense and perilous situation arose, he would depart quietly in search of peace. But he also knew that even though he faced no violence, he would inevitably meet with opposition in some form, with resentment and suspicion and dislike. This was not in the least because he was a Jew—the people of New Mexico knew almost nothing of Jews—but because he was a gringo, and even more because he would be an interloper, an innovator, a disturber of the ancient feudal peace.

Why, then, had he set out upon this adventure? Well, chiefly because now he had money. Deeply buried at the bottom of his panniers he had a canvas bag filled with the strangely assorted gold and silver coins then current in the territory, and in Santa Fe he had still more money on deposit with Wells, Fargo and Company, where he could draw on it for credit when he needed more goods. Money was a tool in his hand. He felt a need to use it.

He knew his money was pushing him into this venture and he also knew he had another and more troubling motive. In his long solitary walking he had thought it all over, questioning himself as all solitaries do. For years the proud Ricos of the northern valley had ignored his existence. As a peddler he had never been able to get past their heavy front doors, to sell them so much as a needle. He was not an aggressive man but there was something inside him that wanted to challenge these lords of the earth, and it was in conflict with something else that wanted only peace. As a peddler he had known much of contentment. Now he had to go starting trouble for himself, risking his money if not his life. Was he then afraid? Yes, he found it necessary to admit that he was afraid and he half-enjoyed the tingle of fear, the thrill of his own temerity. One phase of his life was over and another was about to begin. He felt peculiarly alert and alive, stimulated by the mystery and hazard of new experience.

He rose and prodded his burro gently. He had named it Spinoza because his father had taught him to revere that name and he liked to utter it and to stir the memories of youth that were associated with it.

"Vamos a ver, Spinoza," he said. It was a common idiom of the country—"We are going to see"—reflecting the fatalism of the Mexicans, which was much like his own.

He had been told that Beltrán lived a few hundred yards from the plaza on a road running north. There he would find a long, low building, most of it empty and beginning to crumble in the weather, but at the far end a couple of rooms were kept in good repair and there lived Beltrán. It appeared that the Beltráns had once been a strong and numerous family, with a house nearly as large as that of the Vierras, but the tribe had dwindled and scattered. There were others of the name living thereabouts, but only Aurelio still lived in the ruin of the family homestead.

It was easy to find the building, and Leo noted with interest that while it was in bad shape, it could be made usable by plastering the walls and mending the roof. He went to the one good door at the far end, a heavy wooden door with a big iron latch, knocked upon it and stood waiting and listening with a sharp suspense tightening his guts, a

feeling that much depended upon the next few minutes. There
was a moment of silence, then he heard a slight cough, a
whisper of moccasined feet across a dirt floor, and the door
opened upon an impressive figure of a man. He stood well
over six feet, broad-shouldered, erect and powerful, a man
with no softening comfortable fat anywhere about him and
no smile upon his face. It was a massively aquiline face with
an imposing nose and deep-set eyes. The hair was straight
and black, but Leo knew at once that this was no Indian.
Beltrán was a Spaniard of the lean and taciturn breed which
has been producing fighters and fanatics for a thousand years.
He said, "How do you do" politely enough, but without smiling, and then after a deliberate pause, "What do you want?"

"I am a peddler," Leo said.

Beltrán considered the fact a moment.

"What do you sell?" he inquired.

"I have very beautiful colored pictures," Leo explained,
"of Christ crucified, the Virgin Mary and also the Virgin of
Guadelupe and most of the Saints."

Beltrán shook his head, his hand still upon the door.

"They are all safe in heaven," he said. "I see no reason to
hang them on the wall."

"I have needles and thread, cotton cloth and scissors,"
Leo said.

Beltrán was not interested. "I have no wife," he explained.

"I have a very fine rifle," Leo ventured, feeling that he
had built up to his climax. "Made by Hawken of St. Louis,
with a bullet mold, a canister of powder and a bar of lead."

He could see the flash of interest in the man's eyes, but it
was a very slight reaction, and he shook his head again.

"I have no money to buy a rifle," he said. "You must know
that. I have buckskin and peltries, a few buffalo robes, beans
and chili, but I have not seen ten silver dollars together since

the soldiers left Mesilla. If you are looking for money, you have come to the wrong place."

"I take almost anything in trade," Leo said. "That is the only way I can do business. Usually peltries and buffalo robes would be too heavy for me to handle, but I hope to be here awhile and to ship goods to Santa Fe."

Beltrán again devoted himself to thought for a long moment. At last he stepped back and opened the door wide.

"Come in," he said. "It will do no harm to look at your rifle."

Leo stepped through the door with the feeling of a conqueror who has breached the wall of a peculiarly difficult fortress. It was dark inside the room, which had only one window with wooden bars and a sheet of oiled paper. When his eyes became used to the dim light he saw that he was facing an enormous dog. It stood there looking at him, silent and motionless, except that the hair on its neck lifted a little, as though in preparation for battle. It was a yellow dog with a white splash on its throat, built much like a mastiff except that its head and ears showed a trace of hound. Leo thought it must weigh at least a hundred pounds. In spite of himself, he took a step backward. The brute looked as though it might kill a man with ease and would not be at all averse to the job.

Beltrán, relaxed for the first time, laughed a little.

"Don't be afraid of him," he said. "If you came here alone he would tear you to pieces, but as long as I am here you are safe."

He spoke a low word to the dog. It came forward slowly and with dignity, touched Leo's hand with its tongue, returned to the back of the room and lay down, its head on its paws like a couchant lion, never taking its eyes off the stranger.

"He is a very valuable dog," Beltrán explained. "He knows how to drive deer out of a canyon and how to tree bob cats and lions. He once killed a young mountain lion all alone, and very few dogs can do that."

"He is a magnificent dog," Leo agreed. The animal's unwavering gaze made him uncomfortable, but it occurred to him that this dog might prove to be something of an asset.

"Sit down," Beltrán invited, pointing to a rolled mattress against the wall, covered with a red and black Navajo blanket. The only other furniture was a homemade chair with a rawhide seat and a massive table of hand-hewn timbers.

"First let me unpack my burro," Leo said.

He dragged his panniers into the room, dug out the rifle, which was carefully wrapped in buckskin, and laid it on the table. It was a beautiful piece with a richly figured walnut stock, a bright nickel butt-plate and a blued-steel barrel. Beltrán picked it up and brought it to his shoulder with a practiced gesture, while his cheek lovingly cuddled the polished wood. He laid it down with a sigh.

"I could never afford such a rifle as that," he said.

"You would not have to pay for it now," Leo offered. "I will give you credit."

Beltrán interrupted with an angry shake of his head.

"I am no peon," he said emphatically. "I would rather eat acorns than go into debt."

Leo saw he had made a mistake, felt he had better go straight to the point of his visit.

"You need not remain long in debt," he said. "I want to open a store in this town. I need a room, and you have empty rooms. It will take some building and plastering to make the place ready. If we can make a bargain I will pay you for the work and I will also pay you a rental."

He paused, fished in his trousers pocket, pulled out a large eight-sided gold coin called an ounce and laid it on the table.

"I have money," he explained.

Beltrán sat staring thoughtfully at the bright gold. It was evident that this double proposition had confused him and shaken his defenses. He was being asked to assume a debt and also to work, both clearly against his principles, but at the same time he was being treated as a landlord.

"So you want to open a store here," he said at length. It was hard to guess from his tone what he thought of this proposal.

Leo shrugged his shoulders and spread his hands in a gesture eloquent of man's helplessness in the face of his inscrutable destiny.

"Perhaps the Vierras will chase me out of town," he said.

"Listen!" Beltrán spoke with sudden heat. "They will not chase you out, not if I have anything to do with it."

He stopped short, evidently aware that he had committed himself more than he had intended.

"Many thanks," Leo said. "I will appreciate your friendship, whether we can do business or not." He began wrapping up the rifle. "It is time for me to go, but I will come to see you again."

Beltrán was silent a moment, watching the rifle disappear with evident reluctance.

"Where do you sleep?" he asked just as Leo was about to put it in his pack.

"I sleep anywhere," Leo said.

"You can stay here," Beltrán offered. "There is plenty of room and I have much venison."

"Well, thank you." Leo laid the rifle back on the table. "I have great pleasure."

After Beltrán had tended his horses and chopped wood they prepared a notable meal of young venison stewed with chili and beans. Leo contributed the rest of his wine and cheese and also some coffee. Before they slept that night it was understood that Leo would pay a rental of two American dollars a month for the use of a room and that Beltrán would go with his wagon to Mesilla where the Confederates had left some lumber he could buy for shelves and a counter. Although they had made no formal agreement, the store already had become a joint enterprise, a thing that existed in two imaginations.

5. When Aurelio had departed the next morning Leo went to inspect the premises he had acquired. The room adjoining those in which Aurelio lived had evidently been the sala, the main hall of the old house. It must have been a somewhat pretentious place in its day, for the room was more than forty feet long with two corner fireplaces, and its roof was supported by massive hand-hewn beams, but its size now was its only claim to dignity. Adobe houses deteriorate rapidly unless they are often plastered and their flat roofs kept in repair. The roof of this one supported a lush crop of weeds and its wooden water spouts had sagged and cracked. The walls on the outside were bare of plaster and the whitewash of gypsum on the interior was streaked by leaking rain water. Windows were only gaping holes and the door was missing. The dim interior had a musty smell and was littered with the droppings of small animals. Two bats detached themselves from a roof beam and blundered through a window, and a pack rat stared at him a moment in amazed resentment before it bounded through the door.

It was not an impressive place to look at, surely, but Leo surveyed it undismayed. For the first time in his life he was a householder, and the fact tingled his blood and stirred his imagination. It would cost little to plaster the place inside and out and to mend the roof. He envisioned a long solid counter and shelves behind it, heavy with goods, and a row of bright religious prints hung against the white walls above the shelving, as he had seen them in stores in Santa Fe and Albuquerque. There at the back saddles and harness would hang on a wooden rack, and the room next to this one would have to be a storeroom, for he would take great quantities of stuff in trade—grain and beans to be sold to the Army, and hides to be shipped north. And a third room he would make over for his own quarters, and more rooms could easily be added, if need be. . . . He checked his flourishing imagination with a short laugh. It was well to remember that so far he had nothing but a ruin littered with rat turds and something of a doubt as to whether he could stay there. But he knew he wanted to stay. He had long thought himself content as a wanderer, but now he was suddenly aware of the appeal of solid walls, of a foothold on the earth, of a possession that would spread and grow, a solid extension of his own being.

He had an impulse to make a beginning right now. In the courtyard he found a couple of old water barrels and a long pine plank, dragged them into the room and improvised a table. Then he brought in his panniers and began unpacking the few goods he had left, taking stock of his resources— needles and thread, half a bolt of cotton cloth, scissors, a few butcher knives and a roll of the pictures which had long been his most reliable staple. It was not much, but it would do for a start.

He heard a soft murmur of voices and looked up to see three small boys standing in the doorway, regarding him gravely. He might have known they would find him before long. Let any stranger or any strange thing appear in a Mexican town and the small boys, precocious, polite, avidly inquisitive, would smell it out and settle themselves to contemplate it. They were never obtrusive or noisy. They had a

great capacity for just sitting and looking. He had been dealing with them for years. He said, "Good morning, boys," and
they all responded in a soft chorus of "Buenos días," and
squatted on their haunches, feeling that they had been made
welcome by his greeting.

Leo had made a speciality of dealing with children for
years, partly because he liked them, but also because it paid.
Girls beyond a certain age could be embarrassing, but small
boys were the unofficial ambassadors of a town and much
depended upon knowing how to treat them. He went on sort-
ing his goods for some minutes, ignoring his audience. Then
he casually brought forth a cone of brown sugar, which was
the only native candy of the region. It was hard as a rock,
and he laid it on the plank and ostentatiously smashed it
into pieces with a small hand axe. Then he looked up and
smiled.

"Come to eat," he said, using a universal form of invitation. The boys came forward, shy but eager, took their candy,
spoke their faint thanks, went back and squatted in exactly
the same place, their small cheeks bulging and writhing
beatifically. He knew they would be there now as long as he
was in sight, and it occurred to him they would also
inevitably advertise his presence to any passer-by. This
proved true a few minutes later, when he saw the figure of a
black-shawled woman peering over the heads of the boys,
her eyes noticeably wide with astonishment.

"Good morning, madam," he saluted with elaborate courtesy. "Enter if you please."

The woman came in, dropping her hooded shawl about
her shoulders, showing her teeth in a good-humored smile.

"What is this?" she asked in wonder. "A store?"

Leo shrugged.

"Perhaps," he agreed. "I am a peddler and here I would
like to stop awhile. I am at your service."

She began picking up articles and examining them. Leo unrolled his stock of religious prints and spread them on his pack cover near the window where the light was good. This display at once took her mind off such utilitarian things as needles and butcher knives. A Mexican, he had learned long since, always put beauty before use, always wanted to adorn life and celebrate it. So now this woman exclaimed in low ecstasy over each of the gaudy prints. She was fascinated completely by a picture, which had long been his best seller, of Christ crucified, with much crimson blood pouring from his wounded hands and feet and streaking his face beneath his crown of thorns. These people all seemed to love the color and flow of blood.

"Pobrecito!" she murmured. "How I would like to have it!"

Leo rolled it and tied it with a bit of twine, handed it to her with a slight bow.

"Madam, it is yours," he said.

"But I have no money."

Leo produced the small ledger he always carried.

"Give me your name, madam," he said. "You can pay whenever you wish and in any kind you wish. I hope to be here a long time."

He inscribed her name, Louisa Candelario, put down the amount of her purchase, and she departed, murmuring thanks.

Already and almost in spite of himself, he was a storekeeper and a creditor. The fact gave him a thrill of wonder. It seemed as though this town had been waiting for him, was coming to meet him with open hands.

He felt decidedly that he had done enough for one day and also he was getting hungry. He had begun putting away his goods when he heard the soft plunk of hoofbeats in a dusty road and looked up to see a rider dismounting before the door. At a glance he knew luck had turned against

him. It had never occurred to him that any Vierra would
find him so soon, but his experience told him at once this
man could only be a Rico. The large, well-fed horse and the
heavy saddle trimmed with bearskin and silver, were enough
to make him sure of that, and the man who strode through
the door belonged to a kind he had known for years. There
was nothing distinctive about his white cotton shirt, open at
the neck, nor his blue trousers, but Leo's practiced eye ap-
praised his boots at about thirty-five dollars, his great jin-
gling spurs of silver and gun-metal at half as much, and
knew his wide white hat had come all the way from New
Jersey by way of the Santa Fe trade and was truly the crown
of his pride. The man was of medium height but seemed
taller by reason of his high heels and his lofty bearing. In
his right hand he carried a braided leather quirt, and Leo
knew its handle was loaded with lead so that it could be re-
versed and used as a weapon. The Ricos all loved such whips,
symbols of an often ruthless authority over man and beast—
an inherited authority for most of them, supported more by
pride of birth than by strength.

Leo was a mild and amiable man but these high-headed
caballeros had always aroused in him an irrepressible antagonism, partly because he was a little afraid of them. They
almost always had arms about them, seemed to be perpet-
ually ready to strike or shoot. He had noticed too that a
streak of cruelty ran through the whole class, as it so often
does in those who have others at their mercy. They loved
huge spurs and he had seen more than one of them rowel a
horse until it bled. He had seen also the whipping posts which
were permanent institutions on many of the large ranches,
for most of these people owned a few Indians as outright
slaves, still bought and sold them, despite the law.

So he knew the man who stood before him now was a
proud, truculent man, accustomed to being obeyed, regard-

ing himself as superior by right of birth, and he looked the
part, with his handsome brown face, fine dark eyes, and silky
black mustache, carefully combed. He carried a little too
much fat around his jowls and under his belt for a man of
his age, which was probably not more than forty, but nevertheless he contrived to look both formidable and dignified
as he stood there surveying first Leo and then the skimpy
stock spread out upon the plank, saying nothing. This silent,
unsmiling scrutiny was evidently designed to make Leo uncomfortable rather than happy.

"Good morning, sir." Leo knew that his tone was con-
ciliatory, almost obsequious, and he did not like the sound
of his own voice.

The visitor merely nodded his acknowledgment.

"I am Augustín Vierra," he said, and he spoke as though
this announcement carried a fateful significance.

"My name is Mendes," Leo replied. There was no handshake, nothing friendly about the exchange.

"What are you doing here?" Vierra inquired.

Leo made a gesture toward his merchandise.

"I am a peddler," he said. "I have a few things to sell."

"It looks to me as if you had opened a store," Vierra remarked.

Leo laughed uneasily.

"You can call it a store if you want to," he said.

"You know you cannot stay here without my permission,"
Vierra announced, as though he were stating something
obvious.

Leo felt a faint stir of defiance, if not of anger. He did
not concede the point, but stood looking at Vierra with a
slight smile, as though inviting further explanation.

"There is no need for a store here," Vierra said. "I supply
the people here with everything they want."

Leo again stood mum, for he could see that his silence

was no help to Vierra, who evidently did not know what to say next. His eyes fell upon the outspread merchandise, he approached the board, began picking things up and examining them. Leo now felt sure the crisis had passed, for the moment at least.

Vierra's attention finally fixed upon a butcher knife with a twelve-inch blade. He hefted it, gripped it, tested its edge with his thumb. Leo could see he was a man who loved naked steel and the feel of a weapon in his hand. He had dealt with such men before. He knew that Vierra would never relinquish that blade.

"What do you want for this?" Vierra finally inquired.

"Only a peso," Leo said. The knife had cost him twenty-five cents in Santa Fe, but all business in this country required bargaining, and everything was worth what you could get for it.

"I will give you four bits." Vierra spoke as though he were announcing a decision rather than making an offer, and Leo accepted it as such, nodded his acquiescence.

"To you, then," he said, "it is four bits."

Vierra dug silver out of his pocket, tossed it onto the board with a gesture exquisitely negligent, condescending. Persons of quality always tossed money at their inferiors, never handed it to them. In the case of a peon they would often toss the coins on the floor, and let him chase them. Leo let the money lie, spoke no thanks. Vierra turned toward the door, knife in one hand, whip in the other, paused and looked back.

"I am leaving for the mesa," he said. "My men are rounding up cattle. When I return, perhaps you will be gone."

Leo looked him smilingly in the eyes. He found that his courage was rising.

"Perhaps," he said.

For a moment Vierra stood staring at him, as though about

to say something more, then turned and strode through the door. Leo watched him mount his big, restless horse and ride away. He felt sure he had met an antagonist, that an issue had been drawn, and he felt also a faint suspicion and a hope that the man was not as formidable as he tried to appear.

6. For days he and Aurelio worked together, plastering the old house inside and out, Aurelio wielding a trowel with expert skill, spreading the plaster with long, smooth strokes, while Leo perspired like a work horse, carrying water from the well and wheeling wooden barrows of earth. As he worked, Aurelio talked, and he talked still more over their long midday meal and the native wine they drank with it. He kept saying that as soon as the first frost was white on the grass he must depart for the mountains because then the bucks would be prime and the young turkeys would be down in the canyons. He evidently felt a need to remind himself, and also Leo, that he was not bound but worked only at his pleasure. At the same time it was evident that this refurbishing of his ancestral home gave him great satisfaction. He was truly rebuilding his own past and that of the town, and as he worked he dug deeper and deeper into the past, one memory leading to another. From the days of his own boyhood, when his grandparents had lived here in the old house, he worked his way back through a couple of centuries to the founding of the town. Leo listened with interest and also with amazement, for to Aurelio the whole story of the town was so much local gossip, and he spoke of what had happened two hundred years ago in the same way that he recalled the scandals and accidents of last summer. The beginnings of the town were a legend unwritten, but one that had been handed down from generation to generation with abundant detail. All of the people who lived here now were descendants of the little group who had come late in the seventeenth century, when the Pueblo Indians made their one great revolt and drove the Spaniards out of Santa Fe and the northern valley. Most of the refugees went all the way to El Paso, but this group of a hundred, mostly women and children, had nearly died of thirst on the Jornada. Under the leadership of one Pedro Vierra they had struck out across country and finally reached the river at this point. A few had died on the way, and children were carried by men staggering in delirium, but most of them reached the river alive and threw themselves into it, drinking frantically until Pedro drew his sword and drove them all back from the water, for he knew they would die if they drank as much as they wanted. Then he ordered them to kneel and thank God for their deliverance.

He was a remarkable man, this Pedro Vierra, who achieved leadership and in fact complete dominance by force of intelligence, character and an immense vitality. For he was not an aristocrat or a man of wealth or an officer. Aurelio was very specific about that. These were all poor people who had been small landowners in the upper valley north of Santa Fe. Pedro Vierra had come across the seas as a common soldier, who wore a shirt of chain armor and carried a matchlock in the service of the Emperor, and so had Roberto Beltrán, the forebear of Aurelio.

"We are all cousins around here now," Aurelio said. "When I meet a man on the road, I say, 'good morning, cousin,' and I cannot be wrong."

How, then, had the Vierras come to their present position of wealth and importance? Simply because this Don Pedro had been a great man. Aurelio gave him full credit and admiration. It was Don Pedro who had applied to the Spanish

Crown for a community grant, so that each of the settlers had his strip of cultivated land in the valley and all of them held the range land on the mesa in common. Most of these people had raised sheep in the north, but Don Pedro had understood that it was too hot for sheep here, and had brought in cattle from Sonora and also goats. He had become the alcalde, as a matter of course. The town had always been called Don Pedro's town and finally it became just Don Pedro, a monument to a man of courage and ability and also of great piety. He had procured the assignment of a resident priest to the town, and all the people had joined to build a church and a residence for the man of God. Every man brought a back load of adobe mud from the river every day, and each woman laid one brick a day until the buildings were done. Both of them still stood, in perfect repair, and the whole community every year met to plaster them and held a dance to celebrate the event.

The son of Don Pedro had also been an able man and so had his grandson. These three had founded the Vierra fortune, and how had they done it? This was a sore point with Aurelio. The range land was owned in common, but the Vierras owned most of the cattle and so they used most of the range, simply squeezing out less fortunate men.

"For my part, when I want beef I take it," Aurelio boasted. "And if Augustín saw me put a knife to one of his calves, he would not dare to lift a finger."

But most of the people now were hopelessly in debt to the Vierras. Not only had they lost their range rights, but also much of the land in the valley had gradually passed into the hands of the Vierras by a process of debt and foreclosure which is as old as the idea of owning the earth.

"My great grandfather still had fields of corn and chili and beans and he raised his own tobacco," Aurelio said. "And what remains to me? Just about enough land to spit on!"

He spoke with bitterness. It was evident that in the eyes of Aurelio the Vierras were a family of greedy upstarts, and the fact that they had upstarted about two hundred years ago detracted nothing from their vulgar pretentiousness. Their estate had been handed down to the eldest son in each generation, but the great ability of the first three Vierras had not gone with it. According to Aurelio, the family had not produced an able man for a hundred years. For Don Augustín he had a rather humorous contempt without much animus, but for his wife, the Doña Maria Guadelupe, he had a hatred which seemed to be both obsessive and unreasonable. It appeared that Lupe, as he always called her, came of a Santa Fe family of ancient and aristocratic lineage. Don Augustín had captivated and married her on a visit to the capital when he was in the first flush of his handsome youth and fresh from exploits in the war against the Comanches. The hot southern country and the moribund little town had perhaps been a disillusionment to her. At any rate, according to Aurelio, she felt that she had married beneath her and looked down her nose at almost everyone in town except the Padre.

"She is the one who puts on all the airs," he said. "The old-time homemade furniture was not good enough for her, so she imported chairs and tables all the way from Kansas City and also mirrors. I have never been inside their house, you understand, but I am told the sala is hung with mirrors in gilded frames all the way around, so that Lupe can see herself coming and going and from every possible angle. That woman's vanity is beyond belief. She is the one who insisted on having a coach, the only coach between Albuquerque and El Paso, so I am told. Of course we have no roads here suitable for coaches, and it is always getting stuck. They have made several trips to Santa Fe in it and it took them twice as long as it would in a buckboard. And her clothes! They come all the way from Kansas City, too, long gowns that sweep up the dust and corsets that make her look like a wasp, just as she often sounds like one. And how many children has she borne? Just two! Can that be anything but shameless sin?"

Aurelio explained that Lupe had borne a son and daughter, but the girl had died in her first year.

"The little girl she has with her now is a niece who was born in Santa Fe. Her parents are dead and Lupe seems to give the child small care. Little Magdalena runs wild about the village with an Indian girl who is supposed to look after her."

Leo remarked that Lupe's small fertility might be the will of God, but Aurelio would not have it so.

"You know," he said. "The Navajo women never have children unless they wish. All of them are whores at heart. And how do they manage it? It is quite simple. They take a ball of buffalo tallow about as big as an egg and put it where it will do the most good. Well, when Lupe was first married, Don Augustín gave her a Navajo maid and I have no doubt she learned a thing or two from that girl. She is too much in love with her own figure to have many children."

Aurelio shook his head and made a clucking sound with his tongue, expressive of profound moral deprecation.

"I have known many women in my time," he said. "But I never permitted any of them to violate the laws of God. Of course, everyone knows that the Ricos have no morality. About a year after the wedding the Doña is looking for a lover and the Don is in the market for a nice-looking Navajo girl about fourteen years old. The rich can afford to be sinners because they can burn candles in the church and have special masses said for their souls. Only the poor truly fear God!"

Aurelio was eloquent, both as a moralist and as a gossip, and Leo could understand the bitterness that flavored his words—the bitterness of a proud and isolated man. He despised the common Mexicans for their humility, their feudal dependence, and he hated the rich for their arrogance and for owning the earth. The only thing he seemed to love was the mountains. When he spoke of them his voice was soft with longing.

Leo felt sure he was winning a friend and an ally but one who would require careful handling. He knew he must humor the man's need of solitude and escape.

"You have worked hard, Aurelio," he said. "And we need fresh meat. Perhaps it is time you went hunting."

"Yes, I must go soon," Aurelio agreed. "But not until Don Augustín has paid us his visit. I must be here then!"

"What do you think he will do?" Leo inquired, and he knew that his voice betrayed his nervous suspense. He did not know whether this situation contained the seeds of violence or not.

"Nothing!" Aurelio spoke with the emphasis of complete self-confidence, and it conveyed a great reassurance. "Not while I am here! But when he comes pay him little attention. Just go on working."

They had almost finished plastering the inside of the great room when the Don stopped at the door, evidently on his way back from the cattle range. When Leo heard his footstep and the jingle of his spurs, he felt a qualm of uneasiness, despite all Aurelio's brave words. He could bring himself to face anything by moral effort but not with heroic calm. So now he went on mixing mud with frantic energy.

The dog Choppo was the first to greet the visitor. Choppo had been lying asleep in a corner, but the instant he heard a footstep he was on his feet with his hackles rising and a deep growl rumbling in his throat. It stopped the Don as suddenly as a gun pointed at his head. Aurelio spoke first to the dog—a single low word which caused Choppo to sink flat on his belly with his head on his paws and his eyes on the Don, just as he had done when Leo first met him. Over his shoulder, then, Aurelio gave his polite good morning, without interrupting the smooth sweep of his trowel. When greetings had been exchanged all around, the Don seemed considerably at a loss, and he also seemed unable to take his eyes off the dog, as Leo could observe in a sidelong glance.

"So you are repairing your house, Aurelio?" he inquired at last.

"Yes," Aurelio replied, still busy. "This gentleman wants to rent it."

The Don nodded and stood staring about at the newly plastered walls, as though in admiration or surprise. For a long moment there was no sound but the soft whisper of Aurelio's trowel and the squish and splash of Leo's nervous attack on his mud. Then the Don gave them a quick "Adiós," and they heard the jingle of his inglorious retreat, the thud of departing hooves. When the sound had died away, Aurelio turned from his work and burst into a great laugh that flushed his face and shook his belly.

"What did I tell you?" he demanded. Then he jerked a thumb at the dog in the corner. "That dog hates Ricos!" he remarked. He turned back to his work, made a few final strokes with his trowel, then washed it carefully and laid it aside.

"Now," he announced, "I can go hunting."

---

7. When he opened his store a few days later, Leo had a rush of customers, most of them women and most of them obviously impelled by curiosity. The founding of a store in Don Pedro was news that traveled fast. Everyone

wanted to see the place and the man who owned it and to
stare at the little stuff he had to offer. Few of them had
money, but Leo disposed of most of his stock on credit. He
knew almost all business here had to be done on credit and he
knew also that these people were bound to the soil and had
been trained for generations to regard their debts as sacred.
So he let everyone take what he wanted and before the end
of the second day he had half the names in town on his
book.

Late in the afternoon there came to his door a slender
woman with a little girl of nine or ten years beside her. She
entered with slow and graceful dignity, exchanged greetings
with him gravely, stood for a moment looking at him with a
rather haughty unabashed curiosity. Leo returned her stare
with equal interest, for this, he knew, was no common Mexican woman. He felt sure he was being honored by a visit
from another Vierra. She was dressed simply enough in a
gown of flowered cotton print and a black shawl with a fringe,
but the shawl was of heavy China silk and he could see
rings on both her hands, which were long, slender hands un-
marked by toil. Her hair was piled high on her head, too, as
no peon woman would have worn it, and the head was proudly
carried. She was somewhere in her middle thirties, Leo
thought, but not marked by age as so many Mexican women
were, for most of them fattened early. She was slim and trim
and even a bit hard looking, with shoulders noticeably wider
than her hips and firm pointed breasts pushing against her
frock. Her face was too narrow for beauty but it was handsome, with a finely cut nose and dark eyes under heavy brows
that almost met. Leo was acutely aware of every detail of her
appearance, for it was the first time in all his years in New
Mexico that he had been so close to a woman of her class.
His business as a peddler had been all with the poor Mexicans. Rico women he had seen strolling in the plaza in Santa

Fe when the band played and rolling past him on the road in the Concord coaches the most important families owned, but they lived in a world apart from the one where he sold his trinkets and ate his beans and chili with humble folk, squatting on the floor with a rolled tortilla for a spoon.

There was only the width of a counter between them now. She was so close he could smell the perfume she wore, mingled with a vague odor of feminine presence. He felt a stir of desire toward her, and also of antagonism, such as any man may feel toward a provocative woman who stands beyond his reach. He could understand now the resentment she inspired in Aurelio, with her lofty bearing and her unsmiling stare.

Her eyes fell upon the counter and then suddenly she did smile, making a gesture with both of her long fluttering hands, so that her emeralds and rubies flashed in their settings of heavy soft gold. Her smile, like everything else about her, was a little hard, sardonic and mischievous. She was looking at the few things on his counter.

"They told me you had a store," she mocked, and laughed at him.

Her laugh and her words created a wholly new atmosphere in the room. Leo laughed, too.

"I have a store," he said. "All I need is some merchandise. I will have that, too, when you return."

She picked up a little painted plaster image of the Virgin Mary, of which he always carried a few. Almost every Mexican home had a niche where an image of some saint was kept, and most of them made their own santitos, or bought them from native wood carvers. These were much more distinctive than the cheap plaster saints he sold, but his images had displaced many a santito a hundred years old.

"I will take this," the lady announced, laying money on the counter. Afterward she smiled at him again, said "Adiós" and departed with proud grace and a slight disturbing oscillation of her elegant hips. She left Leo feeling slightly shaken, but also gratified. He suspected the Doña was a forceful person, and that her smile was good promise for the future of his store.

He felt sure now that he was going to stay here. When the last of his customers had gone, he took a smooth board and a bottle of black ink he had in his pack, carefully lettered a sign, and hung it over the door.

LEO MENDES
Tienda Barata

It meant literally "cheap store," but he had seen the same sign in Santa Fe and Albuquerque, and he knew that to the common people it meant a place where they could get what they wanted for less than their lords and masters would charge. It was a defiant sign, a challenge to old and established powers and customs. It was destined to be known all over the valley, across the river in Sonora, and even in Arizona and Texas.

CHAPTER

TWO

1.During the years he walked the long roads as a peddler, Leo thought and remembered much, as do all solitary walkers. He read little if only because most of the time he had neither book nor light, but the past was a book he conned over and over, finding in it always something new, stirring old emotions to a new life, reliving moments that seemed to belong to another person and another world.

When he remembered he always imagined himself as he must have looked. So in his earliest recollections he saw a little fat curly-headed boy, somewhat old for his years, sitting on the floor surrounded by older people. His only sister was four years older than he and his father and mother in those days always had many visitors who were also older people. He remembered the beards of the men smelling of tobacco when they bent over to pat him on the head, and the voluminous skirts of the women sweeping about him on the floor. He re-

membered good food and especially thick hot soup and
stewed chicken and gefüllte fish and sweet little cakes with
tea drunk out of hot glasses. He remembered above all a
pervasive sentimental sheltering tenderness which began with
the clasp of his mother's arms and her kiss on his mouth and
seemed to extend to everyone he knew, so that he had a feeling
of cherished security such as he was never to know again.

Always his life was one of crowds and walls and noises in
a swarming human world, an enclosed world of people
pressed together in mutual dependence. It was also a paved
and cobble-stoned world. He seldom saw a tree or grass and
never a stretch of the natural earth or a glimpse of distance.
Where he lived, near the corner of Broadway and Canal Street,
the buildings, three stories high, crowded down to the edge
of the pavement and all of them had shops on the lower floor
and flats above. The rattle of wooden wheels was a noise so
incessant that he never became aware of it until he left it.
Peddlers shouted their wares up and down the sidewalks and
garrulous women laughed and chatted from window to window. Noise and people were everywhere.

He went first to a private school and then to the Ward
Schools, which were the beginning of public education in
New York, but never to the Cheder, the orthodox school where
boys learned by rote, reciting their lessons aloud. For it was
a rebellion against orthodoxy that had first pushed his father
across the sea, and there were enough like-minded Jews in
New York so that he was never lonely there. In public school
Leo first awoke to the fact that the world could be hostile. He
encountered boys who did not like him and even had a few
reluctant fights, but nevertheless he still lived in a community
which was dominated by the feeling of mutual dependence.
Its basic social principle was that every Jew is responsible for
every other Jew. There were now rich Jews farther up town
who lived apart from poor Jews, but every immigrant was

cared for. No Jew was ever permitted to beg on the streets of New York. In the Jewish quarter, with its forty thousand people, there was almost no crime of violence, although the notorious Five Point Gang, only a few blocks away, practiced mayhem with brass knuckles and billies and the nearby Chinese settled their differences with hatchets. The Jewish community was filled with benevolent and charitable societies of a dozen kinds. It was organized to care for its own. It was a society in which violence rather than desire was considered the source of evil, a society half-consciously pervaded by the Oriental feeling that all life is one.

Leo knew little of his family background before the time of his father, Samuel Mendes. He knew that his name was Portuguese and he had learned on the streets of New York that he looked much like an Italian or an Armenian or any other boy of Mediterranean stock, and nothing at all like the blond German Jews who had come in later than his father, many of them fleeing the troubles of 1848. But his father had come to America from Bremerhaven and it was family legend that his grandfather had come there from the old Kingdom of Bohemia. No one knew when the family had left Portugal or why. Leo came of a race of reluctant pilgrims, of people who loved family life and security and peace and yet had traveled halfway around the world, always in flight from something or in search of something. This was a conflict that ran in the blood, and Leo knew that it ran in his own, for there was something in him that loved the road and something that longed for a home. In Germany and Bohemia most of his forebears had been settled merchants, but his father had told him of a great-uncle who was all his life a peddler and a wanderer, a man who could stay nowhere, despite the incessant efforts of his family to settle him down.

Leo's father, too, had suffered from this same conflict. He had aspired to be a learned man and if possible a rabbi, and

had spent his youth in half-starved study. Then he began to
feel the lure of the new world, toward which men were moving
in a vast migration. The rich and the old stayed home, but
the poor and especially the young poor were infected by the
movement as by a disease. About the same time, Leo's father
was spoiled for an orthodox career as a Jewish scholar by his
reading of the great philosopher Spinoza, who repudiated the
terrible Jehovah of the Old Testament and found God in
everything, in sinner and saint, in bird and flower, in the
spirit of life that unifies nature. He also believed that man's
destiny grows out of seed and soil, like a tree, that he does not
control his fate, but that he is free when he moves upon his
own impulse and in bondage when he is compelled by forces
outside himself. Beginning when he was about sixteen, these
ideas became familiar to Leo. His father was always talking
about them. They became a part of his mind because they
came to him when he was young and soft and because they
were congenial to his feeling.

His father also told him much about the history of his own
people, of their long trials and persecutions, and of their enforced wanderings. Samuel Mendes saw his own emigration
not as an isolated thing but as part of the movement that had
carried his stock from its Asiatic homeland to every part of
the world. He went through long and painful inner conflict
before he could bring himself to leave his familiar world and
face the terrors of the sea. For all of his kind feared the sea,
as they feared all the wild wide places of the earth where men
were not. Fear of the sea kept many of them at home, so that
those who went were in some measure a chosen band, with
more than average courage. The sea had not swallowed Samuel Mendes, but it had scared him almost to death, for he
went through the horrors of a major storm on a sailing ship
with its canvas whipped to tatters and the waves washing its
decks from stem to stern. On shipboard he had met the pretty

little Galician girl who was to become Leo's mother. Both of them had told Leo how they gave themselves up for lost and how they embraced on the storm-tossed boat, clinging to love in the face of what they believed to be certain death.

In New York Leo's father became a bookkeeper and worked all his life for a firm of importers, who valued him highly and paid him a good living. He remained always a scholar at heart, who spent his evenings with his books, except when the whole family went to concerts, for the whole community loved music and tickets were cheap. Before he was eighteen Leo had heard almost all of the romantic Italian opera of the period and a hunger for music followed him all his life.

2.It was a comfortable, sheltered separate society into which Leo was born and perhaps he would have remained in it all his life if the white plague had not invaded his family. Tuberculosis then was the terrible killer of the Western world and it was the curse of the crowded metropolis. First his father caught cold and developed a cough that never left him, refusing for more than a year to admit either to himself or to anyone else that he was doomed. After his death, Leo became the support of the family, taking his father's place in the same firm. His mother died a few years later and his sister married, so that suddenly he found himself a lone man, traveling patiently from his office to his room, day after day. When he began to cough, he too refused to admit to himself that he was sick, and he was far more resistant than either of his parents had been, but he lost weight and energy and he also underwent a slow and subtle change of mind. Little by little, this comfortable, crowded, friendly world came to seem a place in which he was entrapped, with death in its very air, threatening him with destruction. He fell in love with a girl named Rachel Raphall, a buxom magnetic creature, whose warm body and confident spirit seemed to give him life. But he was afraid to kiss her for fear that he carried the deadly infection. They went to concerts together and sat hand in hand, and then he took her home and left her quickly. Finally she opened her arms to him, with a question in her eyes, in the lift of her head, and he turned and fled, feeling that both life and love were denied him. He went to a doctor then, who convinced him that he was doomed unless he moved and that the high dry country of the Southwest held his only hope of cure.

Leo approached the crossing of the plains exactly as his father had faced the crossing of the sea. Young men were then going West by the thousands, especially from New York and New England. The papers and magazines were full of writings about the West; it was a favorite subject for dime novels, and there were serious books full of information about it. All of this literature portrayed it as a land of vast prairies and towering mountains, of buffalo herds and wild Indians, of romance and battle. It stirred the imaginations of many American boys, but it had small appeal to Leo. He did not want to fight Indians or kill buffaloes or see the wilderness. He dreaded violence of every kind and a world unpeopled was to him a desolation. Nevertheless he became slowly aware that west he would inevitably go. Dry air and burning sun would cure him if anything would. Moreover, he longed to be a new man in a new world, and everything new and untried lay westward. For a man in his state of mind, no other direction was possible. He was pulled toward the West as a plant is pulled toward the sun. So he became one more human unit in the great migration of his time, and he carried the long pilgrimage of his people one step farther, to a land where only a few of his kind had gone before him. When he left New York, Leo was twenty-eight years old, with a weak lung, a bad cough and three hundred dollars in cash.

---

3. Eusebio Velarde of Santa Fe was a barber and one of the many Mexicans of the peon class who had profited by the American conquest. His father had lived on the great Perea estate and had been valued for his skill in shearing sheep. Eusebio had applied the same talent to the hair and whiskers of the American Army, with the result that he owned a good house and had money in his pocket. At sixty he was a wiry, active little man. He and his fat wife Teresa had raised five sons, all of whom had married and moved away, so that they were lonely at home.

This last was a fact which proved important in the destiny of Leo Mendes. When he got off the stage at the Santa Fe Plaza, he was a sick and exhausted man. The terrible shaking of the journey across the plains had started him coughing and a paroxysm struck him as he stood there in the plaza. He sat down on a wooden bench, gasping for breath, staring at the blood on his handkerchief—an exotic figure, with his sallow face under its heavy mop of curls, and his tight city clothes. Small boys gathered first to stare at him and then the Velardes happened along and stopped to look, and he heard the woman speak that invariable word of compassion: "Pobrecito!" It meant literally "poor little thing," but Mexican women applied it to all suffering creatures, human and otherwise. The Velardes conferred apart for a moment, then the man came and took him by the arm, helped him up, and said, "Come with me."

Leo had money in his pocket. He could have gone to the fonda, as other travelers did. But just then he needed friends even more than he needed food and shelter. For ten days he had sat staring at a wilderness, longing for everything he had left behind, and then the stage had rolled into this strange little town where almost every man he saw wore a weapon or carried one in his hand and most of the women looked funereal in black shawls hooded about their heads. He had dreamed of warmth and sunshine, but in March, Santa Fe was cold, with muddy snow on the streets and a sharp wind blowing. Then these people had come and lifted him up in body and spirit. It was not an unusual thing for a Mexican to do, but to Leo it seemed an act of Providence. He felt as though in a strange land he had found something of home.

He had learned enough Spanish so that he could speak his thanks after a fashion. He let the Velardes lead him home, insisting only that he could carry his own bag. They took him to their clean whitewashed house, and Eusebio gave him a big drink of native brandy, while Teresa cooked eggs and tortillas for him. After he had eaten he could barely keep his eyes open, and they put him to bed on a pallet of sheep skins covered with a Navajo blanket.

So Leo Mendes was introduced to the society of the common Mexicans, and he found himself surprisingly at home in it. These people, like his own, had a history of oppression. They had the same quick compassion and feeling of responsibility for each other, the same mordant humor and fatalistic outlook. He was not one of them, but they treated him as though he were, and he could understand and appreciate them. He lived with the Velardes as long as he was in Santa Fe and returned often to their house after he took to the road. He soon found that any offer of money would be an insult, but that gifts were welcome, and he hunted the stores and markets for what they could use. Teresa soon was calling him her son. Before summer he knew enough Spanish to carry on a conversation, for he was quick to learn.

4.Santa Fe then was a boom town because it was both an American Army post and the terminus of the wagon trade which had been growing steadily for years. On days when wagon trains arrived the plaza and the narrow streets leading to it were crowded with wagons and six-mule teams, and the air was full of dust, bilingual profanity and the deadly crack of bullwhips. At night the town was a flower of sin and passion. Gambling was its leading nocturnal industry. Leo was amazed to see gaudily gowned women, black robed priests, army officers in uniform and buckskinned hunters all bucking the monte and faro games in the long narrow adobe rooms, hung with flaring lamps, and in the famous Barello place, with huge chandeliers. He was amazed, too, at the piles of gold and silver that lay on the tables, in five or six different kinds of coinage, and even in the form of raw dust and nuggets. Besides the games there were bailes every night where soldiers and Mexicans danced with brown-skinned girls on the sanded floors. Leo saw two men fight with knives over a girl, and one of them fell and was carried out limp and bloody. Every soldier seemed to have a Mexican girl. It was the common joke of the post that to learn the language you had to sleep with your dictionary. Coming home late one night Leo saw a soldier and a Mexican girl grappling on the ground in the dark plaza, and the guttural fury of their desire left him shaken and disturbed. The place seemed overcharged with youth and energy, with passions engendered by the sudden conjunction of two races, erupting into lust and battle, as though conqueror and conquered struggled violently to become one.

Still sick and thin, short of breath by reason of the altitude, Leo wandered about Santa Fe day and night, fascinated,

observant, bewildered, feeling alien to its very spirit—to its
explosive violence and noisy haste—wondering what place it
held for him. There was just one thing he could do here. He
could get a job in any of the stores as a clerk or bookkeeper,
for all of them needed help. The stores were long, dark adobe
tunnels and he repugned at the thought of burying himself
in one of them. All his life had been indoors and there he
had nearly died. Although he feared the wide wilderness he
loved the sun, and he had an abiding intuition that the sun
was his salvation. He felt best sitting in the plaza on bright
mornings, watching the business of the town. The blue sky,
the slightly intoxicating air, faintly perfumed with wood
smoke, the sunshine that seemed to reach down and caress
him like a great warm finger—these he loved. He wanted to
stay in the sun. He also wanted to remain free. The bondage of
a job appealed to him no more than did its immolation. So he
moved inevitably toward the idea of becoming a peddler. In
this country if a man was not a fighter then he could only be a
trader, and only by taking the road could a trader remain in
the open.

Leo went about this business with the inquisitive patience
which was always part of his strength. He learned that some
pack peddlers went about among the Mexican towns but that
few of them got far from Sante Fe and Albuquerque. He
saw no reason why he should not work the whole of the upper
valley as far south as Socorro. He knew he was not strong
enough to carry a back pack, nor would one serve for so long
a journey, so he went to Burro Alley and made a study of
burros, learning to ride and pack one. It was his first intimate
contact with the animal world and he was astonished to discover that he had a fellow feeling for burros and got along
with them well, whereas high-headed prancing horses filled
him with alarm. He visited also all the traders and learned
what his stock would cost him and what profit he could make.

It was not hard to learn what he could hope to sell that was light enough to carry: cotton cloth, needles and thread, knives and scissors, a few simple remedies, pictures and images of deities, saints and prelates—these were the standard merchandise.

His decision and all his plans were made before he told the Velardes he was going, for he knew they did not want to see him go. Teresa sat shaking her head at him and wagging her finger.

"No, no, no!" she said. "In the south the Apaches still raid the valley. You know that. And there are bandits! Did they not hold up the El Paso stage last spring? You must not go!"

Leo was properly afraid of Apaches and bandits, but he had the self-assurance of a man who has carefully considered the facts. He knew there were villages and ranches every few miles in the well-settled upper valley, and that travelers for the most part went safely enough. He doubted the road was any more dangerous than the streets of Santa Fe on a Saturday night. And he had also the courage of his fatalism. If there was a bullet waiting for him somewhere he could only go to meet it.

Eusebio also protested, but more mildly than his wife. He admired courage and recognized the right of a man to take his chances. When he saw that Leo was quietly determined, he fetched from a chest one of his most valued treasures. It was a single-barreled pistol about a foot long with a wide bore, a polished hardwood stock, engraved locks and a huge hammer sitting ready above a bright copper cap. He presented it to Leo butt first.

"You must take this," he said firmly. "Then when the Apaches come, you can fight!"

Leo lifted his right hand, palm out, in a spontaneous gesture of refusal and aversion. It was a moment of self-discovery to him. He knew at once that he was more afraid of this in-

strument of destruction than of any savage or robber whatsoever. He knew he would never carry a weapon or lift
one against his fellow man. This beautiful tool, ready to belch
death, was to him the symbol of everything he feared and
instinctively repudiated.

"A thousand thanks, Eusebio," he said. "I cannot deprive
you of it and neither could I use it." He laughed at himself.
"When I see Apaches coming," he said, "it will be a race, not
a battle."

---

5. South of Santa Fe lies a wide barren mesa,
made of darkly molded lava, sparsely decorated with blue
sage, yellow-flowered rabbit brush, and a few scraggly juni-
pers and piñons on the higher parts. The canyon of the Santa
Fe river cuts through it, and the old road follows the canyon,
but the shorter way was to take the route across the mesa
and descend by a winding trail to the little town of La Bajada.
It was then still another ten miles before the traveler reached
the Rio Grande at the Pueblo of Santo Domingo.

When he set out upon his career as a peddler, Leo was
advised to take the short cut across the mesa, and it was bad
advice for him. On the canyon road he would have passed a
few houses, but on that blustery October day the mesa
stretched before him to a blue horizon of mountains without
a sign of life except a few high-sailing turkey buzzards. He
stopped and stared at the scene before him with a dismay
that bordered on despair, asking himself if he could face life
in such an inhuman void. Men who are born to wide spaces
learn to love them, but he was a child of crowd and pavement
and intimate incessant human contact. It took all of his courage to set his face against this emptiness and push his burro
slowly across it. For one thing, it seemed endless, like the

space beyond the stars. He found it hard to believe he was ever going to get anywhere, felt as though he might be doomed to toil forever on the treadmill of the wheeling earth.

It was his feet that first took his mind off the size and hostility of the universe. Knowing little of walking or footwear he was thinly shod and both lava and obsidian cut like knives. He became aware that his shoes were going to pieces, that his feet were bruised and aching. He sat down to rest but soon saw this was a mistake, for he quickly chilled and stiffened, so that it was hard to start again. Then late in the afternoon the wind became a gale, blowing straight in his face, carrying a burden of coarse sand that stung his skin and blinded his eyes. It seemed to him that any human antagonist would have been better than this brutal conspiracy of storm and space and punishing rock.

His pace was painfully slow. Off to his right he saw to his terror that the sun was leaving him, poised on a black horizon of jagged rock. The western sky was briefly a red warning of disaster and then darkness and cold fell upon him together. He could no longer see any trail. Now he was only following his burro's rump, grateful for this one living presence and also for the fact that the animal seemed to know where it was going. It led him presently to the brink of a precipice, which might have been the end of the world, a dropping off place into some nether void, for all that he could see below. But there was a narrow trail here, cut into the face of the cliff in some places as though it had been chipped out with a giant chisel. Leo shamelessly seized hold of his burro's tail, feeling that in this extremity he had to cling to something alive. They descended very slowly, with zigzag turns, disturbing loose rocks that plunged rattling down the mountainside. As if in answer to this racket there came from below a confused chorus of staccato cries and long-drawn wails, shrill as though with some inhuman misery. It was the evening song of the coyotes

that lived on La Bajada hill, a sound that he was to hear often
for years and finally to love as a voice of the country, but now
it struck him as something terrifying and unearthly. His burro
paused and lifted its head, with ears cocked forward, and
Leo too stood listening. This whole journey had seemed more
and more like a nightmare, ending with a descent into some
inferno, and now, it seemed, he was greeted by a chorus of
fiends. It was too perfect, too theatrical for belief. Suddenly
he threw back his head and laughed, not mirthfully and
not knowing why. Then he shouted into the darkness, en-
couraged by the sound of his own voice.

To his surprise the chorus died away in a few yaps and
whimpers. He went on down the trail, feeling a little better
for this successful self-assertion, but not good. After another
painful half-hour, with his knees steadily weakening, he found
himself suddenly on level ground, crossing a strip of sand.
They forded a shallow stream, cold water soothing his troubled feet. Then he saw dimly before him the angular black
mass of an adobe house, and three lean dogs came bounding
and barking at him, circling about as though to surround him.
He stood stock-still, close to his burro, prepared to scramble
on top of his pack if necessary. At last a door opened and
a beam of yellow light revealed a man, who shouted the dogs
into silence and came toward him, slowly and cautiously.

"I am a peddler," Leo announced weakly. "I am very
tired."

The man stared at him a moment in amazement.

"Well," he said at last. "Come in," and turned back toward
the house, Leo following. He found himself in the usual whitewashed room, with its corner fireplace and scant homemade
furniture. His host was a young man with a very dark skin and
a crinkled Indian mustache. His wife presently came from the
other room, a shapely dark girl, hastily dressed in a blue
cotton shift with bare feet and a heavy mane of black hair

hanging loose about her shoulders. She greeted him with low-voiced Mexican politeness, but with surprise in her eyes. It was evident that neither of these people knew what to make of this late and sudden visitor with his exotic looks and alien accent, but hospitality was almost a religion to them.

"I have money," Leo said.

"It makes no difference," the man replied. "Sit down." He gestured toward a rolled mattress covered with a Navajo blanket just behind Leo. At the word "sit," his knees buckled and he hit the mattress with a helpless thud.

"Pobrecito!" said the woman, smiling for the first time. They both now understood that he was nearly helpless. The woman blew a low fire into life and put a pot of stew upon it, while the man went outside to attend to Leo's burro. He presently returned, dragging the pack saddle and panniers, which he deposited against the wall. With a mighty effort, Leo edged over to within reach of his baggage, searched with a trembling hand and brought forth a large flask of brandy—a parting gift from the Velardes. He uncorked it and held it out to his host, smiling weakly. The man waved it away.

"Drink," he said. "You need it."

Leo bowed, shook his head.

"After you," he said firmly. He had been in the country long enough to learn that he must never be outdone in politeness.

The man lifted the flask, took a long gurgling swig and handed it back, with thanks. Leo then offered it to the girl, who shyly refused at first, with a glance at her husband, then took a tentative swig, batted her eyes, drank a little more and burst into laughter. It was evidently a new experience to her. Briefly they all three laughed together, and laughter seemed to dissolve the strangeness and surprise. Leo lifted the flask to his lips and drank long and deeply, with tears in his eyes. The alcohol seemed to pour all through his body, spreading a welcome relaxation even to his fingers and toes, soothing the ache and twitch of his weariness, leaving him numb but content. The woman brought him stew red with chili and steaming hot, and he could barely keep his eyes open while he ate. When they unrolled a mattress for him he lay down fully clothed and went suddenly to sleep.

---

6. Two years after his first crossing of La Bajada mesa Leo was a famous man in his own world. He was known in every Mexican village and Indian pueblo between Santa Fe and Socorro, a distance of nearly a hundred and fifty miles. The rich and the mighty knew him not, but many hundreds of the humble knew him by his first name and watched for his coming. For Leo became a peddler extraordinary. Nothing like him had ever been seen before in these parts and nothing ever was again, so that long after he had left the valley he was remembered and talked about, and a traveler could follow the trail he had left in the minds of men.

Everything that Leo did was good business primarily and his motto was business first. He cultivated his customers with loving care because it was good business, and he brought to bear upon their humble wants a patient intelligence such as most of them had never encountered before. His approach to a village, perfected by trial and error, had become almost a ritual, seldom varied except when the weather made it impossible. He always carried candy for the children, and the children always first saw him coming down the road, announced his arrival with whoops and squeals, charged to meet him in a body. By the time he reached the plaza he had accumulated a retinue and almost everyone turned out to greet him. There was a rivalry, sometimes embarrassing, for the privilege of being his host for the night, and wherever he stayed a large part of the village would be there that evening. For Leo brought not only merchandise but also news, gossip and stories, all of which he collected with care and retailed with a practiced art. He brought the latest gossip from the neighboring village and he also brought the political news from Santa Fe. In an illiterate world of slow and painful travel he was not merely welcome, he was necessary. Stories of all kinds he picked up along the road and while he walked he perfected and embellished them, sometimes with more regard for art than for truth. When a soldier was killed by a grizzly bear, he gathered all reports with care and fought that bloody battle over and over, first in his own mind and then for his public. Funny stories he loved and the scandals of high life in Santa Fe, where the military was a threat to the purity of wives, he retailed with just the right touch of moral indignation.

When finally the need of his friends for entertainment and edification was satisfied, and he spread out his wares, he made himself even more indispensable. If a man or a woman needed something he did not have in his pack he would make a note of it and bring it on his next trip. He carried from the first a few simple remedies and this medicine chest he slowly enlarged and improved, consulting with an obliging army surgeon in Santa Fe about drugs and symptoms. In the later years of his peddling he carried even spectacles, finding that he could fit the nearsighted with lenses that suddenly enlarged their world, as though by magic. Always he carried one patent medicine labeled simply "painkiller." He knew it was heavily loaded with opium and he gave it chiefly to the old who were dying painfully of incurable diseases.

Most of his business was done in the villages at night, but he made a specialty of attending all fiestas. When the Corn Dance was held in Santo Domingo and the long rows of men

and women danced in perfect time to rumbling drums and a
deep-throated chant, he was there with his wares spread out
on a blanket in the shade and did business not only with
Mexicans and Pueblos but often with Navajos and Apaches,
who came from afar. He always stopped at Bernalillo when
they danced the Matachinas, and every year he saw in some
village the celebration of Día San Juan, the patron saint of
horsemen, when the young men stooped from their saddles
at a gallop to snatch at the head of a rooster buried in the
sand. He stopped also at the sheep camps when they were
close to his route of travel, sold knives and gun powder to
the herders and filled his belly with the good young mutton
they always had. Wherever he went he was welcome and he
had not an enemy in the world. His was the fortunate lot of
one who serves the needs of men and escapes their envy, for
to all of these people he was a homeless wanderer, whom they
could pity as well as patronize.

---

7. For a long time Leo himself had felt that
he was a homeless wanderer. Sick and weak at first he could
barely make his way from one village to the next. The blazing
summer sun more than once made him stagger like a drunk
until he could reach a bit of shade, and the terrible sand-
storms of winter sometimes forced him off the road. Often at
first he felt as though he fought a losing battle, but during
the first year of his travel he underwent a slow change in
body and spirit. He lost his cough, began to gain in weight,
and the growing strength of his légs amazed him. On a cool
autumn day he could do twenty miles and like it. He began
to love the road, first because it had given him back his life,
and he came to love it also for reasons more subtle and various.
At first it had seemed to him that he was nowhere at home,

and finally he came to feel that he was at home everywhere. He lived in the whole valley, had ten times as many friends as any sedentary man, and all of them assured him, "My house is yours." He had friends but he had no ties, for the wandering life is a life of endless escape—a fact which he understood better after he had left it. He was never caught in those tangles of feeling and obligation in which most men are entrapped. No one owned him and he made no claim on anyone. Routine had no part in his life, for every day was a new experience in a different place. When he returned to Santa Fe for a stock of goods, he found that he soon became restless for the road. Walking that had been a toil became a rhythm that soothed his feelings and tuned his thought.

The river ran beside the road, sometimes near it and sometimes nearly a mile away, looping from one side of the valley to the other, washing the feet of the sandhills in a narrow eroding current, then spreading out across the valley in a wide sandy flood plain, bordered on either side by a dense bosque of cottonwood and willow, deep green in the summer and yellow in the fall, with blue mountains standing over it. Bosque and mountains and river were a wilderness to him and he felt no affinity for them. It was the road he loved, with its stream of human travel, its frequent houses and villages. He would never have gone near the river except for the fact that most of the time he had nowhere else to bathe. A strict cleanliness had been one of the disciplines of his life and in this country it was not easy to keep clean. Especially in the hot weather the sun drove him to the river. In the spring it was often a growling muddy torrent two hundred yards wide, but in the summer it was slim and tame and the water gathered in clear pools with sandy shores. At first he stripped timidly, his body pale as a fish belly, washed himself quickly and got back into his clothes. But then he began to loll on the sand and let the sun redden his skin until finally he was deep brown all over and stayed that way from May until November. It seemed as though he had taken on the color of the earth and he came to feel that here beside the river the earth had taken him to her bosom.

When he lay still for a long time the country seemed to come to life all around him. Wild doves came on whistling wings, lit sometimes within a few yards of him to drink. Tiny spotted sandpipers skittered daintily along the sand bars. In early fall more than once a flock of ducks rushed down from the sky with a roar of power, set their wings and came to rest on the water. Shy jack rabbits showed along the edge of the brush, cocking their ears at him, and rarely he would glimpse a coyote, trotting across a sand bar or lapping at a pool. He had never known so much shy and beautiful life lay hidden about him, waiting a moment of quiet to show itself. He had a fellow feeling for it all, watched it with absorbed curiosity.

Experience is the only genuine revelation and his experience of the river was truly one to him. Mountains and deserts and empty distance still appalled him but this intimacy with sand and water, bird and beast, this discovery that sun and river welcomed him with a caress made him feel at home on earth as never before.

One more initiation he owed to the river and also to the small boys of a town called Pajarito. When he went for his bath that day to a place less than a mile from the village, he found the river high and muddy, looking dangerous to a man who could not swim.

He had stripped and was sitting timidly on the bank with his feet in the water when eight boys from the village came tearing through the bosque, whooping like a tribe of Apaches. They all knew him and hailed him as they shed their few clothes and plunged into the river, shouting, "Come on, Leo, the water is warm!" They all came up snorting, dog-paddled across a deep narrow current and emerged on a sand bar beyond, shouting again, "Come on, Leo! What's the matter?" Then all at once they grasped the fact that Leo couldn't swim, that he was afraid of swift water six feet deep. In the village they had always treated him with the deference due an adult and a benefactor, but naked by the river he was just one of the gang and the day of his initiation had come. They swarmed back across the water, beating it to foam, and seized him by both arms, three on a side, and two pushing from behind, laughing and yelling.

"Don't be afraid, Leo," one of them said. "We won't let you drown."

Leo was afraid but he knew that any protest or struggle now would be both futile and a social error. They dragged him out to the middle of the current and gave him a shove. He found himself fighting the water furiously with both arms, blowing and spouting while his delighted instructors shouted encouragement. When he went under the second time, they fished him out and pulled him ashore, and all of them rested on the bank. Diego Gonzales, a boy of about fourteen years, was the oldest of the gang and its informal leader. He addressed himself to Leo now in serious terms.

"You must practice now, Leo," he urged. "It is not right that a man should not know how to swim."

Leo did practice all summer, learning first a laborious dog paddle and finally a competent overhand stroke that enabled him to cut a current with ease. Throughout his learning he fought against his own fear. He was afraid the first time he dived deep and felt the sandy bottom with his hands, and afraid the first time he swam all the way across the river. Moving against his own fear had become a recurrent motive of his life.

8. The Mexicans made him learn to dance just as they made him learn to swim, and this too proved a perilous and difficult business. Bailes were held almost weekly in every village on his route, for all Mexicans love to dance. There was always one building with a wooden floor which would serve the purpose and every village had at least a fiddler, and usually a three-piece orchestra. Almost always the leading fiddler was a blind man. There in Pajarito he used to ride about the village on a white mule in the afternoon, fiddling as he went, to announce the baile. The women would always come first and sit on benches all the way around the hall, while the men crowded about the doorway. Every dance opened with a march around the room and then broke into a swift hopping waltz, the dancers close and nimble. When the music stopped all couples broke apart and the sexes went back to their separate spheres, but anyone present could dance with anyone else and on the dance floor no holds were barred.

Leo began going to bailes and standing near the door with the other men, partly because this was the only music he ever heard except when the military band played in the plaza in Santa Fe, and also because here he saw all the best-looking girls in their bright red skirts and fresh white bodices, with their arms and legs bare and flowers in their hair.

The girls were a growing problem to him. For a long time he had been too sick and weak, too tired at night, to look upon women with longing, just as sickness had seemed to deny his love in New York. So he had become a celibate man, as were many wandering men in the West of that day, some of whom did not see a woman for months at a time. But Leo saw women every day, yet knew they were not for him. The better he came to understand these people the more clearly he saw that he must address himself to the men and leave the women alone. For these were a highly erotic people with a strict morality, which was always violated, a pious people who sinned with passion and confessed and repented with passionate sincerity. Unmarried girls were guarded with fire-arms and sometimes locked up for safekeeping with ferocious dogs, but the boys and girls of a village nevertheless contrived to explore the wonders of love at an early age, as Leo had opportunity to observe. Men were always ready to fight for the purity and fidelity of their wives, yet adultery had almost the status of an institution. Husbands had to be much away from home and wives were sly and cunning.

Desire was not to be denied, and without sin how could there be repentance and divine forgiveness? To these people sin and repentance were the drama that kept faith alive and life exciting. It also made every community a network of intrigue and Leo knew he could not afford to become entangled in that. If once he became an object of jealousy or suspicion, doors would be closed to him, and even whole villages, for the stranger always enjoys less tolerance than the native. For him only one rule was possible—he could never permit himself to be alone with a woman.

It was customary for all the women and girls of a family, down to the age of fourteen, to embrace in public the male visitor who had the status of an old family friend. It was a definite step in his social progress when Leo found himself elevated to this privilege in the house of Fedro Gongora of Pajarito. Fedro had a widowed sister named Desideria, who showed a friendly interest in Leo from their first meeting. She was a plump, smooth, brown girl, full of laughter and good humor, light on her feet in spite of her weight. When she came forward one day and embraced him, the Doña Lisa Gongora followed suit and so did both her twin fifteen-year-old daughters, while Fedro smiled his tolerant approval. Leo

had seen this ritual of greeting performed before and he knew
it was a delicate business. The correct technique was to embrace the girls lightly and kiss them on the cheek if they
kissed first. To kiss one on the mouth or to permit the hand
to go astray would have been a gross and dangerous impro-
priety. Conscious that his business career was at stake, Leo
performed these ceremonies with the lightest possible touch,
with a restraint that was impeccable if not excessive. Desideria
evidently considered it so, for on his third visit after he had
achieved the privilege of an old friend, instead of bussing him
properly on the cheek, she bit him on the left ear when no one
was looking. Leo knew he was being chastised for his back-
wardness, for gross neglect of his social opportunities. He
laughed and made a mental note to beware of Desideria.
But it was Desideria who first dragged him onto a dance
floor. She saw him standing among the men about the doorway
and sent her young brother to summon him.

"Come now, Leo, march with me," she said. "And then you
are going to dance—do you hear?"

Leo heard with trepidation.

"But I don't know how to dance," he protested.

"Everyone has to learn," Desideria told him, as she en-
veloped him in her wide embrace. "One, two, three, four,"
she counted.

Leo did the best he could and better than he had expected,
while other couples stopped to watch and laugh and encour-
age him. Presently teaching Leo to dance had become a community enterprise. It was easy for him to learn. He had a
natural gift of rhythm and the same good feet and legs that
made him a mighty walker served him well on the dance floor.

Dancing like swimming seemed to add a new element to
his experience. After he had learned well he danced with
abandon, with a complete absorbed excitement. Every baile
seemed to start slowly and to rise in successive numbers to a

pitch of intense excitement, when the whole crowd truly moved as one, welded into an ephemeral solidarity by the magic of music and rhythm. When he was dancing, more than at any other time, Leo lost his abiding sense of stranger-hood, felt that he swam in a current of shared experience, flowing to a tune. But he did not escape his separateness for long. Often after a dance he found it hard to sleep and often next morning he would plunge into the cold river to wash away the disturbing memory of clinging, laughing girls.

9. In Santa Fe on summer nights he used to sit in the plaza. Every Saturday evening a Negro band be-longing to the American Army gave a concert, and this event was perhaps more appreciated by the populace than anything else the conquerors had done. The whole town turned out to hear the music. The rich and exclusive came in fiacres and coaches, the old crowded the benches, and the young prome-naded around and around the square, the men going one way, the girls the other, as is customary in all Mexican towns. If a man turned and walked with a girl and she permitted him, it meant they were affianced. But challenging glances and even quick words could be exchanged in passing without hazard of matrimony. Saturday night in the plaza was a mass flirtation. All the town's most gorgeous prostitutes were there, as well as all its finest ladies. The air was filled with the squeal and giggle of feminine excitement, with the perfume of femi-nine presence. Leo, sitting alone, or sometimes with his old friend, Eusebio Velarde, felt as though life was a carnival in which he had no part. For one thing, in Santa Fe women cost money and he was poor. By the time he had bought a new stock of goods and a pair of shoes and a present for the Velardes, with whom he always stayed, Leo had nothing

left. He was a good peddler but cash was scarce. He generally got back to Santa Fe with a few silver pesos, a little coarse gold, perhaps some pieces of turquoise that were worth money and rarely a few good furs. More bulky plunder he could not pack on his burro. It seemed as though he could never accumulate any cash. On the road this made no difference in his way of life, but here in Santa Fe he was bitten by envy. In particular he resented the Ricos, with their expensive-looking women, their silver mounted saddles and pretentious coaches. He was always glad to take the road again, to lose himself among the poor who made him welcome.

He never joined the parade around the plaza because he felt strange and shabby, and for a long time no woman gave him so much as a glance, but one woman did repeatedly capture his eye. She was a large handsome woman of indeterminate age, with a fine brown skin, heavy black hair and a deep bosom. She had the gliding walk of an Indian and also the perfect bearing. She might have carried a cup of water on her head without spilling a drop. She wore always a blue cotton dress, very clean and starched, a black silk shawl about her shoulders and turquoise earrings, set in silver. At a glance she looked like a woman of the people, but her silk shawl and her costly earrings set her apart. So, even more, did her strange manner, for she never looked right or left, never smiled and never greeted anyone. Proud and self-contained, she moved through the crowd as though it had not been there. Leo watched her every time she passed with intense and growing curiosity and also with a measure of fellow feeling. Like him, she seemed to have no part in the spirit of the gathering. Then one evening she turned her head and looked him full in the eyes. She did not smile or nod, just gave him a long cool stare and went her way, but she nevertheless gave him the feeling that he had been chosen, for he had never seen her look at another human. The next evening he saw her again, but this time he was sitting beside Eusebio Velarde and she did not give him a glance. When he asked Eusebio who she was, the old man turned and shook a warning finger under his nose.

"Don't you know?" he demanded. "That is Dolores Pino. She is a witch!"

Leo had heard much about witches and the evil eye in the past few years. He had been amazed at first to learn that nearly all Mexicans believed in witchcraft, just as they believed in ghosts. Those who had the evil eye could cause sickness and even death with a glance, and witches could ride the wind and could also turn themselves into animals. A crowing hen was more than likely to be a witch in disguise, and cats and owls also harbored these malign spirits. He knew that most witches were old and ugly women, but some were men and some were young and comely. Some he knew were persons of power, shunned in public but patronized in dark and secrecy for the potions and amulets they sold and the spells they could cast. This Dolores Pino, it appeared, must be such a person, for Eusebio was full of gossip about her. She was said to be the daughter of a Navajo woman and a young scion of the Pino family, one of the most aristocratic in the territory. This young Pino had captured a Navajo girl about sixteen years old and brought her home for his pleasure. Almost all of the old families had Navajo slaves and Navajos caught as young children became good Mexicans, but those past puberty were often untamable. This girl fought her captor like a wild-cat, and he had great sport subduing her to his desire. So the girl Dolores was born of rape and nursed on hatred. That was her legend. Moreover, her mother stole a horse and ran away when Dolores was a few years old. She proved as un-tamable as her mother had been, and refused to work, so that her lawful owners were not sorry when she left their house. To their great embarrassment she had kept their name and had made it notorious by her practice of witchcraft.

"Many of the Ricos go to see her," Eusebio assured him. "They say that she always knows all about anyone who comes to her door, even his most secret deeds and things he would hardly confess to a priest. And how does she learn all this? They say at night she becomes a black cat and prowls the streets and slips into bedrooms. Mind you, I tell only what I hear, but she is a dangerous woman!"

Leo nodded gravely.

"Why does she never look at anyone?" he inquired.

"Who would want to meet her eye?" Eusebio demanded. "It is an evil eye if ever there was one. They say that once in a long while she does look at a man, here in the plaza, almost always a stranger who knows nothing about her, and then he must rise and follow her—he cannot help himself. And they say also that those who follow her are seldom seen again."

"She must be a terrible woman," Leo said. He thought she must have cast a spell upon him, for he knew very well that if she ever looked at him again he was going to rise and follow her.

It happened the very next time he sat in the plaza, listening to the band. She passed him once without looking, but the next time she gave him that quick, hard stare, and when she turned away a faint smile flickered about her lips. He followed her at a distance, just near enough to be sure he would not lose her in the dark. When she had gone a little way along the Acequia Madre Road she stopped and looked back at him, apparently to make sure he was following. Then she left the road and disappeared in the shadow of some old apple trees. He supposed her house must be somewhere behind them.

Where she had turned he stopped and asked himself if he was going any farther. He believed nothing in witchcraft and he was not afraid of this woman, yet he hesitated there on

the edge of darkness and mystery as he had hesitated to plunge
into cold swift water. Then he saw a light shine through a
window behind the apple trees, and that decided him. He
made his way slowly down a dark, narrow path and knocked
on her door.

"Come in!" she called, and her voice was strong and hearty.

He pushed open the door and found himself in a small,
white, neat room with some very good Navajo blankets over
the bed and on the floor, and a large wooden image of the
Virgin of Guadelupe in a wall niche. The only other furniture
was a heavy wooden table and two chairs with rawhide seats.
Dolores Pino was kneeling before the corner fireplace, blowing on the flame and stirring something in a copper pot. She
threw him a smile over her shoulder.

"Sit down," she said. "I am making chocolate for you."
For an agent of the devil she had a very pleasant manner.
She worked at the chocolate for some minutes, beating it to
a froth with a wooden beater she spun skillfully between her
palms, then poured two cups, and gave him one.

"Thank you," Leo said. "How did you know I was coming
to your door?"

"I always know all about everyone," she said. "I have the
gift of second sight." She smiled at him. "I do *not* turn myself
into a black cat and prowl the town," she added.

"No, I never thought you did," Leo replied, sipping his
chocolate.

"But you have heard that I do," she told him.

"Yes," Leo admitted. "You are a famous woman."

"They tell many lies about me," she said calmly. "You
must not believe what you hear. I am a good and pious woman.
I go to church and confess my sins. I pay my tithes and give
to the poor. And I have never harmed anyone."

Leo nodded.

"But when you look at a man, he must rise and follow you," he said.

"I knew you would follow," she replied. "That is all."

"And why did you choose me?" he asked.

"We are both solitaries," she said. "We ought to be friends. Besides, there are few men I can trust, but I know I can trust you."

"But how can you be so sure?" Leo demanded.

"That I don't know," she said. "I simply see these things when I think about a person. That is why I am feared and hated, and that is why people who would not speak to me on the street come here and pay me good money."

"What else can you tell me about myself?" Leo asked. She laughed.

"I knew you would ask that," she said. "Everyone does." She pushed away her cup and went and got a large white bowl, half-filled with water, and a pot of ink. She poured a little ink into the water and bent over the mixture, staring at it intently for several minutes.

"I can tell you that you came to this country from a great city," she said. "I can see large buildings and great crowds of people. There you had a life wholly different from the one you live now. Also, you move toward yet another kind of life. Perhaps you are a man of many lives. You think now that you will go on walking the roads for a long time, but I see that soon you will stop somewhere and I see people coming toward you from all directions and from great distances, bringing you money and all kinds of other things. I am sure that you are a man of power."

"I can hardly believe in such good fortune," Leo said.

"Is it good fortune?" she asked. "People hate one for what he has and for what he can do. I have learned that over and over."

Leo laughed.

"I know nothing about that from experience," he said. "I have many good customers but none of them has any money and neither have I."

"No one has any money in this country," she remarked, "except the few rich and those who steal from them."

"I can't do any business with the rich," Leo said. "And I don't know any thieves."

"Maybe you will meet with some," she suggested. "Anyway, I am sure you will get money and also that you will rise in the world. I am so sure of it that I would be willing to bet on it."

"I have nothing to bet," Leo said. "And nothing to pay you for all this."

She smiled at him broadly.

"You owe me nothing," she replied.

For a long moment they sat looking at each other in a half-embarrassed silence, filled with a tension of suspense. Leo was acutely aware of her round, strong arms with supple wrists and large well-formed hands, and also of her smooth and perfect yellow-brown skin. He wanted to go and lay hands upon her, but somehow the table between them seemed a barrier he could not cross. He smiled, feeling a little foolish.

"Is that all you can tell me about my destiny?" he asked.

She laughed at him and bent over her bowl again.

"I can tell you that you will come here again tomorrow, just after dark," she said.

"And then?" Leo queried.

She shook her head in mock puzzlement, staring into her bowl.

"That I cannot tell you," she said. "I see nothing but darkness. And now you must go because I have a good customer coming, a young woman who is much in love and has much money."

10. Leo was restless all the next day. He sat in the plaza as usual, taking the sun and watching the people, but wishing all the time daylight would fade. As soon as it was dark he set out for the house of Dolores Pino, forcing himself to go slowly. He had felt sure she was making an assignation with him, but both doubt and desire had been growing in him all day long. It seemed to him now that he had become only the carrier of his seed, that his only object and errand in life was to go to this woman and pour himself into her. He had endured celibacy for a long time with a good deal of equanimity, even with some slight disdain for men who could not live without women, but now that a woman had tossed him a challenge, raised his hope, he seemed to be only a walking phallus in search of a home. He longed for this woman and he also damned her for making herself a mystery. He remembered that she had laughed at him, wondered whether after all she was only playing a joke. She had seemed all friendliness, but he knew there must be a great hatred concealed in her somewhere and a great need for revenge. Perhaps it was one of her revenges to lead men on and then elude them. He had heard of such women, and this was a strange woman. After all, he had been fairly warned against her.

It was a moonless night and the narrow dusty Acequia Road was dark and wholly deserted. It ran beside the great ditch that irrigated the gardens and orchards of the town and he could hear the swift current gurgling along behind its covert of willows. He found the footbridge she had crossed and saw the apple trees beyond and that was all. There was no light! He stopped, feeling at first as simply disappointed as a child denied his candy, and then a righteous anger against this woman who had fooled him. Obviously, she was not even there. He was about to turn away, but on second thought he decided to go and knock on her door, just to make sure. The door, to his surprise, stood slightly ajar. He knocked on it and stood listening, but heard no sound except a faint breeze in the apple trees. Something strongly impelled him to push the door open and enter. He stepped into solid darkness and a silence in which he could hear his own quick breathing. Then, after she had enjoyed his suspense for a full minute, he heard her laugh softly. He did not say anything but went groping toward the sound with slightly tremulous hands. She had made down her pallet and lay there naked, and when he put his hands upon her she did not laugh any more or say a word, but when he had stripped and mounted her she made a continuous guttural sound deep in her throat. It seemed to have in it nothing of her usual voice or of any human voice but to be a subhuman music of desire, of the pure and innocent lust that is common to man and beast. Between their embraces she lay silent, and when finally she spoke it was in her usual crisp and positive way, as though she had come out of a trance or up from some abysmal depth of abandon to resume her personality.

"Put on your clothes," she told him firmly. "I may commit carnal sin, for the flesh is weak and God will forgive me, but no man has ever seen me naked and none ever will."

"I admire your principles," Leo said.

When she lit her candles she was dressed from neck to ankle, but her hair, heavy and black as a mustang's mane, hung loose and wild to her waist. She looked remarkably pretty, Leo thought, and more than ever like a witch. She sat down and began deftly combing and braiding her hair, putting it all in perfect order, serenely repairing the damage of her fall from grace. She smiled at him broadly.

"You see," she said. "Just as I told you, you are a man of power."

"Thank you," Leo replied. He did not feel especially powerful at the moment. He felt weak, hungry, mildly happy and immensely relieved, as though he had been delivered of some burden that had become intolerable. But he was aware that he had discovered in himself a power he had not known before.

When she had finished her toilet Dolores produced a stew of venison, beans and red chili, which she warmed over the fire, and also a bottle of wine. They both ate largely and with great enjoyment, beaming at each other over their wine with the mutual gratitude and approval which is the mood of successful lovers. But there was something more than that between them. They were fellow spirits in a way that both of them could feel, though neither could have explained it. And Leo was aware also that this woman had quickened his destiny whether she had foretold it rightly or not. There was some kind of a power in her for which he felt profound respect.

When he rose to go she gave him her hand but did not kiss or embrace him. She was a flame only in the dark.

"When you are in Santa Fe again," she said, "sit in the same place in the plaza. I will know you are here and I will come."

She did not make any claim upon him, then or ever, but yet always welcomed him when he came. He understood well enough that she was deeply absorbed in her own life, a life she could share with none.

II. On the western edge of the valley, a few miles south of Albuquerque, a small village was built against the foot of a black lava mesa. It was the only town on his route where he had never sold a thing. As he approached he always saw a boy tending goats on the mesa above the town and the boy always descended and disappeared. When he entered the town he saw no one, and if he knocked on a door he got no response. In due course he had learned in other villages that this was a plaza de ladrones, a town of thieves, who lived chiefly by stealing sheep, and that they did not welcome strangers of any kind. He had learned also during his years of peddling that New Mexico, like the country across the border, was full of thieves of many kinds and that stealing enjoyed a measure of social tolerance. After all, the poor must live. Petty thievery was seldom severely punished and the thieves' market in Mexico, patronized and recognized as such, was a standing acknowledgment that larceny was half a privilege and half a crime. On its higher levels it was a profession with a certain social standing. The mounted bandits who stole cattle and horses and sometimes robbed coaches were popular heroes. They were the revenge of the poor upon the rich. For many years a bandit had operated on the road between Socorro and Albuquerque who specialized in holding up the coaches of important people and making them kneel in the dust to deliver their valuables. Such a man enjoyed none of the tolerance a sneak thief might claim. There was a price on his head, but he was greatly admired by the poor and could always count on them to feed him and hide him when he was in flight.

The greatest freebooters of all were the dreaded Apaches. For two hundred years they had been raiding all over New Mexico and Sonora. They took their share of the sheep every year, like robber barons claiming tribute. In Sonora they stole horses and mules by the herd, ran them across the river and sold them in New Mexico. Now they were few and hard-hunted but richer than ever. One of the few Apaches killed

by the American soldiers had on his person nearly two hundred dollars' worth of silver, gold dust and turquoise. The
Apaches even stole Mexican children and held them for ran-
som or sometimes converted them into good Apaches and
taught them to plunder their own kind.

So Leo lived and traded in a world of thieves, but he had
never encountered any thieves. No one had ever held him
up on the road and in the villages he left his pack unguarded
and it was never touched. He understood the reason for this.
He was poor himself and lived wholly among the poor and
served them as well as he could. Only the rich were proper
subjects for larceny in all its branches.

It had never occurred to him that he might do business
with thieves, at least until Dolores Pino had mentioned the
matter to him, and he had not given it much thought then.
It was more by accident than intention that he finally gained
an entrance to the little village at the foot of the black mesa.
He passed that way one afternoon in late summer when a
thunder storm was piling up in the west, booming its great
guns and flashing its white fire. It struck just as he reached
the plaza, beginning with a volley of bouncing hailstones as
large as marbles. A saddle horse tethered in the plaza plunged
against his rope in frantic terror. Leo knew that tied horses
often broke their necks in hailstorms. He ran toward the animal, drawing his pocketknife, and cut the rope, setting it
free. As he did so he saw a door open, showing a man in hat
and serape, knife in hand, evidently bent on the same errand.
The man beckoned him to the door.

"Many thanks," he said, offering his hand. "I am Marcos
Herrera." He was a tall, powerful man, grave and quiet-
spoken.

"I am Leo Mendes, the peddler," Leo replied.

"Yes, I know all about you," Herrera replied. "We do not

care much for peddlers here, but since you have come, let us see what you have."

When the quick storm was over Leo went and took his pack off his burro, which had found prudent shelter on the lee side of the house. He produced first the bottle of brandy which he always carried in case of sudden wetting, snakebite or social emergency, and each of them took a long pull and offered a short toast. Leo then showed Herrera a set of three butcher knives in different lengths, all of them carefully sharpened, for he never sold a knife with its factory edge. Herrera tested each blade with an expert thumb and was obviously impressed. After a little of the customary haggling he bought all three and paid for them with two silver pesos.

It was the first of many transactions. After that Leo stopped at the plaza de ladrones on every trip, and each time he penetrated a little farther into the life of the town, until he knew every man in it and even a few of the women. Moreover, each time he carried away a few silver dollars, so that he began to gather a small surplus of cash.

He had been calling there for six months when Herrera one day introduced a very dark stocky man with a huge black mustache, which completely concealed his mouth, so that his small cunning eyes seemed to be peering over an ambush.

"This is Reinaldo Griego," Herrera said. "He comes from Manzano."

As he took the man's hand Leo felt that this might be a meaningful introduction. For Manzano, a village in the mountains of that name twenty miles to the east, was another town dedicated to the art of gathering movable property. But the men of Manzano were of a different and higher order than the sheep thieves of the valley. They all rode horses and carried guns and were suspected of doing much business with other bandits from across the border who needed a market for wet livestock and other merchandise. Reinaldo had a

drink, rolled a cigarette and conversed politely about many
things, as is the Mexican custom, before he got down to
business. Then he produced from inside his shirt a beautiful
crucifix about ten inches high. The figure was pure soft silver,
mounted on polished tropical hardwood, trimmed with
mother of pearl. As Reinaldo put it in his hand, Leo knew
at once that it had come from far to the south and had probably passed through several hands since it left its owner. He
also knew that this was for him a fateful moment. He was
going to be asked to do something with this valuable trinket.
He knew that if he accepted, other commissions of the same
kind would surely come his way, for all the ladrones in New
Mexico were in touch with each other, more so perhaps than
any other people in the territory, and with their allies across
the border as well. For one thing, all of them belonged to
the sect of Penitent Brothers, which was a highly organized
fraternity. So if he took this bauble he would also take a long
step into a half-hidden world of cunning, ruthless men. He
knew they trusted him. It struck him as a mild irony that he
was becoming a confidant of thieves and a receiver of stolen
goods because he was so completely honest and trustworthy.
And if he refused? Well, then he would lose standing as well
as money and many doors would close in his face and he
might even become an object of suspicion. He knew these
men were ruthless toward those who betrayed them or might
betray them. He had heard that the Penitentes sometimes
buried a man to the neck in a nest of red ants and left them
to do their work. Also, it was easy to stop a bullet along a
lonely stretch of road. Not that he was afraid—no, he was,
not afraid to refuse, but could he afford to do so? What he
needed was time to think, but there was no time to think
except the minute or two that he spent looking at the crucifix,
polishing the silver with his handkerchief, pretending a great
and expert interest when in fact he was wholly absorbed in

his own inner conflict. Perhaps you will meet with thieves, she had said. Well, here they were. What comes to a man unsought seems to be always a part of his business.

"It is a beautiful thing," he said at last.

"What will you give me for it?" Reinaldo asked.

Leo laughed.

"I never have any money," he said, "except when Marcos pays me a few pesos."

"Perhaps you can sell it for me, then," Reinaldo suggested.

Leo nodded and tossed the trinket on top of his pack, hoping both his voice and his gesture suggested a casual mood.

"I will see what I can do," he said. "I have a friend in Santa Fe who may be able to help. I will leave the money here next time I come."

---

12. This was the beginning of a lucrative trade that grew in volume. He was amazed at the variety of plunder it brought to his hands—heavy Mexican jewelry of pure soft gold, some of it set with precious stones; silver filigree work and hand-hammered silver vessels of many kinds, from water pitchers to tiny cruets that held the oil used in the ceremony of extreme unction for the dying; knives and daggers with handles of mother of pearl and mottoes and designs engraved upon their blades; even a few vessels of the curious kind called Chinese cloisonné, bearing an intricate design of colored enamels. All of this stuff he took to Dolores Pino and all of it she sold for a good price, but she never told him where. So he became a broker who knew neither the origin of his goods nor their destination and he would have been most indiscreet to inquire about either. But he felt sure that Reinaldo was a link in some chain of trade that reached far to the south, for he knew most of those luxurious trinkets must have come from the rich Mexican cities—from Chihuahua, Durango, Monterrey and Mexico City. He suspected that most of it had been traded at the border for goods that came to New Mexico by way of the Santa Fe wagon trade and could not be purchased farther south. He had no doubt that all of it was either stolen or smuggled or both, but he was virtuously aware that he could not have restored any of it to its original owners if he had wished. And he was deeply impressed by the way this trade was pouring money into his hands, wholly unsought and unforeseen, except that Dolores Pino had told him it would come. Man's destiny is full of miracles but he is seldom aware of them as such except when they come in strange and surprising ways.

A few months later his growing reputation brought him another lucrative piece of business when a small, quiet Mexican approached him in the plaza at Socorro. This man, who gave no name except Pedro, revealed that he was an agent of the Apaches who had their stronghold in the White Mountains. They wanted knives, skillets, powder and lead, all of which Leo delivered to Pedro in Socorro, receiving payment always in gold. He came to understand that Pedro was a Mexican who had been captured by the Apaches as a child, had become wholly devoted to them and very useful as a spy and purchasing agent. He was the only Apache Leo ever saw but Pedro assured him he was known to all of them and that they would never molest him.

Dolores Pino had warned him that his good fortune might not make him happy and this was true. The money he was piling up in Santa Fe stimulated and disturbed him, filled him with a restless discontent. He had thought often of opening a store in the northern valley, perhaps in a town such as Pajarito, where he could do a small business with old friends.

But as his capital grew his ambition grew with it. In the northern valley he would be too close to the Santa Fe trade and to the powerful mercantile companies, operating their own wagon trains, who were well established in Santa Fe and Albuquerque. In Pajarito he would be just a petty merchant and now he saw the possibility of becoming something more than that. He lived in a world where capital was hard to acquire, but where anyone with even a little money had many opportunities. He had always been a modest man with no vanity and little self-confidence, but he had learned that he contained a kind of quiet power, that he could often get his way by patience and cunning without lifting either his hand or his voice. So he was no longer satisfied to be a petty storekeeper in the shadow of larger establishments and his growing ambition turned his mind inevitably toward the south. He knew that since the Confederates had been driven out of Mesilla, the whole of that region had been in a demoralized condition. The southerners had owned all the business in the lower valley, and no one had become well established there since they had been dispossessed. Then he learned all about the army post of Fort Selden, and the salt lake that drew Mexicans from a large territory, and he already knew that the border itself was a commercial asset of great possibilities. Plainly, opportunity lay to the south. But it was not easy to leave the pleasant and accustomed ways of his life as a peddler, to abandon all the friends he had made along the road. He understood for the first time how much he loved the valley and the river and all the villages where the children ran to meet him, and even more, his visits to Santa Fe when the band played in the plaza and music was the prelude to desire. He was pulled two ways and inner conflict was painful as the gripe. He had been walking the road as a peddler for five years and was thirty-three years old. If ever he was going to make a change, it was about time. But did he truly want to leave the ways and people he had come to love?

It was Dolores Pino who brought him to decision, though not in a way he could possibly have foreseen. He returned to Santa Fe that year in late July after an absence of more than two months, for he had spent much time in Socorro making inquiries about the south. He sat in the plaza that evening, listening to the music and confidently waiting. She had seemed always to know when he was there, but it was also her invariable habit to walk in the plaza on Saturday nights and to go to early mass on Sunday morning. Now for the first time since they had met she did not appear, and he was amazed at how deserted the plaza seemed without her. Next morning he went to the church and searched the kneeling crowd with care. She was not there either. He asked about her that night when he saw Eusebio Velarde, trying to make his inquiries sound perfectly casual, for he knew his old friend did not suspect his intrigue and would have been profoundly shocked if he had.

"No one has seen her for weeks," Eusebio reported.

"What do you think has become of her?" Leo queried, trying hard to mask the anxiety he felt.

"Who knows?" Eusebio shrugged. "There were those who wanted her away from here. She knew too much about too many people."

Leo was silent a long moment, remembering. She had told him more than once that she was hated and feared. He knew that men and women had come to her and asked her to cast a spell upon someone which would cause his death and that she had always disclaimed any such power. But she was believed to hold powers of life and death. Leo tried again to sound as though it were a matter of no consequence.

"Someone might have killed her then," he suggested.

"Yes," Eusebio assented. "Or someone may have given

her money to go. She could find her way across the border."

Leo asked no more, but the next morning he went to the little house on the Acequia Madre. As soon as he saw its half-open door, he feared that she was gone, and when he pushed the door open he was sure. The place had been stripped of everything except the table and the two chairs. The dust, the cobwebs and the flies had taken over, creating their own peculiar atmosphere of desolation. A deserted house has always a feeling of death about it and a deserted house where one has lived intensely is truly haunted. Leo felt as though he stood in a tomb where a part of himself was buried. If she had gone away would she not have left him a message? He felt sure she would have tried, but she could neither read nor write, and what messenger could she trust?

"Perhaps you are a man of many lives." He could hear her voice again speaking the words. He felt sure now that one of his lives had ended and that he must seek another.

I. The Leo Mendes establishment reached
the height of its growth and fame about three years after it
was founded. What had begun as a little one-room business,
trading with the Mexicans of Don Pedro and the surround-
ing valley, then drew its trade from Texas and Arizona and
Chihuahua, from the soldiers of two army posts, from Mexicans who came to gather salt at the nearby salt lake, from
prospectors who were working placer deposits on the Gila
and the Mimbres, from mysterious horsemen, both Mexican
and gringo, who had livestock to sell and needed grub and
ammunition. It was known also to wayfarers of many kinds
traveling the north and south route that followed the Rio
Grande. In the seventies this was a post road, guarded by
United States troops, and carried a weekly stage service from
Sante Fe to El Paso, besides a growing load of freight.

A good many men remembered the Mendes store in later

years and left some account of it in conversation and letters. One of these was a Major MacTavish who commanded the army post of Fort Selden only ten miles from Don Pedro. The major rode to the store one day on a shopping tour. Although his sutler had done some business with Mendes, the major had never before visited the store nor met its proprietor. Mendes waited upon him in person with quiet courtesy, supplied all his needs and then requested the honor of the major's company at supper. The meal was prepared and served by an old Mexican woman who answered to the name of Avandera and who seemed to be a gifted cook. The major remembered that the principal dish was a fricassee of young quail with rice and vegetables, that there was a lettuce salad, a custard of a kind peculiar to Mexican cookery, and a bottle of white wine that had traveled a long way in a wagon. The major had intended to ride back to the post shortly after supper, but he found himself comfortably seated in a rawhide chair with a large Mexican perfecto in his hand and a tumbler of a very old native brandy at his elbow, so that he was persuaded to linger until nearly ten o'clock. He found his host an entertaining man, with a slightly sardonic sense of humor, and one who kept himself well-posted by means of papers and magazines from the states and even from Europe. These periodicals were all from one to six months old, but the major was glad to accept the loan of a generous supply of reading matter in a country where the printed page was rare. He rode back to Fort Selden much pleased with his visit, reflecting that he might very well direct his sutler to call upon Mendes for beef and corn when he needed them, rather than go all the way to El Paso, which was four times as far. Doubtless the possibility of such an arrangement had occurred also to his host.

Mendes may have had a mercenary motive in his entertainment of the major but this was hardly true of another

customer who long remembered him, a prospector known as
Captain Sparks, although what he had captained and when
no one seemed to know. He was a man in his fifties, and one
of some education, who had spent a decade or more hunting
a famous lost mine in the Mogollon Mountains. He would
spend all summer and all of the autumn until snow fell wandering alone with his burro in the high country. For the winter
he would find a job at some ranch, and every spring he would
visit Mendes, who invariably received him as a guest and
supplied his grubstake and all his other needs for the season
of prospecting. He usually brought back a little placer gold
to pay on account, and when he found the lost mine Mendes
was to share equally in the treasure, but both of them understood that the mine was an obsession, a myth and a quest,
and that Captain Sparks was never going to find anything
except the end of his long and tortuous trail.

Captain Sparks was only one of many who came to
Mendes periodically, received whatever they needed and
rode away, leaving nothing but a promise. For the fame of
the store rested largely on the fact that its owner seldom refused credit to anyone, not even to a known bandit or smug-
gler from across the river. Some of these men he never saw
again and never knew whether they were still alive, but his
policy of credit to all must have paid in the long run. At
least Mendes was certainly not getting poor.

Sparks and others described his establishment, which was
all in one great sprawling adobe house with the store at the
front and Mendes' living quarters on the opposite side of a
shaded courtyard. Behind this was a corral with a ten-foot
adobe wall and a great wagon gate, where his customers fed
and stabled their horses. Mendes had three clerks, two men
and a woman, all bright young Mexicans who lived in the
nearby valley. It was said that Mendes himself, finding no
literate population within his reach, had taught his staff to

read, write and do simple sums. All of his visitors remembered also his wagon master, Aurelio Beltrán, who was on the road more than half the time between Don Pedro and Santa Fe, hauling loads of hides, pelts, dried chili and other products of the valley to the northern market and returning with goods for the store. Beltrán was a truculent and commanding wagon master, a hard driver of mules and men and a terror to thieves and marauders. He established his reputation as a fighter by beating off a small band of Apaches singlehanded, using two of the new model 1873 Winchester repeating rifles with such speed and skill that the Indians thought they had run into a cavalry patrol.

Mendes himself was described as an incessantly busy man from early morning until his store closed at night, but he flatly refused to discuss business with anyone after dark. His evenings were devoted to reading and hospitality.

2. Leo had made that rule in self-defense long before the period of his greatest business success when MacTavish and Sparks knew him. At first the store had been a quiet and peaceful place, with perhaps a dozen customers a day and plenty of time for the long conversations which had always been the prelude to business in his peddling days. He had missed the long road beside the river, the incessant change and movement of his wandering period, but otherwise his life seemed not very different for more than a year. Then the business began to grow, rapidly and unaccountably. Customers multiplied and came from farther and farther away and were of more different kinds and wanted more different things. It became necessary to buy first one wagon and then two and finally three, and also to make an annual visit to Santa Fe himself. He had to take over herds of cattle and

horses and then to find a market for them and men to handle
them on the range and on the road. In his office he received
an endless stream of creditors, sellers and petitioners. He
became a banker in spite of himself, lending money to young
men who wanted to buy a few cattle or goats and set themselves up as independent rancheros. He was asked to finance
weddings, funerals and fiestas. More and more people came
to him daily with their troubles, their needs, and their ne-
gotiable assets. To his considerable surprise, he had become
successful and success anywhere and any time is always the
same thing—a sudden focusing of human energies and passions and demands upon its victim. Leo had become the
center of a growing human constellation. Did he own the
store, he sometimes asked himself, or did the store own him?
He could no more escape it now than he could jump out of
his skin. He knew his vagrant years had unfitted him
for all this confinement and pressure and responsibility. In
a corner of his office he kept the hardwood cane he had
always carried on the road, using it alternately as a walking
stick and for burro riding, and he used to look at it once in a
while with nostalgic longing. He had also the leather money
belt he used to wear, and he kept it full of gold coins, with
some vague feeling that a time might come when he would
buckle it on and pick up his stick and walk away from his
laborious triumph. But this, he knew, was only fantasy. Fate
had anchored him here just as surely as it had so long kept
him moving.

3. It was in the third year of his growing pros-
perity that he bought a five-gaited Kentucky saddle horse
for three hundred dollars and learned to ride it. Nothing
had more surely marked him as a man of the common peo-

ple than his seat upon the rump of a jackass and nothing more surely marked his rise out of that class than his Kentucky gelding, his fifty-dollar saddle and the polished half-boots that he wore when he rode.

He had not found this ascension altogether easy. When he saw that he had to have a horse he commissioned Aurelio Beltrán to buy one for him.

"It must be a very gentle horse," Leo explained, "but not a small horse." He knew that dignity as well as transportation was involved.

Aurelio hunted for weeks before he found a six-year-old bay of pure Morgan strain which had been imported by an army officer and found to be not quite tough enough for the work of chasing Apaches across a desert.

"I have tried this horse for three days," Aurelio assured him. "He won't buck—you can't make him. He won't kick, he won't pitch, he won't shy. He will eat out of your hand, stand without tying when you drop the reins on the ground and come when you whistle. He was raised as a family pet and a child of three could ride him. Now let us see you mount."

Despite all these assurances, Leo contemplated his new steed with some misgiving. The horse certainly had a mild eye but he looked incredibly tall.

"I have never ridden anything bigger than a burro," he explained.

Aurelio laughed at him

"Well, you can't afford to ride any burros now," he said. "You are a patrón, a Rico, a hidalgo. You must ride a big horse."

In the face of this irrefutable argument, Leo hoisted himself into the saddle and began his career as a horseman in a slow walk. But he soon became accustomed to his high place. In his burro-riding he had learned the balance which is the

prime essential of good horsemanship and he became a good
horseman with an erect and graceful seat. As he cantered
magnificently down the road, poor men lifted their hands
and bowed their heads in a greeting that was also an obei-
sance. These were the same people, or at least the same kind
of people, with whom he had shared beans and chili, squatting on the floor, whose wives and daughters had bussed him
on the cheek, who had taught him to dance and swim. Now
they addressed him invariably as Don Leo. Quite suddenly,
as it seemed to him, he had become a Rico, a patrón, a gentleman on horseback. Poor men now treated him with deference,
and behind that deference, he knew, was fear, for many of
them were at his mercy.

He had truly risen out of one class without rising into another, for he was no part of the society to which the Vierras
belonged. On his high horse he sat alone. He did not feel
lonely because he struggled with people all day long and
was often dead tired at night, but he was aware that he had
achieved a peculiar isolation.

Riding became incidentally an escape from the bondage
and pressure of his business. In long hot summer afternoons
he would steal an hour and ride down the river to an isolated
spot where a deep pool and a wide sand bar waited for him
like a moment out of the past. He rode there at a fast gallop
and sometimes briefly at a dead run, scaring himself with a
burst of speed that pummeled the earth and tore the air. He
rode fast because he had little time to spare but also because
he loved the feeling of flight. When he had stripped and
plunged and sprawled naked on the earth he felt as though
he had shed the circumstances of his destiny along with his
clothes. It was a relief to be at one with sand and water and
to hear again the sweet untroubled voices of the wild.

4.The first man to invade his social isolation was the Padre, an Italian named Orlando Malandrini. For more than a year before they ever became well acquainted Leo had known the Padre by sight and as a customer in his store. Padre Orlando was a small man with a comfortably bulging stomach, a smooth yellow skin, a bald head fringed with white hair, and small dark eyes of a peculiar liveliness and intensity, which seemed somehow out of keeping with his leisurely gait and his soft speech, as though they had been the living coals of some half-smothered fire. Leo knew a good deal about the Padre by reputation. He was famous for his eloquence, and people came from long distances to hear him preach. He was known also for his ability to extract money from the rich for the benefit of the poor. Especially when there were weddings and funerals to be financed the Padre would demand the money in the name of God, and few had the courage to refuse him. The Doña Maria Guadelupe, although she had the reputation of being a somewhat hard woman in most matters, was a great friend of the Padre, aided his charities and was known to entertain him frequently. But the most important of his friends was the great Archbishop Lamy of Santa Fe, who had come to New Mexico in 1850, had found the Church in a deplorable state of corruption with some of its priests openly living in sin and acknowledging their offspring, gambling in public and getting drunk. The Archbishop had reformed the Church, restoring it to a position of great respect and authority and Orlando Malandrini had been his chief assistant here in the south. He still made occasional trips to Santa Fe to consult with the Archbishop. Both of them now were old men and their reform of the clergy had long since triumphed, but they worked

incessantly to improve the morals of the people—a much more
difficult business. For a long time it had been customary for
many of the poor to live together without benefit of clergy
because marriage was such an expensive business and a Mexican wedding is a feast as well as a ceremony. Here in Don
Pedro the Padre labored incessantly to have people properly
married, to bring the young girls of his flock to the altar in
a state of purity and dedication to God. If the families involved could not afford a proper wedding then the Padre
would go to some person of substance, traveling as far as
El Paso or Mesilla if necessary, and demand the funds to
finance virtue and save souls from purgatory.

It was such an errand of God that brought him first to
Leo's office. One Mercedes Espejo, aged sixteen, was about
to marry Bartolomé Lopez, who was twenty-five years old
and owned fifty goats and several acres of land. The Padre
told him all about Mercedes and Bartolomé, and especially
what a good girl Mercedes was and how her parents had
labored to keep her pure. Leo listened gravely, although he
already knew more about both of them than the Padre did.
He knew that Mercedes was the only unmarried daughter of
an old widower, Manuel Espejo, and that he had truly labored
to keep his daughter pure, going so far as to lock her up
with a savage dog when he had to leave her at home alone,
and also on one occasion shooting at one of her suitors in
the dark with an old bell-mouthed buffalo gun, which roared
like a cannon and almost scared the young man to death.
He knew all about young Lopez, too, for he had loaned him
the money to buy goats, including a fine Angora buck. He
had confidence in the youth and he also knew that Lopez
was already as far in debt as he could afford to go.

"I am not asking for charity," the Padre explained. "I am
only asking that you give the young man enough credit so

that he can have a proper wedding in the church. I will see that he makes good on his debt."

"And why should you not ask for charity?" Leo queried. He felt that this was a time to make a friend rather than a profit.

"Well." The Padre was hesitant for the first time. "I have never seen you in church. If you were one of my own it would be different. I suppose you are not a Catholic."

"No," Leo admitted. "My parents were Jewish and I don't know what I am except a storekeeper. But I would like to help you and also Bartolomé."

"A Jew!" The Padre sounded both surprised and pleased. "You remind me greatly of my friend Bernard Rosenfeld in Santa Fe. He too is a Jew and now a very rich one. When we were finishing the cathedral there, he gave us much money. He always said he did not know whether he believed in God but that he was sure he believed in the Archbishop."

The Padre laughed a soft laugh that gently agitated his paunch. It was evident that he had a very tolerant attitude toward unbelievers in general and munificent Jews in particular.

"Where do you come from?" he inquired.

"I was born in New York," Leo said, "and lived there until I was twenty-eight."

"New York!" The Padre repeated the words and Leo knew by his tone that it had stirred memory and feeling. "You must have lived then downtown on the East Side."

"Yes," Leo agreed. "I grew up near the corner of Broadway and Canal Street."

The Padre shook his head, smiling.

"Think of that!" he exclaimed. "I once lived within a few blocks of you. I must have come to New York about the time you were born. And what brought you to this far place?"

"I got sick," Leo explained. "I fled for my life."

"And I too," the Padre said. "I would never have come if I had not been desperately ill. I came to get well. I got well, and I have been here ever since."

The Padre spoke the last words with a touch of sadness, with something like wonder, as though it was a little incredible that he still was in Don Pedro. It was evident that their talk had stirred deep feelings in him. He brought himself back to business with a quick jerk of his head.

"I am taking too much of your time," he said. "You will let Bartolomé have what he needs then?"

"Yes," Leo agreed. "It will have to be a gift and the gift will have to come from you." He smiled. "I can't afford to be known as one who gives away merchandise."

"I understand perfectly," the Padre said. "Have it your own way, and I thank you in the name of God. Now I must go."

"But come back?" Leo asked, as he gave his hand.

"Never fear," the Padre said. "I will be back. I am sure we have much to talk about."

5.Much talk they did have from that day on and it was a great boon to both of them. Soon the Padre was inviting Leo to supper and he was returning the hospitality as best he could, though he could never quite equal the Padre as a host. The holy man was truly both an epicure and a gourmet. It appeared that his father had been a restaurateur, both in the old country and in New York, so that Orlando had been taught to consider food as an art from childhood. He was especially fond of game and the valley abounded in delicious birds. Although he disliked to kill even an insect himself, he was always sending his gardener with a shotgun to gather the young doves in September and the blue quail when they were prime about a month later, and ducks and geese along the river. From Aurelio Beltrán he purchased turkeys and venison. He even knew where to find mushrooms and he imported his olive oil from New York. His cellar contained many good wines, most of them gifts from his admirers, but his favorite beverage was the red wine made in the valley which he aged in his own casks.

The old woman who did his housework was a creditable cook but the Padre did most of his cooking himself. He cooked with intense concentration, never saying a word until the meal was on the table, and then he ate slowly, as do all good eaters, with the sincere delight of one who knows the value of flavor. Leo, who had relished his beans and red chili for so long, his cheese of goats' milk and his cold tortillas, now found himself considering with care just how long a duck should be hung before it was put in the oven, and also how many years it took for a native wine to become truly potable. He discovered in himself a taste for luxury and felt again, as he had when first he mounted a horse, that he was in process of becoming something else.

His conversations with the Padre also created a new kind of awareness in him, although at the same time they took him back to the past, for they reminded him of those adolescent years when his father had talked to him about Spinoza and read to him the great poetry of the Old Testament and of Maimonides. He had hardly read a book or thought of an idea for years, but now, under the stimulus of wine and the Padre's eloquent talk, he found himself trying to explain how the pantheism of Spinoza had entered his young consciousness and how he had rediscovered it when he learned to swim and lay naked upon the earth and felt his kinship with all living things. The Padre listened tolerantly and nodded sympathetically and poured red wine. Like all Italians, he had a great capacity for wine, liked to sit and sip it slowly

all evening. When he was properly mellowed he would sometimes talk of his youth in New York.

"I was a wild one then," he said more than once. "I was a
shameless young sinner."

He never quite brought himself to be specific about his
sins but it was evident that he loved to remember them. Leo
came to understand his story, little by little, as much by
inference as by direct revelation. He gathered that the young
Orlando had fallen in love, that his beloved had died and
that he had suffered great sorrow and also great illness. It
was then, in his early twenties, that he had determined to
enter the Church, inspired largely by the writings of St.
Francis, who like himself had tasted sin before he came to a
true knowledge of God.

All of this helped Leo to understand the Padre. It explained the rare combination of piety and broad tolerance
which he brought to his holy duties and showed when he
talked about them.

"Of course, all these people are sinners in the eyes of the
Church," he admitted. "There is not much excuse for the rich,
except that their ancestors brought their habits and customs
from a medieval Spain which was very corrupt and partly
Moorish and that nothing here has ever changed. They are
all good Catholics but their attitude toward women is as much
Mohammedan as Christian. The poor, of course, are nearly
all at least half-Indian and some of them are wholly so. The
Pueblos all have churches and they welcome the Padre and
kneel to God, but they also dance to their pagan deities and
worship the serpent as a sacred symbol. Most of the peons are
not much better. They love to confess, just as children do,
but the pagan blood is strong in their veins. They find it very
hard to understand the doctrine of original sin."

"I must admit that I do also," Leo said. He spoke with a
certain diffidence but with a feeling that he must conceal

nothing from his friend. It seemed as though the Padre had become to him a father confessor, even though he had no sense of sin and nothing to confess but his unbelief. "If everything happens as it must, whether you call it fate or the will of God, how is anyone to blame?"

"Yes, yes, I understand your viewpoint perfectly," the Padre assured him. "Let me fill your glass."

It was a characteristic reply. The Padre would listen with unruffled tolerance to anything Leo chose to say, but he would never argue about any point of doctrine or belief, as though those sacred matters lay beyond the reach of reason. Often he would merely nod and smile and pour wine.

Leo had known the Padre nearly a year before he discovered that the man was writing a book, had been writing it apparently for about twenty years. It dealt with the Seven Golden Cities of Cibola which the early explorers had sought in New Mexico. So far as they had any reality the cities were identified with the adobe villages of the Moquis, which had nothing golden about them except the sunlight that fell upon their ancient walls. But the Padre had done much research and had discovered that this legend of golden cities had existed in Europe before America was discovered. The explorers had brought their dream and their quest across the seas along with their arms. All who had sought the golden cities had encountered failure if not tragedy, but it was the Padre's theme that they all lived greatly and achieved much for the glory of God while the dream was alive in their minds.

It was the great moment of their friendship when the Padre consented to read some passages from his book. He read only fragments, and Leo came to believe the book existed only in fragments, that the Padre would never finish it because if he did his own dream would be ended. But the parts he read were eloquent and touched with a vividness that

made the past live again. Leo was moved to question and
protest.

"I cannot understand how you have been content to live
in this forgotten village," he said. "You have great gifts and
surely here they are wasted. Why have you stayed?"

As soon as he had spoken he regretted it, fearing that his
questions had been impertinent, but the Padre merely smiled
and nodded and put the question back to him.

"Why do *you* stay here?" he inquired. "You are a man of
ability who might find your place in a larger world. Well, I
will tell you why we both stay—because it is easy, because all
these people are children and do our bidding, because we
have power over many lives. It is not good! I have been
learning that for twenty years. A man needs to struggle with
his peers and sharpen his mind on other minds. Here we
sleep in the sun!"

Leo sat silent, aware that for the first time he was hearing
a confession from the Padre and also that what the man said
was true. Founding his store and building his business had
been a stimulating struggle, but it was true that the longer
he stayed here, the more completely the people were at his
mercy. He had taken over some part of the easy power the
Vierras had held, their peons were becoming his, and he
could easily fall into their soft and idle ways. The Padre's
words had a sound of prophecy.

"The longer you stay the harder it is ever to leave," he
said, "ever to face life again where life is hard."

The Padre believed that the Southwest laid a spell upon
men, such that it bound them forever to its soil, that many
came to regain their health or make their fortunes, expecting
then to leave, but never did. Leo knew from his own observation that this was true, especially of those who lived
almost wholly among the native people, and also of men who
became enamored of the wilderness. He knew that Captain

Sparks was an able man who had lost his heart to a country. Old-timers said if you stayed ten years you would never go back East. He knew too that men who became accustomed to the warm submissiveness of Mexican and Indian women lost all taste for the women of their own blood. In truth the whole country had a quality of warm submissiveness about it. You might struggle mightily for a while but in time you were conquered by sunshine, silence and sleep. Although Leo had worked hard, he had felt a quality in the country and the people which seemed to mock his effort. No one else ever hurried, no one ever sacrificed the good moment to the future, and the wide-horizoned hush of the barren land seemed in harmony with this wisdom of indolence.

"I remember how empty and even terrible this country seemed when first I came here," the Padre said. "I dreaded the long silent heat of the summers and the winter season when the great winds sweep the valley with sand. I felt lost and isolated, and so I set tó work to create a little world of my own. It was then I had a large cottonwood brought from the river and planted in the courtyard, so that I should have shade, and I planted also fruit trees and vines and made my own little Eden. I sent for books and papers and furnished my study to suit myself. I learned how to use the wines and foods of the country and to practice my father's art of cookery. Oh, I was kind to myself, much too kind, and I came to love this little world of comfort I had made to my own taste. Then came the period when I worked with the Archbishop and that was truly a period of some achievement. When it was over, I told myself, I would leave. For years I had believed that eventually I would go back to Rome, where I was born—to the capital of Christianity where a man might use all the ability he had. But then I became absorbed in the Seven Golden Cities and what is more beguiling to a reflective man than a studious solitude? So here I sat, poring over my papers, doing the work of God as best I could—and here I have sat ever since."

"Do you regret it, then?" Leo asked.

"I do not know whether I regret it," the Padre said. "You asked me why I am here, and I have tried to tell you. It is the first time I have told anyone. I do not know that I regret it, but I think one Orlando sits before you and there is another Orlando who never lived except in my imagination."

It was a warm summer evening and they were seated under the trees in the Padre's courtyard with a bottle of wine on the table between them. Beyond the walls lay the purple mystery of night and the wail of coyotes came faintly from the hills, but here in the courtyard was a little cosmos of friendship and feeling shared. The Padre filled their glasses and they both lit their pipes and sat silent for a long time, each absorbed in his own thoughts but confident of the other's sympathy. Then Leo rose and said good night and walked home slowly under the pale blue blaze of the great desert stars, feeling that he knew the Padre as never before but also that he had a new understanding of his own destiny. The Padre was truly a talented confessor. He had the gift of revealing people to themselves.

---

6. Another evening when they parted after dinner the Padre gave him an invitation, wholly casual in tone but filled with import for Leo.

"I am going to drink chocolate with the Vierras tomorrow afternoon," he said. "Would you like to come with me? I have the Doña Lupe's permission to bring you."

Leo stood silent for a long moment, much too long for good manners, while swift thoughts chased each other through

his mind. The Padre did not pretend that they had asked to
see him, said only he had the woman's permission to bring
him. He had never met the Don face to face since that day
two years ago when he opened the store, and the woman he
had seen only a few times across the counter. They would
receive the devil himself if the Padre had asked it. He had
come to understand that the Padre was the real ruler of the
community, not only because he was the vicar of God but also
because he was a man of quiet innate power. The Vierras
might own the earth but the Padre dominated the Vierras.
Solely because the Padre wished it, they would let him pass
their door. Well, it would never do to refuse.

"I will be very pleased," he said. "Thank you."

On the fateful afternoon he dressed himself with un-
wonted care, for most of the time he thought little of his
appearance. He put on a new suit of a fine brown corduroy
that a Chinese tailor in El Paso had made for him, and a
blue silk shirt and new tan boots of a very fine polished calf.
He had discovered in himself a taste for rich colors, just as
he had also come to like rich foods, as though money had
brought out some Oriental strain in his blood, converting
him into a mild voluptuary after the enforced asceticism of
his years on the road. He stood for a moment staring at himself in the mirror, and this also was no part of his habit. He
saw a rather handsome man with heavy regular features,
dark thick brows, slightly upturned at the outer ends, thick
black hair faintly touched with silver. It struck him oddly
that he looked like a rather devilish fellow, although no one
perhaps had ever felt less devilish. He noticed also that he
was a little bulkier than he used to be when he walked ten
to twenty miles a day. In fact, he did not look like Leo the
peddler any more than the peddler had looked like the pale
and desperate youth who fled the city. He stared at himself,

not because he was vain, but because his good appearance gave him confidence, and he needed confidence now. Then he made a face at himself, mocking his own image, and laughed a short laugh and went to join the Padre.

1.The Doña Lupe received them alone in the long Vierra sala with its gilt-framed mirrors on bone-white walls, its couches covered with Navajo blankets and floors spread with woolen rugs of native weave in black and white checks. A few red upholstered chairs, which had come all the way from St. Louis, and a long hardwood table seemed a little incongruous, but the room had dignity and was delightfully cool on a very hot afternoon. The Doña took Leo's hand for an instant and gave it a firm, quick pressure, which at once reassured and surprised him, for usually the Mexican handshake was limp as an empty glove. The lady then clapped her hands for chocolate and cakes and began chatting brightly with the Padre, leaving Leo merely to listen. In about fifteen minutes she contrived to reveal a great deal about herself—that she had gone for five years to a convent in Durango, that she knew French as well as Spanish, that she had read *Don Quixote* and *Gil Blas* as well as a good many French novels which did not have the complete approval of the Padre. All this was delivered adroitly, with no flavor of boastfulness, but Leo felt that she wanted him to know she was an educated woman in a society where many women, even of the best families, never learned to read. He also felt she was glad of his presence, if only because he was a new listener. With chocolate warming his stomach he began to relax and to feel that perhaps he had found a friendly house after all.

The atmosphere changed suddenly when the Don arrived late in the afternoon. He stood for a moment, staring at Leo with a most unmistakable expression of angry surprise. Then he turned and looked at his wife, still speechless, but Leo noticed a quick clenching and unclenching of his hands, as though it would have been a pleasure to throttle the woman or slap her, while she sat quiet with downcast eyes. Finally he turned to the Padre and extended his hand, then offered it also to Leo with limp reluctance, and sat down with an air of disgusted resignation. It was painfully clear the Don had not been consulted about this visit, but since Leo was sponsored by the Padre, it had to be accepted as the will of God. Conversation after that came slow and hard, and Leo presently rose and bowed himself out, feeling that his career in the society of the Ricos had begun and ended on that afternoon.

About this he discovered in the next few months that he was mistaken. His friendship with the Padre had definitely changed his status in the world, and so had his own growing importance as a man of business. A few weeks later he was summoned to the Padre's house to drink a cup of chocolate with one Don Tobias Barreiro of Mesilla, who occupied in that town a position of eminence and power similar to that of the Vierras in Don Pedro. He already knew Barreiro by reputation as one of the very few Mexicans who were good at business. Barreiro had made money by trading for copper from the Santa Rita mines, shipping it East and selling it at a good profit. He was a fat Mexican in his fifties with a twinkling eye and a hearty manner.

"When you are in Mesilla my house is yours," he told Leo in parting. "Next Sunday we are entertaining friends, including your friends the Vierras. We will be honored if you come."

The Vierras did not have social relations with anyone in Don Pedro except the Padre, but they exchanged frequent visits with the ruling families of Mesilla and El Paso and the valley that lay between, and they were also in touch with the best people of the northern valley where the Doña had many relatives. A few hundred families owned more than half the arable land in the territory, and all of these were known to each other and were further held together in a network of relationship that had been woven by intermarriage among them for two hundred years.

Leo found that now he had become a part of this society, in spite of himself and whether Don Augustín liked it or not. At the house of Barreiro he not only met the Vierras again, but also Gongoras, Romeros, Bacas and Sandovals, whom he knew as persons of consequence in the valley. All of them accepted his presence graciously and without surprise, as they did that of a Spanish-speaking officer from Fort Selden and an equally bilingual Irishman from El Paso who made much money buying and selling hides and pelts. There was nothing snobbish about these people, but anyone who did not speak their language and know their manners would have found it hard to meet them.

The Barreiro party was a typical Mexican party starting about four in the afternoon and lasting until ten at night, including about forty persons of both sexes and all ages from fifteen to eighty. There were games such as drop the hand-

kerchief and blind man's buff for the young, with some of
the elders joining them, and toward the end there was a
brief burst of dancing when one of the guests produced a
fiddle, but the main business of the gathering was eating,
long and slowly and enormously, with much conversation
and much drinking of chocolate and wine poured from silver
pitchers. There were meats of many kinds including chickens,
mutton, roast kid and game, and also cooked vegetables and
raw fruit and sweet little cakes called biscoches and rich
yellow custards. All gathered about a long rough table and
ate and chattered and tossed bones over their shoulders to
be caught by well-trained dogs, which seemed to mingle on
equal terms with the whole company. Long, slow, sociable
eating had always been the chief diversion of these people
and they had a great capacity for food. Leo was amazed
at how much provender a pretty girl of fifteen could pack
into her slender person. The Doña Concepcion Barreiro was
a fat, brown, good-humored woman in her early forties who
had lived up to her name by bearing ten children and rais-
ing seven of them, a high proportion for that time and place.
All of the Barreiros tended to be plump and were much ad-
dicted to laughter, so that the party moved to the tune of
their assorted guffaws, chuckles and giggles, ranging from
the shrill mirth of adolescent girls in the excitement of play
to the rumbling bass belly laugh of the master of the house.
To Leo it was a significant occasion, for when he took his
departure, not only Barreiros but Gongoras, Romeros, Sandovals and Bacas informed him in most gracious terms that
their houses were his.

A few weeks later he received a call from Don Tobias in
his office. After an appropriate chat about trivial matters, Don
Tobias made him a business proposition. He could buy much
more copper if he had American dollars, and he knew that
Leo had them. He proposed a loan, the profit on his trans-

actions to be divided equally between them. It was a good proposition, and Leo accepted it. Nor was he at all surprised to discover that his social progress bore a direct relation to his success in trade.

Among these families of importance, only Don Augustín Vierra seemed to resent him, and that he understood well enough. The Vierras had long been powerful in Don Pedro, but now the Tienda Mendes was becoming more important than the house of Vierra. The town's center of gravity was visibly shifting from the plaza where the Vierra house stood to the side street in front of the store. The hitchrack there was always crowded and so was the Mendes corral, where the horses of wayfarers were fed and stabled free. Don Augustín could not be expected to enjoy this situation, yet social relations between the houses of Mendes and Vierra seemed now to be inevitable. In due course the Vierras gave a party to which all the Barreiros came and Leo was necessarily invited also, because by this time he and Don Tobias were known to be friends and allies. This invitation made it obligatory for Leo to call again at the Vierras for chocolate, and this time Don Augustín seemed to contemplate him with resignation if not with approval. He met the Vierras also at the Padre's house and finally he mustered the courage to serve chocolate in his own sala, so the Vierras entered his home for the first time, as did the Barreiros and the Gongoras. It became apparent to Leo that his importance now made it impossible to ignore him. The fact gave him a mild thrill of egotistical satisfaction and also a faint feeling of insecurity, such as he had known when first he mounted a horse.

2. At every social occasion he attended Leo saw Doña Lupe. Repeatedly he found himself seated opposite her, often a little too far away for ready conversation, but always in such a position that he could contemplate her with ease, and in fact could not avoid doing so. All Mexican women love to be stared at and it is good form to stare at them, even in public and when they are accompanied. So Leo became intimately familiar with Lupe's appearance, with all of her costumes, with her quick, restless gestures and her slightly acidulous chatter; and the longer he looked at her the more he was impressed by the fact that she was a most unusual person and not at all a typical Mexican woman. Certainly she did not conform to the Mexican ideal of feminine charm. The Mexicans all liked their women plump, soft and sweet, and Lupe was none of these things. She had a slender, sinewy, hard-looking body with a visible play of muscle in her well-turned forearm, and her voice had a sharp quality rather than the soft cooing note which most Mexican girls carefully cultivated. Her laugh, too, was sudden and a little shrill, in contrast to the soft feminine chuckle of the Barreiro women. Her figure was strikingly good in its slender way and she showed both originality and taste in adorning it. Mexican women in New Mexico were then undergoing a transformation, for styles and clothes from the States were coming in, and all those who could afford them wore the kind of gowns that were fashionable in St. Louis. So Leo was permitted to contemplate the Doña in a very long gown, with a very low neckline, which revealed her completely from the cleft of her small firm breasts upward, and concealed her from that point to where her skirt dragged the floor. It revealed the fact that Lupe had very pretty shoulders and arms, even though they were so thin that her delicate olive skin was shadowed along the line of her collar bone.

When only a few friends were present, she sometimes appeared in the costume which most Mexican women had worn for generations. It consisted of a red knee-length skirt, a white linen bodice and a bright silk shawl, with no stockings and very light slippers without heels. This, too, was evidently a daring departure from the good form of the moment, for both her husband and the Padre looked at her with visible surprise. Moreover, in her typical, restless way she contrived to toss her pretty slender legs about so that she seemed to be constantly on the verge of an intimate revelation.

Leo found her increasingly fascinating as a spectacle if not as a personality. To his alien taste she was vastly more attractive than the plump virgins with large soft eyes and large soft bosoms, who were the magnets of male attention in all gatherings. He liked to believe, although he was not at all sure of it, that Lupe staged her carefully calculated appearances and costumes for his special benefit, that she was aware of his appreciation, that a very slight intercourse had sprung up between them, a wordless communion in which she adorned and revealed herself for his eyes and he smiled his approval. But for months he saw no evidence that Lupe was flirting with him, and for this he was grateful. He felt sure that a flirtation with the wife of Don Augustín would be bad for business and also hard on his peace of mind.

His peace of mind received its first slight jolt one day when he and Don Tobias, after a business conference, had called to drink chocolate with the Vierras. The two Mexican gentlemen engaged in a lively discussion of cockfighting, a sport which both of them greatly enjoyed. Leo listened for a while, wholly unable to take any part, feeling strongly how alien he was to these two sportsmen, who delighted in the bloody death of a chicken and shook their sides laughing about a cock that leaped out of the pit and ran for its life, pursued by an enraged owner who finally captured the cowardly bird and wrung its neck. He turned away from the story to meet the eyes of Doña Lupe. She did not speak, but gave him a long steady look that seemed to be loaded

with meaning, then smiled very slightly, lowered her eyes
and fussed self-consciously with her skirts. It was a very slight
gesture, but an unmistakable one—a word in the ancient sign
language of sex. Leo knew now that Lupe was flirting with
him, and he felt at once flattered and disturbed, but not
much disturbed. He felt sure this could never be anything
more than a discreet flirtation, not because he believed in
the probity of Mexican ladies in general or of Lupe in particular, but simply because in this tiny and isolated town an
affair would seem, fortunately, impossible.

He had by this time learned a great deal about the morals
of the Ricos, if only because Santa Fe was so full of gossip
about them. All the gringos who came there were properly
scandalized. Everyone had read Josiah Gregg's book about
New Mexico and the wagon trade, and the gringo attitude
was aptly expressed in his dry observation that marriage
here changed the status of the contracting parties, but apparently not their moral obligations. The worst of it was that
the Mexicans did not even practice a decent hypocrisy in
the Anglo-Saxon manner. The women were exquisitely sly
and artful about their amours, but no one pretended that
monogamy was a working institution. So almost every soldier
in Santa Fe had his sleeping dictionary, officers of the United
States Army had affairs with ladies of the first families and
the conquerors enjoyed a delicate blend of moral superiority
and voluptuous delight.

So it was only to be expected that Lupe would practice
upon her guest the traditional wiles and arts of her class,
especially since they had doubtless suffered from disuse here
in Don Pedro and she from boredom. Leo did not feel too
flattered. After all, here he was the invader, the new figure
on the horizon of her life, perhaps the only unattached male
at the moment anywhere within her reach. She wanted him
to feel her charm and power as a woman, to respond to it

as best he could, and this he was determined to do. For if having an affair with Lupe would be a dubious business, to displease her would be hardly less so. In fact, he was rather more afraid of her displeasure than of Don Augustín's possible hostility, even though the Don carried arms and she did not, for she was obviously the stronger personality of the two. So he smiled at the Doña, trying hard to convey the impression that he was thrilled and pleased by the fact that she had flung him a challenge, hoping she would understand that he could not possibly make any better response to it.

For months after that, although he saw the lady several times, there was not another exchange in their silent dialogue and he began to think he had attributed too much importance to a single glance. He found himself about equally divided between relief and disappointment. Most assuredly he did not want trouble—no man ever wanted trouble less—yet there was some perverse part of him that hoped Lupe was not going to ignore him.

When he attended a baile at the house of Don Tobias in Mesilla, he was at first even more convinced that she had forgotten him or had decided that he lacked the spirit of gallantry or perhaps had discovered another subject for her adroit and subtle coquetry.

The dance itself was a new experience to him. He had gone to a hundred dances of the common people, but this was the first time he had seen one in a home of the gentry. The long sala of the Tobias house was cleared for the occasion and decorated with the wild flowers of May. On a platform erected for the occasion sat the same three-piece orchestra that played for all the common dances in the valley and it played all of the same few tunes, but this was a much more elaborate performance than any ordinary fandango. There were square dances of the utmost complication, led and called by a young man from El Paso who had an astonishing repertoire and generalship, handling his dancers like a well-trained army, throwing them into spasms of laughter by his sudden changes of pace and movement, then deploying them into a whirl of waltzing couples. Later, a gifted young woman mounted the platform and made impromptu verses about each couple as they danced past her. It was easy to make verses in Spanish, but her wit and resource were astonishing and she repeatedly broke up the dancing in a burst of applause. Everyone laughed and clapped more and more as the evening lengthened and the crowd madness of music and rhythm seized them all. Leo was again impressed by the great capacity these people had to enjoy themselves, to seize and devour the moment, and now as in his peddling days he felt more a part of society as he capered and swung the girls than in any other phase of his life.

He touched Lupe's hand in the complicated maneuvers of the reels and lancers but she never met his eye, and for hours she eluded his every effort to achieve a dance with her. When he came near her she seemed to be always just floating away in the arms of someone else and she did not even smile at him over a rival's shoulder. He was surprised to find himself a little annoyed. He had never yet done more than touch her hand and had looked forward to the experience of putting an arm around her, feeling that any more intimate contact was forever denied him.

He had almost given up the hope of even that small favor when suddenly she fixed her commanding glance upon him from clear across the room. He was impressed again by her dramatic command of all the looks and gestures by which women communicate their forbidden wishes and seize the initiative which is supposed to belong to men. She tossed her head and flung him a wide smile, showing all her teeth, a smile that said more plainly than words, "Oh, there you are and now come hither." He hurried across the room and she rose and glided into his arms with the quick grace that marked all her movements. She was a perfect dancer, much better in fact than some of the heavily upholstered beauties he had piloted about the room, and she danced well away from him so that he felt as though he were pursuing her around the room with his hands upon her, but never quite capturing her, never feeling the form and pressure of her body. Her dancing had the same elusive coquetry as all her other gestures, and gave him the same feeling of provoked frustration. It did, that is, until just before the music stopped, when suddenly she bent in the middle and thrust herself against him so that just for a moment their legs were tangled and their bellies were tensely intimate. It was no more than many a common Mexican girl habitually did in the cradle waltz, but in this case it was unmistakably a gesture of calculated provocation, long delayed and delivered, like a blow below the belt, with deliberate and perverse intent. A moment later the dance was over and he was bowing to her as she took her seat, amazed at how shaken and disturbed he felt. He was aware that she had been building up a desire in him for months, slowly and artfully, and that this was the final hard thrust of her attack, the challenge that could not be mistaken.

He rode home in the cool of the small hours wondering what if anything Lupe intended. He sensed a touch of cruelty in the woman and of hatred for men in general. Something of that he had felt in a good many Mexican women, who were all treated by their husbands and fathers as articles of property primarily. They had no rights and no freedom but what they stole. In general, they seemed to accept this as the divine order, but with an underlying resentment, and in Lupe the spirit of protest and rebellion was armed with a sharp mind and a restless spirit. Very likely she took pleasure in disturbing his peace of mind and keeping him bewildered and probably that was the only triumph she sought.

If this had all happened in Santa Fe, he thought, it would perhaps have had a different meaning. Santa Fe was a metropolis, even if a very small one, and it seemed to afford a great deal of freedom. He had little doubt that Lupe had made good use of this social license on the several long visits to Santa Fe she had made since her marriage. There doubtless she had lived in the house of her parents with numerous female relatives and he knew that Mexican cousins had various and subtle means of assisting each other in their social adventures. A chaperon could so easily become an ally. Moreover, he had heard that Lupe had been especially popular with the officers of the United States Army. Doubtless they appreciated her slim figure and her sharp and witty tongue as the Mexicans did not, and doubtless also they could communicate with her in French, which all West Point officers knew more or less.

So he rode home slowly, enjoying the cool quiet of two o'clock in the morning with only a chorus of frogs and crickets and the distant call of an owl to break the silence, thinking quite calmly about this disturbing challenge which had entered his life. As always, his strongest desire was to be discreet, and he thought the discreet thing would be simply to see as little of Lupe as possible and also to avoid her peculiarly expressive and disturbing eyes. After all, he didn't have to sit there and stare at her, affording her an excellent opportunity to strike him with a look whenever she wished.

Just as a matter of chance he did not see her again for nearly a month and then only briefly when he and the Padre met at the Vierras' one afternoon, but he did find himself again uncomfortably sitting opposite the lady while the other two were briefly engrossed in their own conversation, and she did again level upon him her peculiarly expressive glance. But this time there was not a trace of a smile upon her lips. On the contrary, she frowned at him, heavily, intently, almost furiously. Her frown was especially formidable by reason of her heavy black brows, which drew down above her fine dark eyes in a gesture that was almost menacing. Leo felt as distinctly chastised as though she had thrown a rock at him. Her look said as plainly as words that he had failed her, that he was a worm and a craven, that he had earned her resentment and also her contempt.

Blame always begets guilt. How, he asked himself, had he offended? What in the name of God did the woman expect? He had heard of more than one Mexican gallant, overwhelmed by passion, who had climbed through the bedroom window of a receptive lady with a stiletto up his sleeve in case of emergency. If she expected him to perform some such feat of romantic gymnastics she greatly overestimated both his daring and his agility. And short of that, what could he do?

It was true that even in the smallest villages the women of the best families apparently did not go uncomforted. He remembered that in the north, which was all sheep country, the lambing season and the shearing season were tradition- ally the seasons of love. Wool seemed to be the only thing that aroused a more passionate devotion than woman. Mex- ican sheepherders had been known to die with their charges in blizzards rather than desert them. If the lord of the estate did not leave home any other time he always did so when the ewes were dropping their lambs and when the wool crop was being clipped, as also in the emergencies of storm and drought. Traditionally, these were the times when lovers ap- peared. He had heard of a famous Mexican soldier who had ridden from Chihuahua to Santa Fe in the spring, stopping at all the best houses, and that he had reported only one faithful wife in the six hundred miles.

Here in the south there were unfortunately no sheep, but there were cattle and hence roundups and brandings. Hus- bands did periodically ride away, so perhaps he was neglecting his opportunities, but he simply couldn't see them. The whole incident made him feel again how alien he was to this society, with its romantic desperations, its horse pistols and daggers, its cult of passionate sin and belligerent honor.

He felt wholly unequal to the situation and somewhat amused by it, but he could not pretend that he was undisturbed. It is in small towns, where people cannot escape each other, that passion becomes obsessive. He wanted no trouble with Lupe, but she had planted a desire in him and it grew. In the long hot nights of that summer, when cooling storms threatened day after day but failed to bring promised relief, she haunted his imagination and even his dreams so that sometimes he woke and flung out an arm to grasp at a wraith. Most assuredly he did not love her. What she had created between them was an erotic hostility, which was no less acute for its lack of all tenderness and understanding. Apparently she had come to hate him and he had come to resent this futile and disturbing tension. He had always thought of himself as a man peculiarly mild and devoid of ferocities, but he had to admit in his troubled, wakeful moments that it would be a pleasure to lay violent hands upon this woman.

His desire for her was a thing that existed and had consequence whether it functioned or not. The part of wisdom he knew was to stay away from her, and he did so for weeks, but the time inevitably came when he found himself one hot afternoon sitting again in the Vierra sala, staring at the woman he had planned to avoid. She had summoned him to meet a visiting family from the north, and it would not have been good business to refuse. The Don, it appeared, had ridden to the lake in quest of salt for his cattle.

It was a day of still cloudless heat with a temperature well above a hundred, the worst kind of weather that afflicted the southern valley. Day after day clouds would roll up over the mountains to the east, while distant thunder and broad flashes of lightning promised a relief that never came. Such weather seems to generate a faint madness in all hot-blooded creatures. Cattle and horses are restless as they fight flies in the scant and crowded midday shade, dogs snap at each other, men sweat and curse and drop their tools.

It was evident that the heat had gotten into Lupe's blood, for her mood was visibly terrible and it seemed to fill and dominate the room. She talked incessantly, both of her long slender heavily ringed hands fluttering in gestures of exasperation. One of her guests spoke a timid compliment about her darkened and relatively comfortable rooms.

"The house is well enough," she said, "but what a country! Why did I ever leave Santa Fe? There at least it is always cool and there are civilized people. Here we have nothing but heat, flies and Indians!"

Such blazing candor was not good form. Her guests laughed faintly and uncomfortably and a little later they tried to leave. They had stopped here only for a rest and to escape the heat. They planned to continue their journey as far as Las Cruces when the sun set and the evening breeze arose. But Lupe was filled with aggressive and indomitable hospitality.

"You cannot go without eating!" she announced. "Supper is on the table. I am having it early so you will not lose time."

She herded them toward the dining room, using both hands as well as her voice, busy and irresistible as a sheep dog. Leo hung back, wanting no share in this party, waiting for a chance to make his excuses and depart. But when the others were all well started for the dining room, she turned and darted at him like a bird at a bug. Her face was only six inches from his and her voice was low but excited.

"I am sending one of my kitchen women to your house this evening, with some melons," she said, making a quick gesture with both hands, which molded melons out of air. "We have some wonderful melons. Will you be there?"

"Of course," Leo said, and before he could speak another word she turned and darted after her guests, while he followed, meek and bewildered, amazed at the speed and dexterity of her maneuvers.

---

3. At home that night he sat in his big rawhide chair, sipping a brandy, although it was much too hot for brandy. He needed something to quiet his nerves. Repeatedly he thought he heard a step or a faint rap at his door and sat listening with painful attention. Once he went and opened the door and made sure nothing was there.

It was ten o'clock, the night was cooling, the town was asleep and the silence was solid as the dark when he heard unmistakably a step and a light scratching on the door, which was often in Mexican towns the signal of the surreptitious visitor. Yet when he opened the door he thought she had truly sent someone else, for he saw a woman wearing a black shawl, hooded over her face as all the village women wore them, with a basket balanced on her head. Lupe let him look at her for a moment, then stepped through the door, dropped her shawl, set down her basket and laughed. It was like her to be as dramatic as possible, he thought.

"For a moment I feared you *had* sent a servant," he said. "I am so glad you came. Please be seated."

It sounded a little too formal, he knew. Perhaps he should have seized her in his arms the moment she stepped through the door, but such a bold attack was beyond him. In fact, now that his great moment had presumably come, he felt wholly unsure of himself, if only because he knew so little about her. It struck him suddenly that so far as any understanding of each other was concerned, they were completely strangers. He had never before seen her alone, even for a moment. To him she had been only a figure in a group and they had communicated mostly in sign language.

"Una copita?" he inquired, meaning a cup of brandy.

"Thank you," she said, taking the cup, putting it down untasted.

There she sat, silent, with a faint smile on her lips. It was an enigmatic smile to him but it seemed more quizzical than friendly—a smile with a faint flavor of disdain. Certainly she was not making it easy for him.

His only approach to anyone was to make friends, by way of much talk, to create a feeling of mutual understanding. It was not her way, at least where a man was concerned. To her a man was always an antagonist, a creature of another species, to be challenged, mystified, deceived. He partly understood that, out of his long observation of Mexicans. Among the common people, where man and woman shared a struggle for bare existence, there was more of companionship, but to the Ricos sex was a game, full of danger and mystery. It was also a sin and its sinfulness was part of its thrill. She wanted to be overwhelmed—he guessed that, too—wanted to keep up a pretense of resistance and defiance. But he was not an overwhelming man. To this situation, he sadly knew, he was wholly inadequate. He had neither the spirit nor the technique.

"It was kind of you to come," he began hopefully. "I have always wanted to talk with you, and I never had a chance."

She rose decisively, with a toss of her head and an audible sniff that plainly expressed her opinion of a man who would see this visit as an opportunity for conversation.

"I came only to bring you a gift," she said. "There are your melons. I hope you will enjoy them."

He was afraid of her and she knew it. Her expression told him that much. He laid a tentative hand upon her arm.

"Please," he said gently. "You must not go."

She brushed his hand away with a sweeping gesture, an emphatic "No!"

Her indignation seemed perfectly genuine. She stood with her head lifted, her brows knit in anger, her mouth hard. Although he was the taller she seemed to be looking down at him from some inaccessible height. Her look pushed him away and down and back into his past so that he was again the humble peddler, who had so long looked up at the Ricos in their coaches, on their fine horses, feeling they were forever beyond his reach.

They stood facing each other in silence for an indecisive moment. Then she smiled a small hard smile which expressed perhaps a challenge and certainly an amused contempt.

The impulse of spontaneous violence he always lacked, but he knew now that he faced a moral crisis, that he had to do something and do it quickly, before she turned away. It seemed to him that if he let this woman go he would be failing her, failing himself, failing the uses and challenges of human life. He would be a man disgraced and despised. Gathering all his strength and courage, he stepped forward with a short laugh, swept her off her feet in what he hoped was a masterful gesture, carried her quickly into the other room, dumped her on the bed, and applied himself earnestly to the business of getting her clothes off. She rolled and squirmed and uttered a series of short explosive noes, but he was now beyond all stopping, determined to strip this woman of her clothes and her pretentions, be the ultimate consequences what they might.

Her resistance collapsed suddenly when his hand explored her naked body. They coupled with a kind of fury that seemed more intense than any tenderness, with her teeth firmly fixed in his shoulder and his fingers punishing her in return. It was as if they were taking revenge on each other for the long painful tension that had sprung up between them, and it seemed also as though all their antagonism was consumed in the heat of this violence. A little later she was kissing him with the utmost tenderness, soliciting him with a skill and grace such as he had never before encountered.

Lupe came of a class and race of women for whom sex had been their whole profession and relation to life for centuries, and they had made an art of it and of every phase of it, from the first faint smile of flirtation to the final spasm. She was the heir of a great and ancient erotic tradition but her silky skin and her gift of touch were her own. She was truly an artist of love. It seemed to him that along with her clothes she had shed her whole social personality, with its prides and poses, had become another creature, all desire, pure and shameless, and one that captivated him completely.

It seemed also, when she left him, that she put on all her manners and pretenses along with her dress.

"When will you return?" he asked her at the door.

"Never!" she told him. "This time I was weak and you were terrible. But it must never happen again!"

She peered cautiously out the half-opened door, listened intently for a long moment, then departed, tossing him a smile over her shoulder, muffling her face in her great shawl.

4.She did come again and many times, but neither too often nor regularly. She was careful to keep desire at a high pitch and to make her visits always an event. She was a conventional woman in her own fashion. Adultery was part of her tradition and it had its own art and etiquette. Leo had the impression that she never came to him except when her husband was away for the night, whether upon some erotic errand of his own or on his cattle range. She was supremely discreet, cunning as a coyote and happily free of guilt. Sin she accepted as a necessary part of human life on earth. For her, every act of passion was both a fall and a redemption, leaving her pure and pacified.

Something of this Leo came to understand, as he might have understood a wild animal by observing its habits, but for months she remained a stranger and a mystery to him, a woman who had revealed her body and her desire but nothing more. Then suddenly one night Lupe began to talk, and once she had started talking words poured from her mouth in eager profusion. She never talked when she had her clothes on, and she never said a word until her ardours were over, but lying naked and peaceful she at last achieved something of self-revelation. Leo guessed that perhaps she had never talked this way to anyone before, certainly not to a man, and he led her on by careful questions, feeling that by her talk she delivered herself of some burden. Mostly, she talked about her youth in Santa Fe and how she had envied her brothers and wished that she might have been a man. She told him about the days of the American conquest, when she was a child, and how the United States cavalry had ridden into town, splendid in blue and gold, confident and powerful, with flying flags and rattling sabers, making Mexicans seem poor and weak, and how she had wished that she too might be a soldier and carry a great shining sword. About her childhood she talked easily and with pleasure, but she evidently found it hard to tell him about her later years. She never mentioned her marriage and she did not confess any of her sins, although in one moment of candor she implied them.

"I never know whether I love a man because I hate him or hate him because I love him," she admitted. "Only you are different, Leo," she added. "You are nothing like a Mexican. You treat a woman as though she were a friend."

After a while she even asked him some questions about himself, and he tried to tell her about his own childhood and about New York, and he understood that she could not imagine a city so large, or one where so many different kinds of people lived. These two were creatures of different kinds and born of different worlds and would never think or feel alike, but lying naked in dark and quiet they had left all worlds behind, had crawled back into the womb of their common humanity, telling each other in muted voices about their so different lives, while crickets made a small nearby courting music and a faraway dog howled his feelings at the moon.

1. There in the southern valley Fort Selden
was the chief visible manifestation of the power and authority
of the United States Government, reminding the people that
they belonged to a great nation, which they might otherwise
easily have forgotten, for the little adobe fort with its tall white
flag pole flying the stars and stripes and its hundred-odd soldiers was almost the only evidence of change since the American conquest. The fort covered about four acres on the eastern
edge of the valley with a bare and shadeless sprawl of adobe
barracks, storerooms, corrals and blacksmith shops. Soldiers
in hot blue uniforms seemed to be nearly always drilling on
the dusty little parade ground except when they were riding
patrols to protect the post road from the Apaches. They were
a tough and truculent crew, many of them wanted men who
had joined the Army to stay out of jail. In Santa Fe soldiers
had a good time, but here they were cut off from the people,

most of them unable to speak the language. In their scant leisure they drank, fought and gambled. A crap game was almost always going on among the enlisted men and the officers ran a famous poker table, which challenged all comers and trimmed the purse of many a traveler. But the post was a boon to the valley. It gave the people a sense of security they had lacked under Mexican rule, and it consumed beef, corn and beans, which were bought from the natives and paid for in gold.

Leo sold the Army much produce that he took in trade and a few cattle now and then, when he happened to acquire them as part of a deal. He had a good and mutually useful friendship with Jack Gibbs, who acted as sutler for the post. Gibbs was a man of fifty, short, stocky, and powerful, with the slow, bowlegged, high-heeled walk of an old rider. A native of Louisiana, he had gone west as a youth, had roped wild cattle in the brush country of the lower Brazos, hunted buffalo in the Panhandle, broken broncos for a living, been a deputy sheriff in Texas and later a teamster for the Army. He had come to the post in that capacity, had taken over the buying of all supplies because he knew cattle and Spanish, and had become also and incidentally a scout and interpreter because he knew the country, a little of the Apache language and enough sign talk to communicate with any Indian.

Gibbs was a man of ability who suffered recurrent attacks of profane exasperation by reason of the incurable inefficiency of most of his fellow beings. He was patient with horses, firm with mules, but chronically disgusted with men, and especially with Mexicans and soldiers. He despised all Mexicans for their laziness, their complete lack of a sense of time, their dilatory attitude toward all the obligations of life. He held the United States cavalry in contempt because few of its recruits knew how to ride according to his standards and because of its complete inability to cope with the wily and elu-

sive Apaches. Apparently he respected the Apaches more than
any other human beings he had ever encountered. He explained to Leo how they always went on a raid driving a herd
of horses before them, three or four horses to every man. When
they camped at a water hole they butchered a horse for supper, washed out its main intestine, filled this with water,
wrapped it around and around another horse, and hit the
trail again with a traveling tank. They carried no supplies,
needed nothing they couldn't pick up off the face of the earth.
An Apache stranded on the desert would cut a switch and
gather a meal of lizards, and he would get water out of cactus.

"How in hell can a soldier catch that kind of a man?"
Gibbs demanded. "It takes a pack mule loaded with grub to
keep every two soldiers alive and they can't hit an Apache
on a horse any more than they could hit a flying bird. Give
me about fifty good cowpunchers with Winchester rifles and
I might give Natchez a run for his money, but this here army
is just something to shoot craps and eat beef."

He and Leo had great respect for each other because they
were both prompt and reliable men in a country where pro-
crastination was traditional and the sense of time was almost
extinct. Gibbs had been heard to say that Leo was the only
man south of Santa Fe who kept his engagements, paid his
bills and delivered his goods on time, and Gibbs occupied
almost the same place in Leo's esteem, so far as his local
dealings were concerned. Gibbs would ride over from the
post about once a month for dinner, and Leo had learned how
to cater to his peculiar tastes. Gibbs was convinced that health
and longevity were sustained by drinking plenty of good
whisky, diluted with water, and eating mostly meat. In his
cattle-chasing and buffalo-hunting period he had often been
compelled to live on a straight meat diet for days at a time
and he had become almost as carnivorous as a mountain lion.
He believed in the virtue of eating the whole animal, innards,

fat and all. His idea of dinner was a big platter of small steaks, a side dish of fried liver, and another of brains scrambled with eggs. The only vegetable he relished was green chili, which he could eat like a native without batting an eye or shedding a tear.

Gibbs liked to talk to Leo because he knew he could say anything with safety. He denounced Mexicans on all occasions but Leo provided his only discreet confidant for his feelings about the military.

It was Gibbs who gave Leo his first news of the disaster which had overtaken Don Augustín when he sold a large herd of steers at the post and received payment in gold. The Don had sold a few cattle to the Government from time to time but had never before delivered them to the post in person. His attitude toward the Army had been somewhat haughty and distant. Although officers of the post had been entertained by the best families in El Paso and Mesilla, Don Augustín had never invited any of them to his house, still distrusted them as foreigners and resented them as invaders. But they had received him at the post with courtesy and even with ceremony, had introduced him to Scotch whisky, persuaded him to stay for dinner, and finally invited him, as a special treat, to join a small and friendly game of stud poker.

Don Augustín, like most of his kind, was a great gambler. He would bet on anything but most of his betting had been on cockfights and horse races. Whether he had ever encountered poker before Leo could not learn, but he certainly knew little about the game, which had come to New Mexico with the gringos. In Santa Fe it had long been employed as a means of separating some of the best families from some of their wealth, but here in the south not so much had been heard of it.

The Don was fascinated by the apparent simplicity of the game and he had profound faith in his own luck. It was a part of his heritage to regard himself as one of God's favored children.

"I knew they were going to trim the poor bastard," Gibbs said. "If the major had been there maybe it wouldn't have happened, but he was up at Fort MacRae, and those young shavetails haven't got no mercy on anybody. They wanted me to sit in on the game, but I wouldn't have any part of it, especially since I had made the deal with him for the cattle. I even tried to get him aside and warn him, but he wouldn't pay me no attention."

"He's never taken advice," Leo remarked. "He just gives orders."

"He thinks he's Godalmighty around here," Gibbs said. "You can't tell those top greasers a thing. And of course they let him win at first. He saw those gold eagles stacking up in front of him, and was he tickled! Then about three more of the boys worked into the game, one at a time, and he couldn't understand it took a better hand to win. He couldn't understand nothing."

"They ought to have stopped the game before he was cleaned out," Leo said.

"He wouldn't quit," Gibbs explained. "He fought it out to his last dollar. The worse his luck got the worse he played. It was downright pitiful. He bluffed on nothing and he raised on the wrong hands and the boys just set back and let him ruin himself. When it was all over they tried to give him back some of his money and he wouldn't take it. Just too goddam proud!"

Leo didn't feel good about that poker game. He wished all that gold had come back to Don Pedro instead of going into army pockets. He knew it probably represented most of the Vierra cash income for a year. The Don would have to borrow. And where would he borrow? The Tienda Mendes had become the bank of the community. The Don would hate to come to him for money. And he hoped the Don wouldn't.

---

2. Ever since that day when he had opened the store, and they had faced each other across his improvised counter, he and Don Augustín had been inevitably antagonists. Their antagonism had never been open. They had never clashed again, but year by year the store had grown in size and importance and year by year more of the people in the valley had come to Leo Mendes for what they needed. The change had been gradual and no one had suffered from it much. Don Augustín still owned his lands and his cattle, he was still the ruling baron and was saluted respectfully by all his henchmen, but now he had to pay some of them in cash instead of goods, and the money always went to the Tienda Mendes. There were also men who worked for Mendes and were not as much afraid of their traditional patrón as once they had been, and there were even a few who had borrowed money from Mendes to buy land or livestock and had achieved a measure of independence.

So Leo had triumphed and he knew the Don resented his triumph, wished him away from there, would probably have been delighted if he had fallen off his horse and broken his neck. Yet these two had learned to tolerate each other, as men always do when they must. The fact that Leo was a friend of Padre Malandrini gave him a privileged position in the community, meant to Augustín that he had to be endured politely. The Don always received him with the same limp and reluctant handshake, which seemed a gesture of resignation rather than welcome, and Leo always listened politely to what the Don had to say, and especially to the stories he loved to tell. The fact that he was a good listener was perhaps the only thing about Leo the Don truly liked.

The Don talked always of his youth. He was no more than forty but yet he spoke of the years before his marriage as an old man might talk of his early exploits, with pride and longing. In the period of the Don's twenties expeditions had gone every year across the mountains to gather a year's supply of meat from the buffalo herds, and every fall they had gone south to Chihuahua on a trading trip, for that was the only way they could get cloth and sugar, knives and chocolate. Now the buffalo herds had been thinned and scattered by the gringo hide-hunters and the wagon trade made it wholly unnecessary to go to Chihuahua. As always, the good old days were gone.

To young Augustín those long expeditions had been the chief delight of his life, the use and consummation of his powers. He was a man of action who could not thrive on peace and routine, nor accept the boredom of middle age. Youth had been all of life to him. He talked about it with eloquence and a touch of exaggeration, but yet his stories were explicit and seemed to be essentially true.

His most famous exploit had taken place on a trip to Chihuahua when his party had been surrounded by a band of Apaches only a few miles south of Juarez. The Mexicans took refuge in an arroyo and held the Indians off with their rifle fire, but they had no water and their powder was running low. Young Augustín had volunteered to ride for help.

"There was nothing else to do," he said. "I had a bay mare that had won many races and I rode her bareback so that if they killed her I would at least fall free and not be gored by a saddle horn. I charged at the Indians in a dead run and all at once the air seemed to be full of arrows and I could hear them whistle. One went through my left arm and one struck the mare in the rump. She almost jumped out from under me and then nothing could catch her."

That was all he said and afterward he sat looking at nothing, wistfully savoring the memory of his great moment. For the first time Leo felt respect for the man, contemplating courage of a kind he could not match. Augustín, he thought, had something of the quality that had made his forebears great pioneers, but he had little use for it here in Don Pedro.

---

3. Leo felt now that he had learned how to deal with the Vierras, taken one at a time, but he had never been comfortable when confronted by both of them at once, and after Lupe's first visit to his house he was more than ever reluctant to face them. He hoped that Lupe would feel the same way and that his social relations with the house of Vierra might be allowed to decline, gradually and inoffensively. But Lupe had other plans. She sent him an invitation only a few days after their momentous encounter and he did not feel that he could refuse. So he found himself again sitting in the Vierra sala, conversing uneasily with the husband while waiting for the wife.

When she entered he looked at her in amazement. She wore a bright blue dress and a yellow shawl spangled with red flowers, which seemed in her restless hands a veritable banner of desire. The change in her look and manner was even more striking than her costume. There had always been something a little shrill and bitter about her, an acrid flavor in her speech, an ironic twist about her smile. It seemed to him now that she had become another woman with a new voice and a new smile. She came forward glowing and laughing, gave him her hand, seated herself between her two men, triumphant, composed and evidently delighted, although neither of them was enjoying the occasion. Her husband looked at her with an evidently puzzled surprise, and Leo wished that her transformation had been a little less obvious. It was evident at least that she was not at all afraid of Augustín, had complete confidence in what she was doing, and Leo found this reassuring. But he did not feel happy. He wished that he were away from there and at the same time he wondered whether and when Lupe would come to see him again, for the memory of her visit seemed to haunt his senses and the sight of her brought desire suddenly to new life. He wished for the moment that Augustín could be somehow painlessly abolished, that he might evaporate and go up the chimney. And he had no doubt that the Don likewise wished that the name and power of Mendes might vanish off the earth. So he sat, making uneasy small talk, contemplating the two-headed monster which is marriage, wondering about it. He wondered what these two said to each other when they were alone, for they never seemed to have any relation to each other in public. He wondered if once they had been passionate lovers, as certainly they were no longer, for the Don's desire had long since turned in other directions and in many of them.

From his own observation and from village gossip he had come to understand the whole pattern of Don Augustín's social life, which was the traditional pattern for the males of his family. For generations they had practiced a kind of customary concubinage among the maidens of the village and the nearby valley—the daughters of those who stood in a relation of peonage to the Vierra family. The Vierra nose was a striking and distinctive organ with a magnificent Roman bridge, and it seemed to be invariably hereditable, at least in the male line. Some men who knew the country claimed they could tell when they entered the Vierra domain by the prevalence of this distinctive feature, which the Vierras had been diligently propagating ever since they had risen to a position of dominance.

The Don sustained this time-hallowed privilege with admirable discretion. Among the many household servants of the Vierra family was an old woman who ruled all the other women of the staff with a jealous tyranny. Such an ancient was to be found in almost every aristocratic Mexican household and she was invariably a walking symbol and compendium of all the feudal traditions and privileges. About once a year this ruler of the Vierra kitchen would select a new girl to enter the Vierra service and she was always chosen for beauty and health as well as for efficiency. Although the fact was never mentioned by anyone and would have been hard to prove, it was known to all that this fortunate maiden was for a time the favored mistress of El Patrón, as all his underlings called Don Augustín. Invariably, after a certain interval, the girl would marry rather well, would have a church wedding unusually elaborate for one of her status, and would bring to her fortunate husband a substantial dowry in the form of a small herd of goats or a few cows. Somewhat too soon for the requirements of a strict propriety she would give birth to a child, which, if a male, would proudly carry the nasal insignia of his exalted origin.

Aurelio Beltrán, with his gift of gossip and his remarkable knowledge of local history, had given Leo a most explicit account of this hallowed Vierra custom. He had the utmost contempt for it, at least as practiced by Don Augustín. In his opinion it was not a sporting proposition for any man to plant his seed in a woman who was wholly at his mercy.

"If I have a girl, it is because she likes me," he boasted. "He can have any girl he wants because she gets three cows and a goat and a wedding in the church when he is tired of her." He chuckled. "All of these girls are supposed to be virgins. Otherwise they would not be worthy of the patrón. Well, I could tell him a few things about some of his virgins."

The fearless Aurelio might scoff but no one else ever dared to mention the amours of the great man, much less to make fun of them.

What Lupe thought of her husband and his gallantries, Leo had never learned. Although they had been lovers for a year or more, she had never spoken of him until the first time she came to call upon Leo after the famous poker game.

He could see at a glance that she was in no mood for play. Her thundercloud brows were tightly drawn and her voice exploded with anger.

"You have heard what happened?" she demanded. "That fool! He will ruin us."

"Perhaps it will not happen again," Leo suggested hopefully. He felt profoundly averse to being involved in the troubles of the Vierra family, but he knew he could not refuse whatever demand Lupe was about to make.

"He will go back!" she said. "He will play again as surely as he has money. You must stop him!"

"You know he won't listen to me." Leo hoped he was making a graceful retreat.

"He will come to you for money," Lupe told him.

"He would hate to do that," Leo said.

"He has nowhere else to go," she insisted. "He does not trust banks. He has tried to borrow from all his friends. Like all Mexicans, they have everything but money."

"I don't believe he will ever come to me," Leo said, shaking his head, thinking with dread of that possible interview.

"He will come, I tell you!" There was always something irresistible about the woman. "I have spoken to the Padre about it."

Leo knew now that he was beaten. He had been learning for years that the Padre was the true ruler of the community, although his power was a hidden one. There was a village alcalde, who was now technically a justice of the peace, and there was a county sheriff, but it was the Padre who told people what to do, rich and poor alike. To all of them he was the agent of God, but he was also one who had authority by natural endowment. Men found it hard to disobey him.

Leo was devoted to his friend Orlando, but just now he felt a justified irritation toward the man. He knew the Padre had probably persuaded the Don to go to him for help and he knew why. Anywhere else the Don went for money he would more than likely be cheated. Leo knew that now he was being appointed banker to the house of Vierra and he knew that his obligations to the Padre and to Lupe were his bond and made refusal impossible. He sat silent a moment, thinking how in this town he had become more and more deeply entangled in a prickly thicket of need and desire, of obligation and demand.

"You will do this for *me*," Lupe said. It was not a question but a confident claim. Leo nodded.

"What do you want me to do?" he asked.

"Let him have the money, but not much at a time," Lupe said. "We will have credit at the store and when he has cattle to sell, you will sell them for him."

She was a shrewd woman. She had thought it all out. Leo nodded, a little wearily.

"If he comes to me, I will do what I can," he said.

She smiled upon him now, suddenly relaxed. She let her shawl drop from about her shoulders and spread her bare arms in a gesture of mock helplessness and of invitation.

"Now he is your peon," she said. "And I am your woman. Do with me what you will."

Leo smiled, somewhat ruefully.

"I feel like beating you," he told her.

She laughed at him, wholly restored to good humor now that she had her way.

"Very well, then, beat me," she said. "But not too hard."

---

4. The Don came to his office a few days later. He was no early riser and it was nearly twelve—a fact which Leo rated fortunate. He rose and offered his hand.

"I am honored," he said. "If there is anything I can do for you, you have only to speak."

The Don evidently found that hard.

"A little matter of business—" he began, uneasily.

"But this is no time for business," Leo interrupted. "It is almost noon. Avandera will be waiting. Come, you must eat with me." He was already on his feet and the Don rose, too. He was evidently reluctant, but there was no escape. To refuse an invitation to eat now would be an insult under his code of propriety, so he let Leo convey him across the courtyard and seat him at the table, which Avandera quickly set for two, while Leo fetched one of his bottles of imported wine and filled their glasses. Then he began talking earnestly about everything except business. He questioned the Don about conditions on the cattle range, raised the always troublesome problem of Apache raids, steered conversation back toward the old days, the days of Augustín's youth, got the man talking at last, as one would get water out of a pump by much labor and priming. After food and wine came brandy and then he persuaded the Don to light a mild cigar, which was an unaccustomed experience for him. When he saw that the Don was enjoying his smoke, Leo felt that the crucial moment had come.

"You spoke of business," he began. "You know that I am yours to command."

The Don looked at the white ash on the end of his cigar for a long moment.

"I need a little money," he said, and it evidently cost him pain to ask. "Perhaps a thousand dollars."

"Money, yes!" Leo spoke as though it were a trifle. "And a thousand dollars if you need it. But not all at once. Cash is scarce. You know that. A hundred dollars now, perhaps, and more later. Meanwhile, you can have anything you need from the store. It will be an honor to serve you."

The Don stared at his cigar and nodded. What else could he do? He was being treated like a prince, but he was the suppliant and could only take what was offered.

"I will pay when I sell steers in the fall," he said.

"Think nothing of it," Leo said. "Take what you need and when you have cattle to sell bring them to me. I will get you the best price in the market, keep what you owe me and give you the rest. It will save you much trouble."

The Don now sat studying his cigar for a long time. It was evident that he did not like this proposition and also that he could not think of any alternative. His was not a business mind.

"Many thanks," he said at last, reluctantly polite. "I will take the money and what I may need from the store. About the cattle, we will see when the time comes."

Leo nodded agreement.

"Very well," he said, "just as you please."

It was all quite vague and nothing was put on paper, but Leo knew it was a safe agreement. He knew that all the Vierra properties would be his security and he knew that the authority of the Padre would stand behind it. He was not worried about money, but he was uneasy about his relations with Don Augustín. He knew that now he was acquiring a dependent who hated his dependence, that he was humbling a proud man.

He poured brandy into the Don's glass.

"This is all between friends," he spoke earnestly. "It shall be just as you wish." He lifted his glass. "Your health!" he proffered.

---

5. At the back of his store, against the wall, Leo had a rack of assorted weapons which had been growing slowly for years and had become the showpiece of the establishment. He always kept in stock a few new rifles and shotguns he bought in Santa Fe, but most of these assorted arms had come to him in trade. A trapper, a prospector or a traveler in need of provender would turn in a gun as a payment on account. Leo knew nothing about such merchandise and could not learn. He invariably called in Aurelio Beltrán to appraise anything in the way of weapons that came to hand and Aurelio was glad to function as an expert. Aurelio, by this time, had become Leo's right-hand man and his trusted friend. He had tried long and hard to teach Leo the importance of knowing how to shoot, had finally resigned himself to the fact that he worked for a man who would not wield a weapon, even in his own defense. So he came to regard this arsenal as his private collection and took great pride in it, wiping all the pieces periodically with an oily rag and displaying them to all inquirers whenever he was in the store. Here were old muzzle-loading rifles and shotguns, even a few flintlocks, and breechloaders of the house of Sharp's, including buffalo guns that weighed fourteen pounds, repeating rifles of the first Winchester model, cavalry carbines and a short, bell-mouthed musket with a wooden stopper in its barrel, such as old-time Mexican buffalo hunters had used on horseback. Side arms were also of great variety, ranging from a muzzle-loading pistol to six-shooters of the new

Colt patent which had become in the last few years the supreme personal weapon of the whole Southwest, taking much
the same place that the rapier had occupied a century before
as an instrument of self-defense, an article of personal adorn-
ment and a necessity of social life in its more turbulent moments. Here too came to rest a great variety of cutlery, most of
it designed for use on the human anatomy. There were Mexican fighting knives of fine, brittle steel with mottoes etched on
their blades: "Do not draw me without cause nor sheath me
without honor," or "At your service, day and night." Machetes
from far to the south came here by way of trade, passing
through many hands, and the collection included several
cavalry sabers, a pearl-handled dagger, a fine old gentleman's
sword with a jeweled hilt and even one sword cane—a type of
weapon then common in Europe and not unknown in Mexico
City, but quite rare in this territory.

Toward all these instruments of homicide Leo had a profound aversion, as rooted and inescapable as his fear of snakes
and spiders, and he could not fail to see how completely this
set him apart from almost all of his male fellow beings. For
this was an armed world and a world that loved and wor-
shiped weapons. Probably every second man who entered his
store bore a weapon, whether it was a six-shooter proudly
worn on the hip by some passing Texan, a blade discreetly
concealed on the person of a humble Mexican sheep herder,
or a rifle in the hands of a professional hunter. And all of them
stopped to look at Leo's collection of firearms and cutlery
which had achieved almost the status of a minor museum. It
was good for business, no doubt of that. Humble customers
were content just to look at the stuff across a counter but a
customer of importance often wanted to examine a gun, would
almost always toss the piece to his shoulder and snap the lock.
Leo had repeatedly warned Aurelio to make sure every gun

was unloaded, but even so, he flinched every time one of them was lifted and snapped.

He dreaded these fire-belching barrels, but even more he disliked the sight of a naked blade. He thought if he had to face death one way or the other he would far rather be shot than carved up with a Bowie knife or pierced by a sword. The two swords in his collection were especially tempting to customers. A man would want to examine the sword cane, would whip out the steel and flourish it with childish delight. The blade was a little over two feet long, triangular in shape, with a needle point and grooves on all three faces to facilitate the flow of blood when it was plunged into the human body. This delicate instrument bothered Leo so much when it was in the hands of a customer that he finally retired it and also the rapier to his office and laid them on a shelf, thinking to take them to Santa Fe on his next trip.

The collection of weapons was especially tempting to Don Augustín. He had seldom entered the store before he established a credit there, but afterward he came more and more often and almost always he carried something away—a bridle, a bit, a rope or a knife; once a forty-dollar saddle, and again a pearl-handled six-shooter. This extravagance worried Leo. It was evident the Don could not resist anything that tempted hand or eye, and that he had no adequate awareness of the debt he was piling up. He lacked a sense of money just as he lacked a sense of time, because he had grown up in a society where neither was important. He was wholly unable to deal with the world that was creeping up on him, a world in which men were always counting their dollars and their minutes.

Leo dreaded the day when he would have to present the Don with a bill. Although he knew he would get his money in the long run, he feared Augustín might drive steers to the fort again that fall, sell them and lose the proceeds. He was reassured about this when he discussed the matter with the indispensable Beltrán. Aurelio was delighted with the whole deal.

"Now Augustín can learn what it is to be in debt," he rejoiced. "People around here have been owing those Vierras money for a hundred and fifty years. They never get paid up and neither will he. Now he is going to learn how a poor man feels."

"But how about the steers?" Leo queried. "He might sell them himself."

"Don't worry," Aurelio told him. "When he rounds up fat cattle in October, I'll be there. You tell me how many steers you want and I'll cut them out of the herd and drive them to the post myself. Augustín won't say a word."

This happened exactly as Aurelio had predicted. He sold the steers and the proceeds were credited to the Vierra account. A few days later the Don called to collect his share of the money. Feeling embarrassed and apologetic, Leo brought out his ledger, made up an itemized bill, explained that the price of the steers still left the house of Vierra far in the red. The Don stared at the paper a long time in silence, shaking his head once or twice, obviously bewildered. It seemed evident that the figures meant nothing to him, but he read slowly the long list of things he had bought, most of them unnecessary things.

"In the old days," he remarked, "we made almost everything right here on the place. We had hardly any money. When we went to Chihuahua we traded horses and mules and buffalo robes for what we needed."

"Yes, I know," Leo said.

Augustín began to wander aimlessly around the room, looking at this and that, glancing out the window. He somehow suggested a man entrapped and seeking a way of escape. Leo watched him with a feeling of growing tension which he

could not quite understand. Presently Augustín noticed the
two swords on a shelf over the desk and picked up the sword
cane, while Leo ardently wished he had never put it there.

"What is this?" the Don asked. He had evidently never
seen one.

Leo reluctantly explained that the cane contained a blade
and that it began where the shaft was circled by a silver band.
The Don obviously was fascinated by this ingenious toy. He
glanced at Leo with a faint smile.

"Don't worry," he said, "I won't buy it."

After some fumbling he discovered how to give the handle
a sharp twist and draw the sword. Now he was truly delighted,
as he seemed to be by any kind of blade. He flourished the
weapon with a deft hand, lunging at an imaginary foe, felt
the needle-sharp point with his thumb, bent the blade carefully in almost a half-circle to test the quality of its steel. Then,
suddenly, he stepped in front of Leo, who sat in his office
chair, struck a pose like a fencer, leveled the blade straight
at Leo's heart and held it there, not more than six inches away.

"Now, Leo," he said, "what if my foot should slip? This
blade would go through you like a knife through cheese."

He was smiling broadly as he spoke. It was all a good joke,
of course, and he was obviously enjoying it, but under the
threat of that deadly point Leo could feel the beating of his
heart. It was so quiet for a moment that it seemed to him he
could hear it. He felt sure of only one thing—that it would be
a grave mistake now to make any move or utter any protest.
He smiled up at the Don, hoping his smile did not look as
forced as it felt.

"One cannot live forever," he remarked.

Augustín held his menacing pose for a few seconds more,
then dropped the point and relaxed. It seemed to Leo that
the man's whole body slumped as he turned away.

"You are no coward, Leo," he remarked. He sheathed the

weapon and laid it back on the shelf, while Leo drew a deep breath. It had been a trivial incident but he felt somehow sure a crisis had come and gone.

When the Don offered his hand in farewell Leo went and got the sword cane and presented it to him handle first.

"This is yours," he said, "with my very good wishes."

I.In the early days of his storekeeping, before he could afford to hire clerks and retreat into his office, the children of the village had been a half-welcome problem to Leo. Just as children had always run to meet him when he was a peddler, because he was the new thing in town, the man from the outside world, the bringer of news and goods, so they came to the store because it was now the most interesting place in their little world, the place where they saw strangers and strange objects and incidentally where some sweet nourishment might be had. Leo kept for their benefit a supply of cheap colored candies which he bought by the wooden bucket in Santa Fe, and this he used as a bribe to get them out of the store when they became too numerous or too noisy. He would distribute candy and then shoo them out the door with both hands, as one might shoo chickens.

"Hurry up!" he would shout. "Run! It is time for you to be home."

They always went, understanding quite well that the price of candy was to do as they were told. But there was one little girl who sometimes came with the others, but never departed with them when they were chased out the door. This was Magdalena Vierra, the niece of Doña Lupe and the only child in the Vierra household while the son and heir was away at school. Had there been the usual large Mexican family Magdalena would probably have spent more time at home. As it was, the village children were her only possible playmates and she had been given or had taken to herself a good deal of freedom. She had first appeared in Leo's store a few weeks after he opened it, but she was so quiet and unobtrusive that he did not become much aware of her presence for months.

She was a dark, skinny child about ten years old when first he noticed her, with a handsome face, large gray eyes and a notably large but shapely mouth. She always took her share of the candy, but when the other children ran laughing out the door she calmly stood her ground or seated herself with infantile dignity on a sack of sugar or a packing box. There was nothing defiant or self-conscious about this gesture. Although she seemed to play with the other children on equal terms, she also seemed to have a precocious awareness of herself as an aristocrat, a person of superior birth and innate privilege. She was perfectly polite, but she took no orders and Leo found that he could not bring himself to give her any. So she quietly established her right to come and go as she pleased, and she spent much time in the store, sitting quietly for the most part, looking and listening. For those large gray eyes seemed to be supremely watchful, expressive of a wide and innocent curiosity. When Leo began to spend more of his time in the office, she also invaded that, his only place of retirement, examined everything in it, often sat and listened while he talked to visitors, so that some strangers assumed she was his daughter.

"A nice little girl you have there," one would say.

"She is not mine," Leo always explained. "I wish she was."

Magdalena had one almost constant companion in the person of Benita Apodaca, the granddaughter of the old woman who ruled the Vierra kitchen. She was about two years older than Magdalena and the relationship between them was of a kind that only a feudal society could produce. Benita, who could have passed for a full-blooded Navajo, had been formally assigned to be Magdalena's body servant and guardian. She would truly have defended the child with her life, if necessary, and she was strong enough to whip almost anything of her own weight. Most of the time these two played and roamed together as good companions, but neither of them ever forgot the nature of their relationship, their respective places in the hierarchy of Mexican life. Magdalena evidently felt no need of Benita's company in the store, would always send her home if they arrived together, and Benita would always go without question, like a well-trained dog.

Magdalena's parents, a young couple on their way, with their infant daughter, to visit relatives in Chihuahua, had been killed by Apaches south of the Rio Grande, and the child had been brought to Don Pedro by the survivors. Lupe, who had lost a daughter of her own, had sworn to be a mother to the orphan child of her favorite sister. This was a customary gesture in Mexican society, where many women died in child-birth and motherless children were always taken over by relatives. Lupe had perhaps been actuated more by tradi-tional obligation than by maternal instinct, for it was ap-parent that she treated her niece ·for the most part with good-humored indifference. She was much more interested in her son, five years older, a bright boy who bore the whole burden of the family ambition. He was sent to school first in Santa Fe, then in St. Louis, where he would learn how to cope with a gringo world, while Magdalena received only what education Lupe could give her at home. She had a lesson for an hour every morning and then was committed to the care of Benita for the rest of the day. The two girls ran wild and free as far as their legs would carry them. Benita took to the country like the savage that she was, and Magdalena was a willing follower. They were forbidden only to go to the river, which was supposed to be dangerous in high water, but Leo soon found evidence that in the hot weather when it was low and almost clear, the river was their favorite resort. On one of his rides he found their barefoot tracks on a sand bar beside a clear pool, just the kind he had often enjoyed himself. Then, a little farther along, in a spot concealed from the road by a rank growth of cottonwood and button willow, he found tracks which at first puzzled him but finally proved to be the imprints of small buttocks where the girls had sat naked in the sun. This, he knew, would have been an even worse misdemeanor than running away to the river.

One baking hot day in August Magdalena came to his office by the back door, peered in cautiously to make sure he was alone, and then entered quickly, slamming the door behind her, panting from a hard run. Her long black hair, which was free to the wind as a horse's mane, now hung wet and maculate with clay and sand.

"What happened?" Leo asked.

"I can't go home as I am," she said breathlessly, ignoring the question.

Leo got a towel and a basin, helped her wash her hair, and tried to dry it, discovering for the first time that a mop of feminine hair holds water like a sponge.

"Sit down," he said. "You can only wait until it dries."

She dutifully sat, giving him a grateful look.

"I like you," she said, "because you never tell me what I ought to do or what God wants me to do."

Leo laughed.

"God only knows what God wants you to do," he said. "But what did *you* do? Did you fall in?"

"No; I jumped," she said. "But it was deeper than I thought and my head went under, and I got my hair wet and then I fell . . ."

It was a breathless and confused explanation, which left Leo a little alarmed and she evidently saw alarm in his eyes.

"It's not dangerous," she assured him. "It's just a little pool."

"But you can't swim," he said.

She nodded her head rapidly three times and grinned a proud and guilty grin.

"We're learning," she told him. She paused a moment and then went on, evidently moved by some infantile need of confession. "We watched the boys to find out how they do it. Of course they couldn't see us. And then we practiced. Don't tell anybody!"

"Of course not," Leo said. Certainly he couldn't tell anyone. That would have been rank treachery, for he was being treated now as a confidant and an ally. He knew that spying on the boys at their swimming hole would be regarded by the Vierras as even more of a delinquency than jumping into the river.

"But you must promise me you won't go into deep water," he said.

"I promise," she told him, nodding solemnly. "And I won't get my hair wet again, either." She held up a bare foot.

"I think it has a thorn in it," she said.

He dutifully found a thorn and extracted it with the point

of his pocket knife, feeling as though he had acquired the duties of a parent without any of the authority.

His responsibilities increased when the girls began hunting along the irrigating ditches and the river pools for almost any small creature they might catch alive. Half-grown birds, beautiful green leopard frogs, tiny rain toads, mud turtles, blue-tail lizards, horned toads, pollywogs, even a water snake, were all captured and brought to town in a small tin bucket with a lid punched full of holes. They caught also a great many kinds of insects, including tumblebugs, ant lions, water beetles and even one tarantula. The girls were both arboreal and amphibious, climbing all kinds of trees, wading in pools and ditches, pursuing their prey with piercing squeals of excitement which Leo could sometimes hear from the back door of his establishment.

When he did so he knew that he was probably in for trouble. Magdalena had been quick to learn that he was a soft and tolerant person, one who had great difficulty in saying no, so she brought all of her plunder to the store. None of it was welcome at home, and there was no good place for it in the house either, but Leo reluctantly assigned them a corner of his storeroom and let them establish there a minor menagerie, with an old bird cage, a large sand box and a tub of water for the accommodation of amphibians. He soon regretted his generosity, for now he had to sit in judgment on the fate of a great variety of living creatures, some of which aroused a strong compassion and others an equally strong aversion. He ruled that young birds had to be taken back to where they were found, although they might be kept for a day or so if they could be fed. Frogs and turtles also had to be returned to the ditch after a period of observation. He firmly declined to accommodate a live water snake, even though Benita wound it around her neck to convince him it was completely harmless. Lizards and horned toads became the only permanent residents of the storeroom, after they proved their ability to make a living by catching flies and had become so tame they could be stroked with a straw.

In all this business Leo found himself functioning somewhat reluctantly as an authority who had to make decisions and be firm while at the same time he achieved something of a return to childhood, for all of these strange creatures interested him almost as much as they did the girls, and they took him back to the days when he had spent much time along the river. His interest even moved him to search Santa Fe for a book on natural history, and he finally found one designed for children and illustrated in color. It seemed not to shed much light on the local fauna, but the girls evidently found it edifying, seeing pictures of elephants and tigers for the first time.

Leo knew that he was abetting Magdalena in a variety of adventures that neither the Vierras nor the Padre would have approved. He felt some faint twinges of conscience about this, but was sustained by a strong sympathy for her freedom and her delight in it. He knew that if her destiny was typical this was the only freedom she would ever have, except such as she might achieve by stealth and cunning. A Mexican girl was often allowed to run at large as a child, but the stroke of puberty suddenly and permanently transformed her life. She then became a lady, and a Mexican lady was more an institution than a person. She first took communion and then made a social debut, more or less formal according to the wealth and social importance of her family. After that she was forbidden ever to see any male person alone, except members of her family, or to go abroad unaccompanied or to engage in any physical activity except dancing. By the time she was sixteen, if lucky, she might be married, often to a husband chosen by her parents and always to one approved by them. Mexican women in general accepted this destiny with grace and resignation, as the will of God, but Leo felt that it was probably going to be difficult for Magdalena, with her rebellious temper, her love of action and her versatile curiosity. For curiosity in particular there seemed to be no place in a life of faith and status. It was essentially an unquestioning life.

2.Magdalena had been frequenting his establishment for a year or more when he first noticed that she was learning a few words of English and trying to use them. She seemed to have an affinity both for the language and for those who spoke it, as though she had been moved by some intuition that her own life would be lived in a world dominated by gringos. When English-speaking strangers came to the store she looked and listened and would always give them her wide smile if they noticed her. The only gringo she saw frequently was Jack Gibbs. He always lifted his hat to her, called her señorita, and asked about her health with grave courtesy. Magdalena evidently found him fascinating and always listened to his abundant talk with close attention, no matter which language he used. Often he mixed the two languages, flavoring his Spanish with some good Anglo-Saxon profanity and sprinkling his English with Spanish words, in a fashion then not uncommon. Magdalena could seldom have understood what he was talking about, but she learned to imitate some of his typical expressions with comical precision. One day when she had become annoyed with Benita and sent the girl home, Leo was astounded to hear her remark, "Goddam these greasers, anyway."

Her aptitude for language did not surprise him. He had long known that an illiterate Mexican would learn English much more quickly than an educated gringo would learn Spanish. It occurred to him that with a little help Magdalena might grow up bilingual, as he knew that some children in Santa Fe were doing, and this would be a great advantage to her.

"Would you like to learn English well?" he asked her, and she nodded eager agreement. He had found long since that Magdalena hated advice and admonition, but would go through with anything that had won her assent. He began his pedagogical effort by addressing her always in English and then translating into Spanish whatever part of his remarks she could not understand. They were soon communicating in a linguistic mixture which slowly became almost pure English, although hers had always a charming Mexican accent. He knew that she must learn to read and write the language and on his trips to Santa Fe and Albuquerque he hunted for books that might catch her interest. This proved difficult. Magdalena was a gifted talker but no student. She was bored by Mother Goose rhymes and also by the classical fairy tales. The few juvenile stories he found were all designed to elevate the character and morals of the young, and these she repudiated decisively. She had no taste for self-improvement. Leo at last offered her some of the dime novels of Ned Buntline which were then just beginning to flood the market, most of them based on the exploits of Kit Carson, who was still living in Taos as an old man and read the Buntline versions of his own exploits with amused astonishment. These epics of slaughter and gallantry delighted Magdalena. She had been raised on tales of Indian battles, had always known the Apaches and the Comanches were the natural enemies of her people. When one more redskin bit the dust, she took a hearty satisfaction in his finish, and her vocabulary throve on a diet of blood and thunder. Within a year after he began teaching her, they were speaking to each other wholly in English and this seemed to create for them a separate and confidential world, for most of the time there was no one else in the store who understood the language.

---

3. Every time Leo came home from a trip to Santa Fe it seemed to him that Magdalena had become a different person. It was not of course that she had truly changed much while he was gone but simply that he noticed her growth in mind and body after an absence. This was the first time he had ever been able to observe the unfolding of a human consciousness, and he found it a fascinating spectacle, the more so because he knew that he had some share in it. He did not know exactly what part he had played, but if he and his store had never existed Magdalena would surely have been a different person and much more a typical Mexican girl. As it was, her personality had acquired a distinctly gringo flavor, with her sharp and irreverent humor, her impertinence and her ready flow of English.

He delighted in the growth of her mind, but her physical growth disturbed him, because he knew it would take her away from him. Very gradually over a period of several years Magdalena had established herself as a part of his life. At first he had been only vaguely aware of her as a quiet little girl sitting in a corner. Then she had begun to make demands upon him and to occupy his time and attention, and now when he was away he thought more of Magdalena than of anyone else and spent much time in Santa Fe hunting out suitable gifts to bring her. She had become somehow necessary to him, and it was her growth that was going to take her away, bury her in that Mexican world of rigid custom and obligation, of a discipline that was not a personal thing but was inherent in the form and pattern of an ancient way of life. Moreover, he knew that most Mexican girls became young ladies suddenly and early, as though this hot country had forced their growth, imposing an early womanhood upon them, but Magdalena still did not look in the least like a young lady in the making. She had grown straight up, like a sunflower after the summer rains, becoming impressively tall but thinner than ever and also more active. She loved to run and seemed to be built for speed, but her body held no promise of that soft voluptuous quality which most Mexican girls achieved so early. Then suddenly, the next year, she began to widen, taking on beef, as Jack Gibbs observed, like a yearling in a cornfield. But to Leo she seemed still very much a child.

"You're getting fat," he told her when he came home from Santa Fe that year. He picked her up under the arms and hoisted her above his head, while she giggled and squirmed with pleasure. It was the nearest thing to a caress that had ever passed between them and this privilege of lifting her off her feet was shared also by her good friend Jack Gibbs.

"A little more weight and I won't be able to lift you," he remarked as he sat down and began unwrapping a package of dime novels he had brought her, while she came and stood beside his chair, leaning against him, as she always had done. His arm encircled her body almost automatically, so that he was hardly aware of the contact until suddenly his hand discovered her small firm breast.

He had never even noticed that Magdalena had breasts, so completely had she always been a child to him. He turned and looked at her and their eyes met in a perfectly mutual surprise. Her face was flushed, her lips parted and her eyes were wide with a look of wonder. He knew, without thinking but with great certainty, that now everything was different, and that this was the end or very nearly the end, that Magdalena, the beloved child, was already gone. What she was thinking he could not guess, but her mouth seemed an open invitation, and he kissed her lightly. Then both of them began laughing. It was not a laughter of joy or delight but simply the relief of a tension that had become intolerable. She squirmed in his grasp, pulled away from him, gave him a soft slap that was more a caress than a reproof, then broke away and ran to the door. With her hand on the knob she turned and laughed again, and he knew that he was looking at another person, a woman, all challenge and coquetry, as though his touch had transformed her in a moment. Then she turned and went, closing the door behind her. He could hear her running feet all the length of the empty store, and he knew that her running was at once a flight and a dance of triumph.

4.When he saw the Padre a few days later he learned that Magdalena's childhood had truly come to an end and also her freedom. The next Sunday she would take communion in the church. Within a week she and her aunt would go to Santa Fe for a long visit with Lupe's numerous and important family and then Magdalena would be placed in a convent.

"She does not want to go," the Padre said. "She wept and made a scene when they told her. She is not a bad child, but she lacks obedience. I think they let her run wild too long here in the village, with only that Indian girl to look after her."

Leo solemnly agreed, reflecting with a mixture of pride and guilt, that Magdalena's insubordinate temper was probably due as much to his influence as to Benita's. He went to the church the next Sunday and saw her arrive in the family coach, clad in a long white dress, her first long dress, looking surprisingly adult and dignified, saw her kneel at the altar and accept the wafer and receive the blessing that made her the bride of Christ. He walked slowly home, feeling saddened and bereft. He almost wished that Magdalena had never moved into his life and especially that their one intimate moment had never occurred. It seemed to be her kiss that had printed her image on his mind so that he could not be free of it. Now she was truly gone into another world where he could not hope to follow.

He thought that probably he would not see her alone again for years, but in this he was mistaken. She came to the store a few days later, quite properly accompanied by Benita, and quite properly she made a few small purchases. He was sitting in his office with the door open and she threw him a smile, then turned to the one clerk and asked for what she wanted. It was near the end of a stormy October day, with a great wind howling down from the mesa. The store would close within an hour. He sat watching her, wondering whether he would have a moment alone with her. He saw her receive her package, hand it to Benita and dismiss the girl, and then slowly, high-headed and smiling, she came toward the office. He was aware of the pounding of his heart, amazed at his own excitement, wondering how she could have become so suddenly such a different person and their relationship such a different thing. They were conspirators now, moving toward a stolen moment. He called out to his clerk, "You may go now, Federico."

The man spoke a low good night and went to the door, glancing back at them curiously as he closed it. Leo rose to meet her, feeling curiously unsure just what their relations now had become. She settled that question by kissing him firmly on the mouth, but it was evident that her mood was indignant rather than amorous.

"You have heard?" she demanded, as soon as they were seated. "I have to go to Santa Fe and they are going to put me in a convent!" She spoke as though the hardship and injustice of such a fate were perfectly obvious.

"I know," Leo said. "I can't tell you how sorry I am. I don't know when I'll ever see you again."

"I'm not allowed to come even here now, alone," she explained. "But I had to see you once more, and tell you . . . I never knew before how much you were to me, you and this place. I never knew until they told me now I can't go anywhere alone, and I must go to Santa Fe and I must go to school and I must be a lady."

She paused for breath and made a comical face, which somehow expressed her low opinion of ladyhood and they both laughed a little.

"You know how much I will miss you," he told her.

"I have been happy here," she said. "Here, and running around with Benita, but always coming back here and to you, and knowing that I could tell you anything and that whatever I did, you would not mind and not scold me, and I never knew how good that was until now, and now they are going to take me away and shut me up and . . . I don't want to go!"

The last words were delivered slowly and with an emphasis that expressed a stubborn refusal, a precocious and untamed strength. She sat breathless, smiling at him, with a tear showing in her eye.

Before either of them could speak again they heard the front door open and close and a step coming down the resounding length of the quiet store. The door to the office was only a little ajar so that neither of them could see who was coming. They sat looking at each other in silence, with sudden alarm and surprise in their eyes, and guilt—the inevitable guilt of lovers who have offended against the laws of the tribe, the immemorial taboos.

He knew only that the step was that of a woman, but he felt intuitively sure who the woman was and he rose and opened the door and greeted her with an elaborate hypocrisy.

"Lupe!" he said. "I am so glad to see you. Magdalena is here. She came to tell me good-by."

Lupe was not to be surpassed in politeness. She had her feelings under perfect control, smiled and gave him her hand ever so lightly and briefly, turned to Magdalena.

"I have been looking for you," she said. "And I thought you might have come here. We have company at the house and it is almost time to eat and you have not dressed."

Magdalena said nothing, but her face flushed and her brows drew together in an irrepressible frown. It was clear that she was not frightened or penitent, but filled with a rage that flooded up darkly into her face and quickened her breathing. Leo, dreading a scene above all things, pulled up a chair.

"Sit down, Lupe, please," he said. "This is the first time you have ever done me the honor of a visit to my office."

She looked at him with a faint smile that seemed to mingle amusement with a little compassion. He felt somehow sure that not much of her anger was directed toward him, that the battle line was drawn between the two women. This was the ancient war of the generations. Lupe was here to enforce the sacred proprieties as they had been enforced upon her when she was young. She had let her niece run free, as a child. Now that Magdalena had reached the verge of womanhood, she must accept the disciplines of her kind and class. And beneath this righteous assertion of power and duty lay the inevitable rivalry, the hatred of the aging flesh for the rising challenge of youth. Leo noticed for the first time that Lupe showed age in her neck and wrists and in the hardness about her uncompromising mouth, while Magdalena had the flushed and vivid freshness of life newly created.

"Well, for a moment," Lupe said smoothly. "It is late and we must go soon."

So they all three sat for a tense uneasy moment, each of

them filled with feelings that could not possibly be expressed, keeping the peace only by saying nothing they meant.

"So you are going to Santa Fe," Leo said. "I am afraid then I will not see you here for a long time."

"Yes." Lupe again executed her controlled smile. "It will be a long time."

She rose.

"Come, Magdalena!" She spoke with sharp authority.

For just a few seconds, Magdalena sat perfectly still and unsmiling. They were tense seconds. Leo wondered if the girl could be about to make an open rebellion. Then she rose, and both of them shook hands with him. Magdalena spoke for the first time since her aunt had entered and she spoke in English, which was half an insult to Lupe, who knew hardly a word of it.

"Good-by, Leo," she said. "I don't know when I'll see you again but be sure I'll never forget you and I thank you for all the nice things you have done for me."

He followed them to the front door where Lupe said adiós and Magdalena said good-by again, and he stood watching them disappear in the darkness with a feeling of sadness and loss. He knew that Lupe would never come to see him again and he did not feel at all sure that Magdalena would ever return to Don Pedro. Very likely she would stay in Santa Fe until she married, and if she did return, Lupe would never set her free this side of the altar. The two of them seemed to be locked in a struggle that locked him out.

I.Strangers who came to his store had been
one of Leo's diversions and also one of his problems ever since
the year he came to Don Pedro. He was a villager, yet he
lived on a major thoroughfare, for the post road from Santa
Fe to El Paso was only a mile away. More and more travelers
turned aside to visit the Tienda Mendes as its fame grew and
also because he had a good corral and camping place. Seldom
a week passed that he did not look across a counter or a table
at some man he had never seen before and sometimes at men
of kinds wholly new to him. Prospectors, cowboys and army
officers were the recurrent figures, but one month brought an
engineer employed on a border survey, an ethnologist from
Washington, a missionary who hoped to convert the Hopi
Indians into good Baptists, and a very expensive-looking Mexican from across the river, who, he learned later, was a famous

bandit. He rode a saddle heavy with silver, wore a fifty-dollar sombrero and had beautiful manners.

Any man who faces many strangers learns to form a quick and fairly reliable opinion of them, at least so far as their relation to him is concerned, and Leo had come to take pride in his ability to judge the new customer. He asked himself two questions about every man—could he be trusted, and was he worth talking with? Some of them, such as the bandit from south of Juarez, were loaded with money, but others had not a dollar, and almost everyone needed something. Leo seldom turned a man away empty-handed and never let one go hungry. To do so would have been to violate the unwritten code of all frontier countries. He sometimes gave credit to men he had never seen before. A deflated cowboy or prospector often would offer a gun, a knife or a pair of spurs as security. Leo would take one good look at the man and then decide whether to accept the pledge or refuse it, making a bet with himself, in the latter case, that the customer would come back and pay. Generally he won. He had come to believe that he could tell by the expression in a man's eyes, by his voice and the character of his speech whether he was honest. One who looked straight at him and spoke slowly was generally a good credit risk, especially if he used profanity. A smooth, fast talker with a roving eye often was not.

One kind of man he faced repeatedly was a horseman, wearing always a huge hat, high-heeled half-boots and a Colt revolver, usually low on his right hip. The rest of his costume was just pants and a shirt with a jacket or jumper in cold weather, but the hat, gun and boots were invariable. Almost all of these men also had the same slow drawling speech, the same reticence about themselves and the same courteous manners, especially toward women. Their great hats seemed to rise automatically at the sight of a skirt. They all called themselves cowpunchers or cattlemen and they were of a type that was to become almost a stereotype, firmly fixed in the popular imagination. But underneath their uniformities of dress and manner these men were exceedingly diverse and hard to judge. Some of them were wandering cowboys in search of a job, some were ranch owners or ranch foremen or professional trail-drivers. Others were rustlers, cattle and horse thieves, experts with the running iron, man-killers when necessary. So it was often hard to guess whether such a man was engaged in larceny or honest labor, and he was little likely to say a word about himself in either case. One day a boy, not more than seventeen and rather small, came into the store and bought supplies, including ammunition for a six-shooter which he wore oddly right over his belt buckle. He had two huge buck teeth, a wide grin, an easy flow of talk. He introduced himself by the name of Bonney, and told the usual nothing about his own business, but did mention that he had been born in New York City. Leo invited him to dinner, as he always did any stranger who seemed to be interesting. They had a pleasant chat about early memories, and Bonney promised to come again, but never did. Not until the man was killed about four years later did Leo become aware that he had entertained the famous Billy the Kid.

It was the summer Magdalena and her aunt went to Santa Fe that he first met Robert Coppinger in the same casual way. He happened to be alone in the store when he saw the man dismount at the hitchrack, noticed that he rode a big gray gelding, worth easily a hundred dollars and led a blue-buck-skin pack horse, which looked almost as good as the saddle horse and doubtless served as a spare mount. Leo was accustomed to notice such things, just as a good hotel man will notice the baggage of an approaching guest. As the stranger walked toward him he knew that he was looking at a very tired man who had just made a long ride in very dry country. Fatigue showed in the way he walked and the fine dust that covered him from hat to boots was the mark of long desert riding. He was a tall man, over six feet, with dark hair and blue eyes, bright against his weathered face. He said, "Howdy," introduced himself, pulled out a tobacco sack, shook the last few crumbs of its contents into a little yellow paper, rolled a cigarette deftly with one hand, lit it and threw the empty bag on the counter.

"I'm out of smokes," he remarked as he exhaled a blue cloud through his nose. "I'm out of damn near everything."

Leo noticed that he did not use his left hand, that a rude and dirty bandage showed at his wrist, and that the bandage was bloodstained. He suspected that the man needed help but didn't want to ask for it. He risked a question.

"Hurt yourself?" He nodded at the injured arm.

"I got nicked," Coppinger said.

"Better let me look at it," Leo suggested. "I have an old woman working for me who used to be a midwife. She's pretty good on cuts and bruises."

Coppinger was silent a moment, blowing smoke.

"All right," he said. "Thanks."

Leo led the man back to his living quarters, called Avendera, and they explored the wound. It was an ugly jagged flesh wound that might well have been made by a bullet. Avandera washed it in hot water, doused it first with pure alcohol and then with iodine, causing Coppinger to grit his teeth, then put on a fresh bandage. She worked in a small room with a board floor, equipped with a large wooden tub, a mirror, a shelf loaded with soap, brushes and shaving equipment. This was Leo's bathroom, by far the most elaborate in Don Pedro, if not in the valley. It was one of his eccentricities that he bathed daily, even in cold weather.

"You can shave and have a bath if you want," he told his

guest. "Avandera will bring you hot water. Come back about six and we'll eat."

"Thanks," Coppinger said. "Why do you do all this for me?"

"I hope you'll be a good customer," Leo told him.

"I'll try to," Coppinger promised. "Right now I'm not a cash customer. I haven't got a buck in my jeans. But I've got two good horses. You can hold one of them against what I owe you."

"All right," Leo said.

Over a drink before supper Coppinger felt moved to explain himself a little. He was a horse trader and horsebreaker, working back and forth across the border. He bought horses in Chihuahua, many of them unbroken, brought them across the river, converted them into good saddle stock and sold them at a profit. It was a fairly common occupation at the time. Much live stock crossed the river. Some of it was honestly acquired and much of it was stolen, so much that "wet horse" had become almost a synonym for a stolen one.

"I was coming back with six head of two-year-olds," Coppinger said. "They were a little hard to handle. I got them across the river all right and camped on this side. That night somebody raided me in the dark. I don't know who or how many, but we traded shots and I got winged. They didn't get my saddle horses because I had them hobbled, but they ran off all the others."

"Tough luck," Leo said.

"When it got light I trailed them up the river to where they crossed," Coppinger continued. "I knew I probably couldn't catch them but I was hoping some of the two-year-olds might get away. I had to turn back because my horses were playing out and so was I. I work out of El Paso most of the time but I came here because it was the nearest place— and I needed to get some place quick."

"I'm glad you came," Leo said. He was wondering whether Coppinger was an honest man or a horse thief and a liar, and that question sat uncomfortably between them throughout the meal. Afterward Coppinger refused Leo's offer of a bed, went to sleep in his own blankets in the open-face shed that adjoined the corral. Next morning he came into the store and bought a few dollars' worth of supplies which Leo put on the books. At noon Coppinger had gone without saying good-by, but he left his blue buckskin in the corral. Leo now felt sure he had met an honest man, and also one who was somehow impressive, commanded attention without trying, conveyed the feeling that he should be given what he wanted.

2. Six months after his first visit Coppinger had established a headquarters at Don Pedro, the second gringo ever to live there. He had evidently found the Tienda Mendes a better place to trade than any other within his reach, but he had also formed a useful alliance with Jack Gibbs at the post. With the help of Gibbs he had sold several saddle horses to army officers for fancy prices and when he had time to spare he often helped Gibbs handle cattle. He had moved into the village much as Leo had done, renting a tumbledown house on the edge of town for about a dollar a month. Behind it he built a circular corral of long cottonwood poles laid end to end like a rail fence, with a snubbing post in the center. This was the necessary instrument of his profession.

Coppinger was in town less than half the time, but when he was he attracted plenty of attention. His horse corral, like Leo's store, quickly became a place of interest. He would come back from each of his trips with three or four unbroken horses and work them over, one at a time, day after day,

until he had converted them all into good saddle stock. He
was a greatly gifted horseman, the best the town had ever
seen. Sometimes he would hire a man to help him, but most
of the time he worked alone. A horse of high value he would
"break gentle"—an impressive exhibition of patience and of
the skillful use of hand and voice. A horse that had never
known hemp or leather would be driven into the round corral
and roped. Then Coppinger would give the rope a hitch
around the snubbing post, brace his weight with one foot
against it and let the horse convince himself, once and for all,
that a rope is irresistible. The half-wild animal might lunge
against it hard enough to throw himself, fight it like a wild-
cat with his fore feet, almost choke himself to death, finally
subside into heaving, snorting pop-eyed surrender. This was
his essential defeat and his only experience of violence. After
that he could be blindfolded and saddled. He was slowly
accustomed first to an empty saddle and then to a saddle
with a bag of sand on either side. He was worked first with a
hackamore and then with a bridle. He was rewarded with
oats and even apples, and always he was wooed with the
low and soothing voice of the good horseman, gentle as the
voice of a mother with a frightened child. When finally Coppinger carefully mounted him, he might tremble but he seldom bucked, and ten days later he would be a working horse.
But few horses were worth that much time and trouble. On a
forty-dollar cayuse Coppinger would do a fine exhibition of
bronco-busting, letting the horse buck until he was tired.
These were the events that drew the largest crowds, sometimes most of the population of Don Pedro. Small boys came
first, then women came in search of their children, and they
were followed by men worried about their wives and daughters. For Coppinger was a handsome man and it was well
known that men who are good with horses are almost always

good with women, who also respond to a deft and patient use of hand and voice.

So Coppinger was a stimulating and somewhat disturbing figure, bringing new life to the sleepy village. He was distrusted the more because he was a Texan. Between Texans and Mexicans there was a traditional hostility, going back to the Alamo and, even more, to the ill-fated Texan invasion of New Mexico in 1841. Most Texans showed contempt for the Mexican male, especially as a fighting man, but this attitude did not apply at all to Mexican women. Texans had a chivalrous attitude toward all women and a fine appreciation of feminine beauty. A good many of them, including the great Colonel Bowie, had married Mexican women, and a great many more had bestowed their informal attentions on Mexican wives. It was said that a Mexican woman who had once had a gringo lover, Texan or otherwise, would never afterward endure a Mexican husband, who treated women strictly as property and granted them no rights whatsoever, while Texans in particular were imbued with that worshipful attitude toward the feminine presence which had long flourished in the Southern states. So the handsome drawling Coppinger might easily have made much trouble for himself and others, but he was evidently determined to avoid this, for he behaved himself in Don Pedro with great discretion. His attentions to women apparently did not go beyond the respectful lifting of his great hat when he met them on the street. All day he worked hard, so absorbed in horses that he seemed oblivious to the human race. In the evening he might ride over to the post to see Gibbs or drop into Leo's office near the end of the day for a drink and a chat, sometimes staying for supper. Between these two slowly grew a friendship, based upon a mutual sympathy neither could have explained, and bridging a difference which gave them always something to talk about, made each a perpetual surprise to the other. One

thing they did have in common in that both of them here
were aliens and invaders. Both belonged to the future and
were engaged in destroying the past. Both were vaguely aware
they didn't quite belong in this lost fragment of the Middle
Ages and became more conscious of the fact when they were
together. This gave them a certain fellowship, but it left them
still about as far apart in tradition and experience as any
two men who spoke the same language. So Coppinger was
amazed and even shocked to discover that Leo lived in this
land of hostile Apaches and professional bandits without any
weapon he could use. The guns in his store he never touched
and did not even know how to load them. As for Coppinger,
he put on his six-shooter when he put on his shirt and would
have felt naked without it.

"Don't you know you can't trust a greaser?" he demanded.
"They'll work for you, sure, but they'll steal anything that
ain't nailed to the floor and put a knife between your ribs
for two bits." This, Leo knew, was the standard Texan's con-
ception of a Mexican.

"I never had any trouble with them," Leo said mildly.

"You just never met up with any good thieves," Coppinger
told him.

Leo laughed.

"I've met some of the best thieves in the territory," he
said. "In my peddling days I did quite a little business with
them. They were the only customers who had any cash."

"Keep it up and you'll stop a bullet sooner or later," Coppinger warned. "You ought to have a loaded shotgun right
there in the corner."

"If there's a bullet with my name on it I'll stop it anyway,"
Leo said. "I believe that what's going to happen is going to
happen."

Coppinger pondered this proposition gravely for several
minutes. It had evidently stirred some memory or idea, but

he finally decided against any reply and changed the subject. Although fast in action he was slow in speech and cautious about either committing or revealing himself. Yet he did reveal himself, slowly, over a long period. He was in some ways a ruthless man, who would not hesitate to shoot in a fight or drop a rope on a horse that didn't wear a brand, but he had one ethical principle he held inviolable, and that was his feeling of obligation toward anyone he had accepted as a friend. He paid cash on his bill at the store whenever he had it, and made some return for every favor. After dining at Leo's table he insisted that Leo come to his home for a meal. He had equipped it with a bunk, a table and two chairs—all homemade—but the floor was still adobe and he did his cooking with a Dutch oven and a skillet in the little corner fireplace.

"It ain't much compared with that place of yours," he apologized when Leo came in. "But you're sure welcome."

"It's all right for me," Leo said. "For years I took all my meals squatting on the floor and chasing my beans with a tortilla."

"If my mother could see this dump she would think I had fallen pretty low," Coppinger remarked.

"What you need is a woman to fix it up and cook for you," Leo suggested.

Coppinger shook his head hard and repeatedly, like a horse trying to shake off a rope.

"Women are just fine when you're going some place else pretty pronto," he said, "but let them once get their hooks into you and you might as well be tied to a tree. That's why I never look at a woman around here."

Like most men of his kind he could make excellent biscuits in a Dutch oven and he had also a pot of frijoles and a pan of young beef cut in small collops, rolled in flour and fried. With good whisky and coffee almost strong enough to

stand alone, they had an ample meal. Over it Coppinger began talking about meals his mother had served in the old
Coppinger homestead on the Guadelupe River near the gulf
coast of Texas. Starting from nostalgic memories of fried
chicken and blueberry pie, he gave Leo a detailed account
of the world that had produced him.

The Coppingers were a numerous tribe who owned thousands of acres, worth about a dollar an acre, and thousands of
little scrub longhorns, worth about a dollar a head. Coppinger's father had a two-story house with long galleries on both
floors, and before the war he had five or six Negroes working
around the house all the time, and there were dances and
picnics and hayrides and great community roundups and
buffalo hunts in the panhandle and horse races in town on
courthouse days. His words welling up from deep springs of
memory and longing, Coppinger spoke more and better than
ever he had before and Leo listened with absorbed interest.
He always liked to hear a man talk this way, felt as though he
were sharing another life, getting outside his own skin. It
struck him how much the Coppingers' life in Texas was like
the life of the Vierras here in Don Pedro, with the same wealth
of land and cattle and little money and the same easy command over slaves and servants. Coppinger and Don Augustín
had looked at each other, the one time they met in the store,
with instinctive hostility, yet they were men of much the same
kind except that Coppinger had a restless energy the Mexican lacked. It was easy to see that Coppinger loved the world
of his boyhood and Leo wondered why he had left it.

"Are you going back?" he ventured. "It sounds like a good
life."

Coppinger was silent for a long moment as he nearly always was when confronted by a question, slowly rolling and
lighting a cigarette, apparently considering whether to go on
with his story.

"I had a little trouble back there," he began at last. "I've never told anybody anything about it, haven't thought of it much now for a couple of years, but something you said the other day about a bullet with your name on it brought it back to mind."

He paused again, and Leo felt sure now that he was about to hear a confession—that Coppinger had something on his mind he needed to talk about.

"We had lots of feuds in Texas, starting right after the war," Coppinger went on. "Plenty of them are still going strong. I know the Coppinger-Shelby feud is still popping and that's why I'm not going back, not any time soon. If I did I'd be right back in the big trouble. Don't ask me how it started, because nobody seems to know exactly. Before the war that was a peaceful country, but after the war everything went bad, especially for Confederates. My father was a Confederate captain and I was seventeen, wearing my first gun and riding my first good horse, when he got back from the war. The country was full of freed niggers and some of them were pretty uppity and quite a few of them got killed. There were Union troops stationed in our county and they seemed to be there just to bother us. A squad of them was stationed at a ford on the Guadelupe River and they disarmed everybody that crossed the river, just for the hell of it. Then there were Union sympathizers. We called them scalawags and that's where the word got started. These Shelbys were scalawags, although we had been good friends with them before the war. Ed Shelby and me grew up together, went swimming and stole watermelons with the same gang. The first trouble with the Shelbys took place about a year after the war. One of them killed an uncle of mine, in an argument about the war, I believe. In these killings nobody ever seems to know exactly what happened or why. Anyway, after that a cousin of mine killed a Shelby and feeling got real bad. The country was full of bad feeling anyway on account of the war and the freed niggers and the Union troops, and it seemed to get into everybody like malaria in a wet summer. It was a funny business, that feud. We used to still go to some of the same parties, Shelbys and Coppingers, and dance with each other's girls and be awful polite, but everybody knew trouble was going to bust out again sooner or later. Then somebody spread the word that Ed Shelby was gunning for me. I doubt that he was but there's always some bastard that wants to start something. Most likely the same man told Ed I was gunning for him, which I wasn't. I was working with horses, like I am now, and I didn't want any part of the feud, but yet it came to be a settled thing that there was trouble between Ed and me, and everybody was talking about it, and some even made bets on what would happen when we met. If I had pulled out then, I would have been rated a coward, and I never could have gone back. Lots of people did leave the country on account of the feuds, but not those that were directly mixed up in them. It's a strange thing but people are more afraid of what other people think than they are of hot lead. I'm frank to say I went out of my way more than once to avoid Ed, but the day came when we met. It was bound to happen. He was coming out the door of a store in the town of Cuero, just as I was getting off my horse out in front. I'll never forget that minute. There were quite a few people on the store porch and all of a sudden the word went around that Ed and I were both there, and those people scattered like flushed quail. One man dived head first through an open window and another crawled under the porch, and I remember a woman ran screaming out into the road to catch a little kid and drag him behind a tree. And then Ed saw me and we both started to draw, but I beat him to it by about a fifth of a second. I remember the roar of my six-shooter. I never knew when I drew it. That's a thing you do without thinking, like you jump when you're scared. The gun went off and the first thing I knew about it was when I heard the noise. But what I remember best is the expression on Ed's face when the bullet hit him. He didn't look hurt and he didn't look scared. He just looked surprised, with his eyes wide and his mouth open, as if he couldn't believe he and I were standing there trying to kill each other. And then he fell on his face and I knew he was dead. They're always dead when they fall that way."

Coppinger was silent for minutes after he had finished his story and Leo felt as though any comment would be an impertinence. He understood that Coppinger had been moved by the oldest code in the world, the code of private vengeance, the code of the Old Testament—an eye for an eye, a tooth for a tooth, a life for a life. Forebears of his own who followed their flocks across the desert, they too had known only the simple justice of the price in blood.

"I had to do it," Coppinger said at last. "It's like you said the other day. That bullet had his name on it and he was walking toward it all his life. I knew I didn't want any more feuding and I made up my mind to go. I knew lots of people would call me a coward even then, but it looked to me like it took more nerve to go than it did to stay."

---

3. One day that fall a gang of Mexicans from across the river came to the lake to make salt and afterward stopped at the store and camped in Leo's corral. He took some of the coarse salt in trade—he could always use it as stock salt—and the Mexicans acquired coffee and sugar, a few yards of cotton cloth, a knife and some powder and lead for their old muzzle-loading guns. This was an event that happened about once a month from September to May.

Perhaps a thousand Mexicans depended upon the lake for salt and came there every two or three years. This gang numbered about twenty-five, including three women and half a dozen young boys. They were very poor Mexicans, explaining that drought had nearly ruined their crops that year and Apaches had driven off a herd of goats. Leo could see they had nothing to eat except atole, which was corn meal toasted and made into a thick gruel. They had no horses, only burros, and most of those were pack animals which went out to the lake loaded with kegs of fresh water and came back loaded with bags of salt.

Salt and water, Leo thought, as he watched them move into the corral and unload their animals, man is made of salt and water. With salt and water and a little corn meal a man can live and these men seemed to be down to the rudiments of human subsistence. Leo felt a strong sympathy for them because for years poor Mexicans had always offered him food, even when they had only atole and salt. He told Aurelio Beltrán to drive a yearling steer into the corral and give it to them. It was a good-sized animal and fat.

"That ought to last them until they get home," Leo remarked. "They can dry what they don't eat now."

Aurelio laughed.

"I can see you never starved," he said, "as I have done when I got lost in the mountains. A starving man can eat fresh meat like a wolf. Tomorrow morning a crow won't be able to pick a meal off the bones of that calf."

They stood watching while the Mexicans butchered the animal, knocking it in the head with an axe, hanging it up by the heels and cutting its throat. They wasted nothing, catching every drop of blood in a bucket, and several of the men drank cups of hot blood. It was a cultivated taste and very nourishing. They did not wait for the meat to age, they barely let it cool before they started eating it. The whole troop of them sat up all night about a fire, toasting bits of beef on green twigs or tossing them onto the red coals to broil, scraping off the ashes and eating them sprinkled with the coarse salt of the lake. As their bellies filled with red meat they felt better and better. Their singing and laughter woke Leo at two in the morning, and the next day they looked like different people, the children especially fairly bulging with food and full of pranks.

The day after the Mexicans left, Coppinger came to visit Leo in his office. He said he wanted to talk business.

"I've known that lake for years," he said. "But it never struck me before that it might make a nice little business proposition. How many Mexicans make salt there—first and last I mean?"

Leo, feeling profoundly uneasy but trying not to show it, guessed that perhaps a thousand Mexicans depended on the lake for salt.

"You know it's in Texas, don't you?" Coppinger asked.

"Yes, it's just over the line," Leo agreed. "Some people seem to think it's in New Mexico."

Coppinger nodded gravely.

"That's probably one reason nobody has grabbed it," he said. "Texas has no public land, but anybody can buy that lake from the state government and buy it cheap because it's arid land."

"I know," Leo agreed. "But it belonged to Mexico until a few years ago and under Mexican law all salt deposits are public property and free to everybody. All these Mexicans depend on the lake for salt. They feel it belongs to them."

"But they're wrong," Coppinger interrupted. "It belongs to anybody that wants to buy it and fence it, and now's the time to grab it. If you'll put up the money—and it won't take much—I'll build the fence and manage the place."

Leo sat shaking his head sadly.

"I wouldn't want to do it," he said. "The salt wouldn't be worth the trouble."

"Trouble, my eye!" Coppinger protested. "Leave it to me. I'll take care of the trouble. A man's got to take what he has a right to. And if we don't do it, somebody else will. I'll bet I can go to El Paso tomorrow and raise the money."

While Coppinger talked, Leo thought fast. He was profoundly averse to having anyone fence the lake. He knew an old man whose father and grandfather before him had come there for salt. To them it was the salt of the earth, the salt of God, to which they had as much right as to air and water. But it wasn't only sentiment that disturbed him. He knew that all the Mexicans who came to the lake for salt would resent any effort to shut them out, and that some of them were smugglers and bandits from across the river, who could use a rifle.

"We'll string a wire fence around it," Coppinger went on, evidently feeling that he had the best of the argument. "When a gang of Mexicans come we'll put them to work at a dollar a day digging salt for us. They can buy what they need. It'll be good for 'em. The trouble with these goddam greasers is they put nothing on the market and they take nothing off. They live from ground to mouth. We've got to have business in this country, and they've got to learn it."

Leo understood Coppinger's philosophy well enough. He had lived with it for years. He knew it was no use to argue against progress and business and the right of every man to take what he could get. He knew it would be even more futile to warn Coppinger that fencing the lake might mean violence. Coppinger would never back down from a threat of violence. It was necessary to make a practical argument.

"In just a few years there's going to be a railroad through El Paso," he said. "Then your salt won't be worth what it cost to fence it. It's only a coarse salt with alkali and gypsum in it. Good salt is dirt cheap wherever you have a railroad."

"That railroad's a long way off," Coppinger remarked. "The railhead is somewhere in East Texas and moving slow."

The two men sat looking at each other for a long silent moment, Coppinger stubborn and self-assured, Leo showing his pain as plainly as a man with a toothache. Not only was the salt lake now in danger, and perhaps the peace of Don Pedro, but also his good relations with Coppinger. For he knew he could not yield.

Coppinger also looked unyielding, but then gradually his expression changed. He smiled, a slow-spreading smile that finally became a broad grin, making him look very boyish and wholly friendly.

"You would hate to see that lake fenced, wouldn't you?" he demanded.

Leo hove a deep sigh.

"Yes, I would," he admitted.

"All right, then, we won't fence it," Coppinger said. "You're a friend of mine and you don't want it fenced. That's enough for me. We won't fence it."

Leo laughed with relief and also with amusement. That was so like Coppinger. He would cheerfully take the salt out of a Mexican's mouth, but he would also do anything or forgo anything for a friend.

"Come on over to the house," Leo said. "We'll have a drink on that."

He felt that their friendship had been tested and proved.

I.The grand ball the Vierras gave for their niece when she returned from Santa Fe was the most impressive social event the lower valley had seen in years. The long sala was cleared for dancing and its rough board floor was strewn with fine white sand from the river bars. A platform was built for the orchestra and the room was festooned with the goldenrod which then was yellow along all the valley roads. There came all the first families of Mesilla, Las Cruces and El Paso, bringing coachloads of women in their voluminous skirts, with bare shoulders and flowers in their hair, while gentlemen rode alongside on their best horses. The famous long mirrors of the Vierra sala captured and multiplied the largest and most colorful throng it had ever held, for these black-haired women liked strong reds, yellows and blues, and their arms were burdened with gold and silver and their hands were bright with jewels. Probably most of the rubies and emeralds south of Santa Fe were there, and so were most of the brightest and most expensive shawls and some fans that had come all the way from Europe. It was an all-Mexican party except for three officers from Fort Selden and Leo Mendes, who had not seen much of the Vierras for many months, but was too important a person to be ignored on an occasion such as this. He knew almost everyone in the room and about half of the men owed him money.

Magdalena let her aunt and uncle receive the guests. She chose to make her appearance after they all had assembled and it was a greatly effective appearance. The door from the hallway was a step higher than the room and she stood there, lifted a little above the crowd, until everyone had become aware of her. Leo at first could hardly believe this was the same Magdalena he had known so long. Although she was only sixteen years old, in this society she was a grown woman, ripe for marriage, and she looked fully equal to her status, as a good many Mexican debutantes did not. She seemed to have reached a full-bosomed maturity all at once, and this was not only a matter of body but also of bearing and spirit. She looked down upon the crowd with her wide, all-embracing smile, with the most complete self-assurance and delight in her own beauty. For she *was* beautiful. In that moment at least it seemed to Leo that she was the most beautiful woman he had ever seen. Perhaps her mouth was too large for classic perfection, but her arms and her shoulders, budding out of the tight blue bodice of her gown, were truly perfect, and her happy vitality seemed to reach across the room and touch him like a caress. He had thought of her less and less while she was away, believing she would surely marry in Santa Fe, that she had gone out of his life for all time. Beyond his reach now she certainly seemed to be, but he knew that she had more than ever the power to disturb him, as no other person had ever done.

When she came down onto the floor, he observed how all the young men in the room began to move toward her, detaching themselves politely from other women and from groups until she was completely surrounded by gallant young Mexicans in tight black suits, and army lieutenants in the blue of military full dress, with golden epaulets on their shoulders. She seemed wholly equal to all of them, talking in two languages and with both hands, throwing back her head to laugh with joy in the consciousness of her power. For beauty is power and it had been suddenly bestowed upon her, young as she was, making her all at once a threat to the peace of men and a disturbing presence in any group.

Leo did not feel that he could push through that cluster of eager youth to claim a share of her attention, but presently she saw him and threw him a smile across the room and came to greet him.

"You are the one I have been looking for," she told him as she gave him her hand. "I have thought about you so many times."

Later they danced together and he was so conscious of her body in his arms and of the tickle and fragrance of her hair in his nose that he could find little to say. He had never before felt so helpless in the presence of any woman. But Magdalena was not at all tongue-tied.

"I must see you alone," she told him. "I have so much I would like to tell you, so many things I can't say to anyone else."

---

2. She came to his store late in the day, just as she had done once before, very properly accompanied by Benita, who carried a basket to hold her purchases. She contrived to keep a clerk busy until all of the other customers had left. Then she sent Benita home, came to his office, held out her hand to him and seated herself with a deep sigh of satisfaction. The door to the store was open, but he was acutely conscious that unless some unexpected intruder came they would presently be alone, and the prospect filled him with an excitement that made him feel at once intensely alive and quite foolish. He was trying to tell himself, over and over, that Magdalena now could not possibly be any of his business, but he knew that he could never get her out of his mind as long as she was in the town. She relaxed in her chair and gave him her wide, slow smile, with a touch of mischief about it. That smile was the one thing about her that seemed wholly unchanged by the years since first she had come to see him.

"It is so good to be here, where I can say what I please and do what I please," she said. "It seems to me I have hardly ever been alone since I left here except when I slept, and all the rest of the time I have been with teachers and chaperons and suitors and I always had to say the right things to them. What can you say to a teacher or to your aunt, who is there to see that you behave yourself, or to the young man you never see alone and who has no sense anyway? And all the girls in the school were so silly, and what can one virgin tell another?"

Her confession came in a rush of words, springing from some long-denied need of candid utterance.

"You must have had many suitors, there in your grandmother's house," he suggested. He had always felt sure she would come back engaged if not married.

"I had plenty," she said, "and all of them were alike. They would come and sit, and of course we were never alone, and some of them read me verses they had made for me, and one of them played a guitar, but none of them said anything but foolishness. A Mexican boy never says anything but foolishness to a woman. There was one, Alfonso de la Guerra, that all of my mother's family wanted me to marry, and he was good-looking and so proud of himself! He thought he was wonderful and he thought everyone else thought he was wonderful. And so one day they left us alone for about five minutes and he came over to me and took my chin in his hand and lifted up my face and he was going to kiss me and I slapped him so hard that my aunt heard it in the next room and came running and he stood there turning purple, and afterward all the women of my mother's family scolded me."

Leo laughed.

"So you are not engaged," he ventured.

"No. And they were all telling me that I will soon be too old, and I should be grateful to a boy like Alfonso, whose father is rich, and I did not tell them so, but I made up my own mind—I will *not* marry a Mexican! They are all alike and they just shut you up in the house and leave you there and do what they please. How I wish I could have been an American! I met a few there at the dances and I saw the American women in the streets, and they go about alone and with men and do what they please, and a Mexican girl cannot even walk across the plaza alone and cannot see any man alone until she is engaged. It is terrible to be always followed and watched and guarded, especially when you are not used to it and when you see others who do what they wish."

She paused for breath and smiled at him.

"I can say all this to you," she said. "And there is not another person I could say it to."

Leo knew now that she had truly come back to him, and he knew that what she had come back for was the freedom and happiness she had known with him as a child and had lost in the world of her own people. He knew that she was asking him to rescue her and provide her with a refuge as he had done in the days when she hunted frogs and turtles and ran away to the river. And what could he do for her, what could he say?

She glanced over her shoulder at the empty store and rose and went to the door, and he followed her, thinking she would leave. But she closed the door and backed up firmly against it so that any intruder would have been barred. Then it was just as it had been before she went away, except that he had a good deal more girl in his arms. When he kissed her she turned her face away in mock resistance.

"You are just the same as ever," she said. "And I am the same bad little girl, running away from home and doing what I shouldn't."

Both of them laughed and then became serious, facing the hard realities of their situation.

"I don't know when I can come to see you again," she said. "It's not like it used to be."

He understood that only too well. They might have a few casual moments together now and then, but that was all. And what could either of them do? He might call upon her as a suitor, properly chaperoned, and how absurd that would be, after all their easy years together. And he would not be at all welcome as a suitor—that he knew. He tried to imagine himself calling on Magdalena, with Lupe perhaps presiding over their conversation. He shook his head sadly.

"I wish I could marry you," he said.

He had not intended to say that, heard his own words with a kind of surprise. He had meant to say only that he was sorry he couldn't ask her to marry him, that it seemed so obviously impossible for him even to approach her as a suitor.

Magdalena didn't take it that way. He might have known she wouldn't. Nothing she wanted ever seemed impossible to her.

"And why can't you?" she demanded. "How I would like

to get out of that house and come here and live with you!"

"How I wish you could," he said. "But your family would never approve, and neither would the Padre—"

"There must be a way!" she interrupted firmly. Her indomitable spirit was impressive. "Now I must go or someone will come looking for me. But I will see you again. I don't know when, but I will!"

She kissed him again—a firm, possessive kiss, which told him even more clearly than her words that he was neither renounced nor deserted—then hurried away, smiling at him over her shoulder.

Leo sat a long time, puffing a pipe desperately, trying to digest the fact that he had proposed to Magdalena and that she had accepted him. He was sure of only one thing—that he was completely absorbed in her, as though her destiny had become the chief concern of his own.

---

3. His problem took him inevitably to the door of the Padre's house. He had known for a long time how this man presided over all destinies in that community and especially over all marriages and all deaths, but he had never thought to come there himself as one seeking advice and permission. For so long he and Orlando had discussed everything on equal terms, as the two most powerful men in the village, settling things between them, but now he had fallen to the estate of a suppliant, explaining with some embarrassment how he had asked Magdalena to marry him without exactly intending to do so, and how she had accepted him.

He was relieved that Orlando did not seem at all shocked or indignant nor did he seem wholly surprised. Nothing in fact ever seemed to surprise him. He nodded his head slowly several times and filled and lit a pipe before he spoke.

"Do you think such a marriage would be wise?" he inquired.

Leo spread his hands in the gesture that so often expressed his doubt and puzzlement.

"My friend," he pleaded, "I ask you to understand that I am of a painfully divided mind. I love this girl as I have never loved anyone else, but I am not at all sure it is wise or right for me to marry her. She is sixteen and I am forty and there are many other difficulties. . . . I have my doubts but Magdalena has none. She always knows what she wants and she always feels it should be given. How then can you expect me to refuse her?"

The Padre nodded solemnly.

"You know that to marry her in the Church, you would have to become a Catholic," he said, "and I could not ask you to do that. I know you too well. You have not the believing mind. I think you have no faith in anything but life itself."

Leo sat pondering this in silence for a long moment. What did he believe in? He had never asked himself the question. He had been too busy. For years he had gone about among these people who all had a perfect faith in God. He knew that God was as real to them as any man in the village. They lived in His presence. They begged His help. They sinned and asked His forgiveness. He knew God was real to Magdalena. He had seen her cross herself more than once, in a perfectly spontaneous gesture of submission to the power that ruled her life. She was full of rebellion and defiance, but she was the child of God. He had no God. Certainly he believed no more in the terrible God of the Old Testament than he did in the God whose presence filled all the little adobe churches up and down the valley where the red candles burned to speed souls through purgatory and the people knelt and bowed their heads before the sacred image. For a few excited adoles-

cent years he had believed in the God of Spinoza who was
present in all things living and made them all in some sense
one. Yes, that perhaps was his God—the God he had known
when he lay naked beside the river and felt himself a part
of the earth, when he danced and felt that music and rhythm
made him part of the dancing whole. If his father had never
talked to him about Spinoza he would still have experienced
these things, but he would never have associated them with
the idea of God. The Padre was telling him he could not
marry Magdalena without accepting her God. He knew he
could not do that. If he had been a younger man, perhaps it
would have been different, but he knew he could not now
embrace any creed or kneel to any God.

"No, I have not the believing mind," he agreed. "It would
be hypocrisy for me to join a church. But are there not special
dispensations for such cases as mine?"

"Yes," the Padre agreed. "The Archbishop has power to
grant a special dispensation, but I am sure he would never
do it without the consent of the Vierras and of Magdalena's
relatives in Santa Fe, and that, I am sure, would never be
given. They all want her to marry into one of the important
families there in the North. In fact, I believe they have already
chosen a young man for her."

"But how can she be happy with a young man chosen by
someone else?" Leo demanded.

"My friend, you do not understand," the Padre explained.
"For these people marriage has long been a family matter,
not a matter of personal choice. Often girls are affianced
before they are five years old and it is very rare for one to
marry without the complete approval of her family. And marriage in the eyes of the Church is not an act of self-indulgence
but a holy sacrament, an ordeal accepted for the sake of
family and race and God. Happiness is not the object, but
there can be a great happiness in obedience, in renunciation,

in the surrender of your own little will to the mighty will of God."

Leo sat silent, feeling what massive forces were arrayed against him. He had known all about the marriage customs of the Ricos for many years, but never before had he understood how completely man is at the mercy of his own institutions, what formidable barriers they may set between him and his desire.

"I suppose I could marry her in a civil ceremony," he said at last.

The Padre responded to this with asperity.

"You could, if she were willing," he agreed. "In that case, she would not be married at all in the eyes of the Church. She would be living in sin. She could not receive the sacrament or go to confessional so long as the marriage lasted. Of course, I could not sanction such a marriage and neither would her family. Although she has lost both of her parents, you must understand that all of her uncles and aunts, and they are a numerous tribe, feel responsible for her welfare."

"But do such marriages happen?" Leo asked.

"Yes, a good many," the Padre admitted. "Desire is such an overwhelming thing. And there are emergencies that make a quick marriage necessary. But I hope you will not consider anything so rash, so impious."

Leo could make no reply to this. He knew he was beaten. He knew he was not going to elope with Magdalena in defiance of the Church and her family and the whole world to which she belonged. He was not a man of defiance, of desperate measures. But what could he say to Magdalena? How could he face her again?

The Padre smiled at him kindly.

"My friend, I wish I could help you," he said.

"You can help me this much," Leo replied. "Will you see Magdalena alone and tell her something of what you have told me? Perhaps, at least, you can make her understand the difficulties. It is very hard for her to believe that she cannot have what she wants."

The Padre nodded agreement.

"I will send for her," he promised. "I will see her as soon as possible. She is not all a bad girl, but she is headstrong. I am told the sisters in Santa Fe found her difficult, and so do her relatives. You understand that I cannot advise her about her marriage until she asks me, but I hope I can make her see that her first duty is to her family, and that she cannot live in the Grace of God without obedience."

After this talk, Leo went home and spent several hours trying to resign himself to the fact that Magdalena was beyond his reach and out of his life. He poured himself brandy and lit a pipe and painfully went over all the reasons why this marriage was impossible. The fact that her whole family would be firmly opposed to it seemed a sufficiently formidable difficulty by itself, but the obvious disapproval of his friend Orlando counted much more heavily with him. Doubtless he must somehow contrive to forget her. For the first time since he had come here, it seemed to him that it might even be necessary for him to leave Don Pedro for her good and for his own peace of mind. Certainly to stay here and meet her—in the store, on the street—that would be hell. He knew Magdalena would not be impressed by the beauty of renunciation. He knew she would feel that he had failed her.

He poured himself another drink and this was the sure sign of his painful inner conflict. He drank little except when trouble weighed heavily upon him, and then often alcohol seemed at once to relieve his feelings and change the state of his mind. So it was now. Having proved to himself with the most irrefutable logic that he could not possibly marry Magdalena, he nevertheless found himself thinking about her, not unhappily, and that she was now a woman grown and ripe for love. He was one who waited and trusted his intuitions, and he had trusted them more ever since he had known Dolores, the witch, who was always so sure what was going to happen. So now, in spite of all reason and all difficulties, he felt that his beloved was coming toward him, like a woman in a dream, and his vision seemed to set him free from the hard logic of apparent necessity and to lift him out of his misery.

4. Magdalena remained out of his life for nearly a week. Then she appeared again in the store, followed by the faithful Benita. While she was busy with her shopping she threw him a smile, broad and cheerful, showing all her teeth.

Leo returned the smile, wondering if his amazement showed on his face. He knew that she must have seen Orlando and that he must have lectured her quite properly upon the virtue of obedience and her duty to the family which would include, above all, marrying with their approval. He had not doubted in the least that the eloquent Padre would make a deep impression on her. He had thought of her as going through the same agony of doubt and inner conflict that he had known.

If she had suffered anything of the kind it most assuredly did not show in her face or manner. When her shopping was done she came to the door of his office, leisurely and relaxed, radiant with smiles, apparently untroubled.

"I can't stay," she said. "I just wanted to greet you."

"Did you call on Padre Orlando?" he asked. "He told me he was going to see you."

"Yes, I did." She nodded as though in delight. "And I am going to see him again tomorrow evening, and I hope many other times. He feels that I have been neglected and that I need instruction, and I am sure he is right. He is going to teach me the importance of obedience and of respect for my elders. He is a good man and I love him. Whatever he tells me I say, 'Yes, Father,' and we get along together just fine."

Again she gave him that wide and joyful smile which seemed to be the overflow of an unconquerable vitality, of a love of life and a capacity for living which could not be denied. It was evident at least that the Padre had not reduced her to contrite despair, and Leo was glad of that. He sat warmed by her smile, glad of her presence, feeling fatuously in love and not knowing what to say.

"I am going to see him again tomorrow evening," she repeated. "And of course I must go alone. It seems to be the only place I can go alone—to the Padre's house and to the Church."

Belatedly, it occurred to Leo that she must be giving him a hint. He could feel his blood jump at the thought, but he managed to speak in a casual way, as though what he proposed were nothing out of the ordinary.

"Would you have time to stop and see me on the way home?" he asked. He was not quite sure what she had in mind.

She nodded rapidly, glancing over her shoulder to be sure no one was near. This was the only gesture that betrayed any uneasiness.

"Yes," she promised. "I will come to your house. I must see you, and that is my only chance. That is why I asked the Padre to give me so much instruction."

Again she flashed her shameless and undaunted smile.

"I will probably come about eight," she said as she turned to go.

5. She had seemed wholly untroubled that afternoon, but when she came to his door the next evening she was a very serious girl—for the first time, it seemed to him, since she had returned. There was no smile upon her face now, no challenge in her eyes. She let him take her in his arms and gave him a kiss that was restrained, almost chaste. Then she held him off, looking at him gravely.

"Did the Padre scold you?" he inquired.

"No; he was very kind to me," she said. "I told him all my sins—how I had slapped Alfonso and spoken impudently to my aunt and stuck out my tongue at the mother superior and that was all I could think of . . . and now . . . and now, here I am!"

She was not highly articulate, but Leo could understand the conflict that wracked her. To come here at all was an act of rebellion against Church and family and tradition, against all the powers that ruled her. He felt a great admiration for her courage, a great tenderness. He led her to his couch and took her hand and stroked her hair, kissing her gently, feeling warmly full of compassion and protective tenderness. She put her face against his shirt and wept softly, then sat up, wiping her eyes.

"What a fool I am!" she said. "What am I crying about? This is where I have wanted to come, all the time. Ever since I left Santa Fe I think I have been coming toward you and your house."

Along with her tears she had apparently shed all of her doubts and inhibitions. She smiled at him now, and it was a smile full of challenge and invitation, making him aware beyond all doubt that Magdalena had come into her womanhood and that she was demanding his response to it. When they kissed again it was a long complicated kiss, a clinging, open-mouthed, all-claiming woman kiss. After a moment she pushed him gently away and they sat looking at each other in mute acknowledgment of their mutual need. In that kiss, he knew, Magdalena had offered herself, and he knew also that this was her supreme assertion that her body and soul were her own. He knew that if he failed her in this moment he had lost her. Church and family and the world counted for nothing now. They were alone with their crisis and it seemed no concern of anyone else.

He took her by the hand and led her to the door of his bedroom, docile and willing. It didn't seem necessary to say anything. Magdalena's kisses always seemed to convey far more than her words. She turned to face him now, assenting with her eyes, with a gesture of both hands.

"But let me be alone first," she asked. She made the sign of the cross in a swift gesture, stood for a moment looking over his head at nothing. "If this is a great sin," she spoke softly in Spanish, "may God forgive me. I can do no other."

When he had closed the door behind her he felt as though she had withdrawn from him completely, even though he knew she would be waiting—had withdrawn into a world of faith and mystery he could not share. He wondered if she were praying now to be forgiven, or if she would perhaps invoke the Virgin of Guadelupe, that purely Mexican deity, soft, passionate and forgiving, whose image presided over so many bedrooms.

He sat down and waited for a while, feeling that he ought to think, that he ought to be sure he was aware of all the possible consequences of this moment, but he found that he was quite incapable of thought. His blood was pounding, his whole being seemed flooded with desire, his mind contained nothing but the image of Magdalena. It seemed to him this moment was its own justification and this fulfillment the one supremely important thing in the world.

When he opened the door she lay there on top of the coverlet, at full length on her back. She had taken off everything except the white linen shift that reached nearly to her knees. She lay very still with her eyes closed and her breathing barely lifted her breasts.

He went and lay beside her, resting on an elbow, and kissed her lightly, reverently, almost with awe, as though she had been a sacred symbol. At first she made no response, but then her lips parted to receive him and her hand found his body. Suddenly she sat bolt upright and began to pull off her shift over her head, rocking from side to side to free it of her weight. She balled it up and threw it across the room, as though she were discarding with it all her doubts and fears, and turned and flung herself upon him. Then it seemed to him that both of them were free of the past and of the world and that this was their wedding.

1.Within two years after his marriage, the
home of Leo Mendes in Don Pedro had become almost as
famous as his store. Like the store, it was mentioned in the
letters and memoirs of various persons, for many Americans
were entertained there. In fact, for a year or more most of
the guests at the Mendes establishment were Americans, including army officers from Fort Selden, business men from
El Paso, some large cattlemen who were moving in from
Texas, and a variety of travelers. All of them were impressed
by the charm and beauty of Magdalena Mendes, one of the
few Mexican women in the valley who spoke English as well
as Spanish.

Because she had been married outside the Church, the
old Mexican families in the valley towns at first showed their
disapproval by neglecting to call or to invite her to their
houses, although all of them had known her since childhood

and were friends of her family. The Doña Magdalena accepted this situation with a good deal of equanimity. She let it be known that she greatly preferred gringos to Mexicans anyway, and she also refused to be embarrassed by the fact that her marriage presumably lacked divine sanction. "I am sure God loves me," she announced. She had also somehow retained the friendship if not the approval of the famous Padre Orlando Malandrini, who had apparently consented to her sudden marriage, even though he could not give it his official blessing.

The disapproval of the local aristocracy did not last. No one truly disliked Magdalena; old friends relented one by one. The fat and happy Barreiros were the first to come to her house, and they were followed by the Gongoras, the Sandovals, the Romeros, the Bacas and most of the other first families of the lower valley. The fact that some of these families had business dealings with Leo Mendes and that some of them owed him money may have been a factor in the change. Moreover, the Mendes house became, more than any other in the valley, a place where two races met and shook hands and danced together, where army officers met Mexican girls and travelers from the East saw Mexican society. Major MacTavish recorded that parties at the Mendes house had made relations between the Army and the local people a great deal easier.

---

2. Leo had gone to the Padre like a penitent, admitting what had happened, and the Padre had agreed that there must be a marriage at once and that under the circumstances it could only be a civil ceremony. He had undertaken the difficult business of explaining this to the family, for which Leo was profoundly grateful. The Vierras did not protest—and Leo was uncomfortably aware that there were more reasons than the Padre knew for their silent assent—but they remained aloof and resentful for months.

This estrangement came to an explosive end one day when Leo and Magdalena were walking across the plaza and met Lupe face to face. The two women stood staring at each other for a long moment, full of suspense for Leo, then suddenly rushed into each other's arms, fairly bathed each other in their mutual tears, ignoring him completely, finally going off arm in arm to the Vierra house, Magdalena turning to wave him a tearful farewell. After that, they seemed to be the best of friends, going about together in the Vierra coach, visiting in Las Cruces and Mesilla. Leo suspected they were good friends for the first time in their lives, now that Magdalena had an establishment of her own and was no longer at the mercy of her aunt. It was harder for him to understand that Lupe seemed to feel no resentment toward him. She treated him with a slightly patronizing friendliness which had something proprietary about it. She had renounced all personal claim upon him, but she accepted him as a family possession and asset, which last he most assuredly was. He had been banker and broker to the house of Vierra now for several years, and his unconventional marriage did not long interrupt that relation, for the Vierras had come to depend upon him, as had so many others.

So now Leo had become fully a Mexican gentleman and the head of a Mexican family. The long social climb that had started the day he drove his burro into the plaza had reached its apogee. Just as he had once looked and sounded exactly like a paisano, pushing his burro down the road, now he had all the manners, idioms, costumes, servants and social prerogatives appropriate to his station in life. But he did not feel like a Mexican gentleman. He knew he did not belong to this world nearly as much as he had belonged to the road and the river and the homes of the humble. There, too, he had always felt himself a stranger, but he had played his part with confidence and success. As the head of a Mexican household he knew neither. In particular he lacked the gift of autocratic authority which is the first essential of a patriarchal lord. For the Mexican family was made in the image of the Old Testament. The head of a household regarded himself as the regent of God and felt that the good order of society depended upon his absolute power. He could chastise a grown son, lock up a frolicsome wife, have a slave whipped at the post, make a peon crawl at his feet to beg for mercy. Authority was his by divine right and a weak man would often exercise it with more severity than a strong one.

This feeling for power over others Leo lacked completely. He had acquired power in spite of himself—the power of money and debt, and the power of an employer over his underlings—but he had never learned to like it. His orders always had the accent of request and his instinct was always for compromise rather than ultimatum. When he had trouble with a local customer he often asked the Padre to mediate, and when an employee proved difficult, Leo would let him go. Worst of all, he lacked the air of command—the peremptory voice, the menacing brow and flashing eye, the sweeping gesture. With admiration and awe he had watched Don Augustín manage his vaqueros on a roundup. No military command could have been more absolute. The Don knew how to make men move, and he could denounce a laggard or a bungler so that the man drooped in his saddle with shame.

This gift of command was the product of an ancient tradition, rooted in faith, nourished in isolation, handed down from father to son—and it was one custom of the country Leo could neither acquire nor imitate. He might get his way, he generally did when it was necessary, but always by patience and persuasion.

He could not make anyone do anything and no one knew this better than did Magdalena, for she had learned it early. She had come to his house as a child because he set her free, and now she had come to stay. Her time was her own and she came and went as she pleased. The household also was hers by right of conquest, and she made it over and organized it to suit herself. She was full of energy and ideas and Leo was too busy to get in her way even if he had possessed the necessary spirit of authority. So he found himself suddenly the head of a typical Mexican establishment with six or seven servants, whereas he had done for years with the services of Avandera alone. She was the only holdover from his bachelor days and the subject of his only firm demand. He had insisted that Avandera remain, and that she should be the head of the household staff and have the keys to the storeroom. He knew she was loyal to him and wholly trustworthy and thought it might be well to have at least a reliable ambassador in his own house.

Most of it no longer looked like the same house. Magdalena had enlarged the sala and had it completely refinished and refurnished. Somewhat to his surprise she did not demand shiny new furniture from St. Louis, but stuck to the charming half-Moorish mode of the Mexican past, with couches covered by Navajo blankets all around the room, walls freshly whitewashed, and skins of wild animals for rugs. Like her aunt she loved huge mirrors, but had only four of them, which made the room seem larger and brighter and caught the eyes of all women and many men, for it was a rare guest who could resist the appeal of his own image. Here she presided almost every afternoon, serving the traditional chocolate, but also El Paso brandy, for she had learned that gringos liked their brandy and did not care much for the cloying cup of thick chocolate. Sometimes there would be only one or two guests, and sometimes a dozen or more. It was amazing how Magdalena could draw people out of a wilderness where there seemed to be so few.

Often a party of young officers would ride over from the fort, knowing they would be welcome, and often Mexican mothers would bring their daughters all the way from Mesilla to flirt discreetly with the young men in blue. Leo had a man in his employ who was a notable performer on the accordion—an instrument for which Mexicans seemed to have a special aptitude. Magdalena would sometimes summon him from his work, give him brandy and cakes and let him play for her guests. Often his music set them dancing, although dancing in the afternoon was no part of Mexican custom. Then the restless young would clinch and whirl while half-scandalized mothers looked on, often smiling and tapping a foot in spite of themselves, finally rescuing their flushed and giggling daughters from the eager arms of the invaders, taking them home reluctant and excited.

Magdalena loved to dance and she was an accomplished dancer, who seemed able to express all of her moods and graces in the way she danced and to infuse her own spirit into her partner, as a good rider communicates himself to a horse. She could waltz with perfect decorum, as she did with Major MacTavish when he attended one of the evening dances she gave almost every month, and when the party achieved a high level of gay abandon she could go into a spinning cradle waltz with a Mexican partner that would have made any gringo dizzy. She knew all the forms and maneuvers of all the old square dances which were a necessary feature of every large party, but best of all she knew how to make a party move. Leo watched her with amazement, wondering at her power to change the atmosphere of a crowd and room as soon as she entered. She seemed to have more life in her than almost anyone else and she seemed able to com-

municate her abounding vitality to others. Where she was
things had to happen.

Leo was soon aware of himself as a husband with many
rivals, for Magdalena drew young men to her house without
trying, and she drew them to her side in the same way, their
eyes shining with admiration and desire. That was a world
in which men greatly outnumbered women, one in which
wilderness-faring men went months without a glimpse of a
skirt, and a feminine flame such as Magdalena warmed and
stirred them all. But she seemed to have no favorites, if only
because she was the favorite of so many.

Everyone who came to her parties could see that young
Lieutenant Hilgard of Boston, Massachusetts, was rather
painfully in love with her. He was a professional soldier,
twenty-four years old, who had gone from the well-disci-
plined society of Back Bay Boston to the still more disciplined
life of West Point, and from there suddenly to a world of
shimmering desert and blue mountain, of wild Indians and
bandits, of military boredom broken by moments of violent
and deadly action, and by glimpses of a society where love
was an art and abandon a thing to be cultivated. Lieutenant
Hilgard was a good-looking young man, slim and strong,
with a wave of blond hair carefully combed, a handsome
aquiline nose, bright blue eyes, a delicate pink and white
skin and a somewhat tight and uncomfortable mouth that
seemed to make his smile slight and difficult. He was a rigor-
ous disciplinarian who imposed upon his platoon the same
hard pressure he put upon his own feelings. In three minor
battles with the Apaches he had shown himself a born fighter,
the kind of man who tastes ecstasy in action and feels neither
fear nor pain. But on a dance floor he was as stiff as a flagpole.
Having learned to waltz at West Point he waltzed correctly,
holding the girl discreetly away from his brass buttons, em-
bracing her gingerly with a large silk handkerchief in his

right hand, his left arm rigidly extended. Among whirling, hopping Mexican couples he piloted his partner with a stately grace, making no concessions to the customs of the country.

Magdalena evidently felt it part of her duty as a hostess to limber him up. Without seeming to take the lead away from him she moved in upon him like a boxer going into a clinch, persuaded him into a series of dizzy spins, impairing his dignity and wrecking his composure. He was a severely self-disciplined man but his delicate skin betrayed his feelings. At the end of the dance he wore a bewildered grin and a heavy blush, while Magdalena stood laughing at him and clapping her hands for more music.

"Huerito (little blond one)," she said. "I will make a good Mexican out of you yet."

After that Leo noticed the lieutenant's eyes followed her almost all the time and he danced with her as often as possible. It seemed as though he came in the afternoons only to look at her, never saying much, warming himself in the presence of a woman whose spontaneous vitality was probably a new experience to him.

3. During Leo's bachelor days Coppinger had often come to his house in the evening for a drink and a chat, but now he never appeared there and Leo saw him rarely in the store. Coppinger knew he was welcome any time, but he was evidently shy, so Leo finally sent him an invitation to one of Magdalena's afternoon gatherings.

Coppinger came, and it was evident that he had dressed carefully for the occasion. His jeans and his shirt were clean, his boots were polished and his great spurs of silver trimmed with gun metal had been rubbed to shining perfection. He looked handsome, but also strange in a roomful of Mexicans.

He and Magdalena stared at each other for a moment when they were introduced, as though in mutual surprise. Then she smiled upon him and gave him her hand.

Coppinger sat uneasily with his great hat on the floor beside him, refused chocolate and brandy and asked for coffee. In his own house he could be a charming and even an eloquent man, but it was evident that he could not be happy in a group of Mexicans. For one thing he spoke Spanish with a flat Texas accent and Leo suspected that he did not know the language well enough to follow the rapid chatter of the other guests. Moreover, he looked and sounded supremely Texan and the ancient hostility between the two breeds was somehow faintly present in the room. Some women looked at the handsome stranger with a good deal of interest but most of the men evaded his eye. Magdalena, always the good hostess, went and sat beside him, chatted with him a while in English, shook hands with him again when he left. Afterward she questioned Leo about him, wanted to know what he did and where he came from. Leo told her what he knew about Coppinger's horse-trading and his ample Texas background. He suggested that she invite Coppinger to one of her dances, but she firmly refused.

"He can't even speak good Spanish," she said. "I don't think people would like him."

Leo couldn't guess whether she felt a genuine aversion to Coppinger or whether she feared he might be a disturbing presence. Generally she was eager to meet gringos and had nothing against Texans. But her attitude toward her male guests always puzzled him. She seemed to embrace them all, with her smile if not with her arms, but yet to hold each of them away, at whatever distance she wished.

Evidently Coppinger was out, at least for the time being. Fearing he might be offended, Leo called on him at his house and was relieved to get a cordial welcome. Coppinger poured whisky and they sat late, talking horses and country and weather and about the railroad that had reached Raton Pass and would soon have a railhead in Las Vegas. It was sure to transform the territory, but this remote southern part of it was beyond the reach of its influence. Coppinger was full of plans for going north to the rich grass country near Las Vegas, and there starting a horse ranch.

"All I need is a homestead with permanent water on it," he said. "There's a million acres of empty range up there. I'll get me a blooded Kentucky jack and breed mules. Settlers need mules. And I'll turn out trained cow ponies. I can finish about forty head a year. There's good money in it."

Leo reflected that probably this was true, but it would also take quite a chunk of money to buy blooded stallions and jacks and build fences. All Coppinger had was a debt at the store which had been slowly growing for several years, despite the fact that he gave Leo cash when he had it. It occurred to Leo that it might be a good proposition to back Coppinger in the north, but he said nothing. Such matters required thought and inquiry. So he listened to Coppinger with care, making mental note of all the essential facts, asking a few questions, and then switched the talk to something else before he rose to go. Coppinger took his hand with a broad grin. Obviously he had enjoyed talking about his dream. Doubtless it seemed more real to him now that he had explained it to somebody else.

"See you again, Leo," he said. "Any time you get fed up on Mexicans and women, there's always a bottle and a piece of meat waiting for you down here."

4.Don Pedro, like nearly all other Mexican towns, had always celebrated Día San Juan, for St. John the

Baptist was the patron saint of horsemen and in this country
almost every man was a horseman. The day was the twenty-
fourth of June, and it was usually a day of still and cloudless
heat. Everyone was supposed to bathe in the morning and
many of them did, men and boys splashing in the river, and
women bathing in secluded acequias, chastely clad in long
cotton slips. Many men also washed their horses in the river,
especially those who had good horses and who expected to
join the game of gallo, which was always played in the afternoon. At night there were always dances and much feasting
and drinking of native wine.

Leo had seen the whole performance many times, and
always it had been a fiesta of the people, with few if any of
the gentry taking part. Here in Don Pedro the vaqueros, who
did the hard riding and roping of the open range, were the
ones who gathered to play gallo and crowded the one dance
hall on the plaza at night. But this year it was to be different.
Magdalena had invited a large party of her friends for supper
and a dance, and the young men of the best families would
play gallo for the amusement of the ladies in the afternoon.
This day truly fine horses would be seen in action, the best
in the valley, and also fine horsemanship; for all the young
men of the best families were good riders.

Most of the horses showed Barb or Arab blood, prancing
graceful horses with narrow muzzles, small ears and arching
necks—the descendants of the mounts that had carried the
conquerors—and every horseman used his best saddle, often
silver mounted, and usually set on a red and black Navajo
blanket. Bridles were woven of horsehair, tasseled and
trimmed with silver sequins, equipped with curb bits that
could almost break a horse's jaw. The young men, with their
huge silver spurs all polished and shining, sat their mounts
proudly, making them prance and rear for the delight of the

spectators who sat in the shade on the long porch of the Vierra house.

The best horseman of them all was young Adolfo Gongora of Mesilla, who had become in recent months Magdalena's boldest and most ardent admirer. Leo had known Adolfo for years, had watched him grow from late adolescence to young manhood, and had always prized him as a perfect specimen of the young Mexican gallant. He seemed to have in an acute form all the qualities that Mexican society admired in the male. He was proud, brave, belligerent, passionate and dangerously hot-tempered. He had seriously wounded a man in a fight with knives in a Juarez dance hall and had challenged another to a duel with six-shooters. They had agreed to meet in the plaza at dawn and to start shooting at each other on sight. The other young man also belonged to an important family, so the duel was prevented by family interference. But bloodshed was always a contingent possibility in the life of Adolfo, for he contemplated himself with complete seriousness and was always ready to defend his dignity. He seemed to have no occupation other than being a Gongora and living up to his personal reputation and his family status, except that he was a great fancier of game chickens. He once had a favorite red game cock that he often carried under his arm about the streets of Mesilla, ready to back it against all challengers. When it died a bloody death in the pit he looked truly sad for several days.

Adolfo felt that he had a divine right to pursue any woman who pleased him, and he pursued Magdalena openly. So far his pursuit had consisted chiefly of coming to all her dances, claiming much of her time, sweeping her about the floor in a whirlwind of passion, wooing her with nimble feet and a firmly possessive arm. It was a violation of Mexican etiquette ever to speak to a woman while dancing with her and Adolfo was not one to depart from custom, but he always whispered

a hot and urgent word in her ear as he led her to her seat and
she always threw back her head and laughed, which seemed
to displease him perceptibly. She laughed also when Leo ventured to twit her about this latest of her many followers.

"But he is redeeculous!" she said. It was a favorite word
of hers, and Leo knew she had learned it from him, and also
probably the attitude it implied. For the Mexicans were thor-
oughgoing romantics, and like all such they had small humor,
especially about themselves and their emotions. But Magdalena had somehow acquired an alert sense of the ridiculous.
And there *was* something funny, as well as something dangerous, about Adolfo's intense and bellicose self-absorption.

This flavor of absurdity was slightly intensified by the
fact that he was not quite tall enough for the ideal of the
romantic hero. In his high-heeled boots he stood little more
than five feet six, so that most men looked slightly down
upon him, and when dancing with some large women he had
the appearance of a lively but minor appendage. Moreover,
he had always that touch of cockiness, which is so often the
mark of the man who feels slightly dwarfed by his fellows.
But on horseback Adolfo was magnificent, for his shortage
was all in his legs. He sat high and proud and preferred
large horses. On this festive day he rode a big roan which
pranced and fought the bit, eager for action.

What followed was a scene of innocent and customary
cruelty. A live cock was buried to his neck in a pit of loose
sand; the horsemen lined up at a certain distance and each
in turn rode at the rooster as fast as he dared, stooped from
the saddle and tried to snatch it out of the sand. It was a
difficult feat, for the terrified bird ducked and twisted and
all the riders missed more often than not. Adolfo rode faster
than any of the others and missed his mark three times, which
was no wonder for he was handicapped by his tall and restless
mount. On his fourth try he touched the bird but his horse

suddenly swerved, frightened by some flash of movement in the crowd, and Adolfo suffered the most terrible disgrace that can strike a horseman. When his horse went left he went right, turning a somersault on the ground, coming up covered with dust and shame. Fellow riders caught his horse and he was back in the saddle in a moment, punishing his mount brutally with spur and bit, whirling it around at the starting line, charging again at the mark faster than ever, while ladies gasped in dread.

But the miracle happened. Adolfo plucked the bird out of its living grave and dashed across the plaza at a dead run, waving his trophy above his head, pursued by all the other horsemen. When he beat them all to the end of the course, he was declared the winner and rode back, dusty but glorious, to salute the crowd, with a special bow for his beautiful hostess. Everyone applauded wildly. The day had been saved and also the dignity of Adolfo and the honor of the house of Gongora. San Juan, protector of horsemen, had smiled upon his favorite.

At the baile that night Adolfo seemed to be filled with an aggressive excitement. He pursued Magdalena more persistently than ever, so that he and Lieutenant Hilgard almost monopolized her on the floor. Then came a dance that both of them claimed and quick hot words were exchanged. Leo became aware of trouble first when he saw other dancers pause and look, some of the men with grave expressions. For this was a kind of thing that happened again and again at dances and often exploded into violence. Men had been killed in such quarrels and family feuds had been started by them. He noticed too that the young lieutenant was standing rigid and silent, almost like a soldier at attention, but his face was flaming crimson and his hands were clenched, while Adolfo was voluble in a low and menacing voice.

Leo had witnessed a good many dance-hall brawls but

this was the first one he had ever seen ended by the lady in the case. Magdalena, calm and smiling, walked between the rivals, pushing them back with a wide and easy gesture of both arms, like a swimmer in troubled waters. She stood there holding them apart, with a hand on each, smiling first at one and then at the other.

"Now you two boys must shake hands," she said.

Adolfo was the mercurial one, a man who could change his mood and expression in a second, as the lieutenant certainly could not. Adolfo suddenly stepped back, smiled, held out his hand, which the soldier accepted somewhat stiffly. Then he bowed from the waist, first to his hostess, then to his rival, consigning Magdalena to the embrace of the Army with a gallant gesture.

"Sir, the dance is yours," he announced.

The danger was passed and everyone laughed with relief.

It was three in the morning and roosters were crowing when the party ended. Magdalena bade her guests good-by at the door, while Leo was busy for another half-hour, ordering their horses and carriages made ready, seeing them all properly started for home.

When he went to their bedroom Magdalena lay waiting for him, naked on top of the bed with her eyes closed, as she always did after a dance. He knew that then of all times she brought him her most ardent desire and he understood also that she was spending upon him all the cumulative excitements of the evening, with its pursuits and rivalries and intimate whirling waltzes. All of this stimulus now reached its necessary and relieving climax in the dance of dances, the rhythmical roll of her body, her gasping cry. Afterward she went easily to sleep like a pacified child, but Leo lay awake beside her for a long time, wondering that he should possess such a charming creature, wondering how truly and

securely he did possess her. For Magdalena seemed to belong
to life and to the world and to give something of herself to all
who came within reach of her voice and hand.

---

5. Later that summer Leo and his wife went
to a dance in El Paso which was an event unique and important in the annals of the lower valley. So far as Leo could
learn, it was the first entertainment ever given by gringos to
which all the leading Mexican families were invited. It was
organized by officials, surveyors and engineers connected with
the Southern Pacific Railroad, which was creeping across the
barren lands of West Texas toward El Paso, and it was designed to create good feeling for the corporate invader among
the native people. So it was an elaborate entertainment in
El Paso's largest hall, with a bar in an adjoining room for
the convenience of gentlemen, and "favors" for ladies.

All the ladies and gentlemen of the leading families in El
Paso, Mesilla, Las Cruces and Don Pedro came in their
coaches, the women wearing all of their jewels and their most
expensive gowns and shawls. The most perfect politeness pre-
vailed throughout the evening, but as a meeting and mingling
of the races the occasion was not a complete success. Too
many of the gringos knew no Spanish and few of the Mexicans,
especially among the women, could speak English. Moreover,
there was a confusing conflict in etiquette. The Mexican gentlemen tended to congregate about the doorway, as they had
always done, or in the bar, while the Americans all considered
it proper to sit beside the ladies—a procedure which flustered
and embarrassed Mexican girls. They were accustomed to
such attention only from fiancés and relatives. So there were
a good many dumb and embarrassed couples at first and later
a reluctant but inevitable segregation of the races.

Magdalena, with bilingual volubility and indestructible good humor, perhaps did more than any other woman on the floor to make the party move. She danced with every male American in the hall and charmed all the American women, most of whom were middle-aged wives of railroad people. Robert Coppinger was of course among the guests, for he knew every gringo in the lower valley, and he proved himself a gallant man in a situation where he had the moral support of his own kind. He was a handsome figure in the tight-fitting black suit which all frontiersmen favored on formal occasions, with a white shirt, a huge black tie and fancy boots. Leo was not wholly surprised to observe that Coppinger knew all the square dances as well as anyone present. Doubtless they had been the dances of his Texas years, as they were in all frontier communities. But Coppinger could also waltz with surprising grace whenever he could find a partner who struck him above his midriff. In his high-heeled boots he towered over everyone in the room.

Leo noticed that Coppinger's eyes followed Magdalena with a curiously intent interest, as did the eyes of so many other men, but he seemed to have no luck in getting a dance with her. She was the busiest woman on the floor. It was near the end of the evening before he saw them waltzing together. They made a striking couple, for Magdalena was one woman tall enough to match his height and stride. In this number, at least, the two races seemed to be getting together with great success—about as close together as they could get on a dance floor. When the music stopped they violated Mexican etiquette by standing in the middle of the floor, talking until the next dance began. Then they shook hands and Coppinger surrendered her into the arms of another partner. He stood looking after her for a moment, then came over to where Leo was standing.

"Your wife is a wonderful girl," he remarked. "She's so

popular I thought I would never get to dance with her—and I did want to tell her good-by."

"I hope you're not leaving us," Leo said.

"I'm riding north day after tomorrow," Coppinger replied.

"Looking for that homestead?" Leo inquired.

Coppinger nodded.

"This is just a scouting trip," he explained. "If I find anything I like, I'll file on it now, come back here and round up my horses and pack my stuff and pull out."

"I'm sorry to hear that," Leo said.

"I'm sorry to go," Coppinger told him gravely. "This southern country gets into your blood. But I've hung around here too long now."

While they were talking the orchestra was playing "Home Sweet Home," people who couldn't speak the same language were telling each other good-by with awkward friendliness, and the first great gringo-Mexican party in El Paso history broke up into its separate components and went its separate ways.

CHAPTER

TEN

I.All over the West railroads were bringing change, more sudden and complete than any part of the country had ever seen before. In Kansas the railroad wiped out the buffalo herds and planted the prairie to wheat in just a few years. It could also wipe out a human society, shattering patterns of life that had looked as permanent as the hills, replacing them with something wholly different, and men were often destroyed or transformed in the process.

The Santa Fe broke through the mountains at Raton Pass and reached Las Vegas in the summer of 1879, while the Denver and Rio Grande was creeping down the river to Espanola and the Southern Pacific pushed toward El Paso in the south. Even three railroads couldn't change most of the Southwest much or quickly, but they did make over the towns they touched. Las Vegas had been a quiet little Mexican plaza for generations. Now it woke up to find it had become a track-end

206

town like Dodge City and Abilene—not as big and not quite as noisy but with the same apparatus of cattle chutes and loading pens, saloons and games and honky-tonks, much of the same population of whores and gamblers which had followed the rails all the way across the prairies, and the same annual invasion of trail-driving cowpunchers, full of liquor and packing guns. All of this was down by the railroad tracks and was called New Town, while the bewildered Mexican part of the settlement became Old Town and steadily shrank.

---

2. Leo looked at the new Las Vegas with astonishment, feeling suddenly that he was an old-timer, a part of the past, confronted by challenge and disturbance. He couldn't pretend that he liked it—the noise and dust and crowd, the pounding of cowboy boot-heels on new board walks, the chatter of cheap pianos, the blowsy painted girls, the frantic feeling of a place where men worked too hard all day and got drunk at night. He stood on a street corner and stared, like any bewildered Mexican. Wasn't he more a Mexican now than anything else? He understood for the first time how completely he had become a part of the slow-moving, soft-spoken life that lived in the quiet adobe towns, in the old recumbent houses, the life of the long siesta and the leisurely meal, a life that had gaiety and passion about it but no hurry at all and little violence. This new life had come to destroy the old one and the whole push and weight of an expanding world was behind it.

He resented the change, and yet he already had a part in it. He had sold cattle for shipment East at a fat price, Beltrán had driven the herd north and he had come to close the deal and do his annual buying. The yelling men with prods and whips, driving frightened red longhorns into stock cars, were working for him as well as for the future.

Aurelio Beltrán liked the new civilization even less than Leo did. He had been waiting for Leo three days in order to turn over to him the money and the bill of sale for the cattle, and he was filled with disgust.

"The gringos are ruining this country!" he announced, as they stood on a street corner surveying the scene. "First they kill all the buffalo. Now they cut down all the trees. And what a noise they make! A man can't sleep in this town. And they do nothing but chase money. Everything here is for sale. You can buy a woman for two dollars, but who would want a woman that way? And their whisky is a taste of hell all the way down."

He refused an invitation to stay for dinner. Although it was late afternoon he mounted his horse and departed, determined to ride most of the night and camp on the desert where he would hear nothing but the coyotes and see nothing but stars.

---

3. For years Leo had bought most of his merchandise from Heine and Kelly, who had long been leading merchants in Santa Fe, doing both a retail and a wholesale business, and who now had opened a new store in Las Vegas. Heine was a German Jew, in his fifties, the inside man of the firm, the architect of its success, with a great gift of foresight. He lived in his office and in the bosom of his family, a small quiet man who sent all of his seven children to Europe to be educated and his daughters to New York to be married. Kelly was an Irish Catholic, a bulky bachelor in his forties, a laughing man who loved dances and girls. He was the outside man, both a salesman and a buyer, celebrated for his quick and accurate judgment of wool in the hand, cattle on the hoof and timber on the stump. He was the one who hired and fired, and nowadays he had to hire not only clerks and book-keepers but also cowboys, loggers and sometimes a man who could use a gun. He had always the appearance of relaxed good humor, was always ready to tell a story or hear one, but his smiling manner covered a restless, aggressive spirit. He had an incurable itch to make men work and things move and change. He gave Leo a hearty greeting, a hard handshake and a huge cigar.

"Thank you, Joe," Leo said. "Your cigars get bigger and bigger."

"Everything's getting bigger and bigger around here," Kelly said. "The country's full of money—railroad money, government money. Besides two stores, now we've got two sawmills cutting ties, and government contracts for beef that would bulge your eye."

He paused and looked at Leo thoughtfully for a moment.

"What the hell are you doing down there in that desert?" he demanded suddenly.

"I've got a good store," Leo said.

"A good store!" Kelly's voice was derisive. "I bet we turn over more money in a month than you do in a year. All the money is up here now."

"We've got a railroad coming too," Leo said defensively.

"It'll never touch that little town of yours," Kelly said. "And without a railroad now you're nowhere. Ever since you and I started in business out here, the trouble has been trans-portation. It wasn't a question of what you could sell but of what you could haul. Your wagons were always stuck in the mud except when they were stuck in the sand. Nothing ever got anywhere on time. Now all that's over. Everything comes by freight right to the door. What we need now is a good man to go East and buy for us."

"I hope you find him," Leo said.

"I've found him already," Kelly said. "You're the man. You know merchandise and you know the market out here. Any man that's smart enough to go into a dead town like you did and make money is too smart to stay there."

Leo sat shaking his head, smiling, but feeling cornered and uneasy under Kelly's persistent attack.

"I can't leave my store," he said. "I've got a lot of money on the books."

"Don't worry about that little store," Kelly interrupted. "We'll buy it and send somebody down there to run it. How much do you want for it?"

Leo still shook his head.

"I don't want to work for anybody," he said. "I never have."

"You don't have to," Kelly told him. "You've got money. You can buy into the business. You can have anything you want. Good men are scarce out here. The Mexicans don't understand business, and every gringo is busier than a cat on a sand pile."

"I'd have to think it over, Joe," Leo said, moving toward the door.

"Don't think too long," Kelly advised. "You know what I think? I think you've gone native down there—too much poco tiempo, too much siesta, no competition. It happens to lots of good men. You better dig yourself out before it's too late."

Leo liked Kelly but he was glad to escape him now because Kelly's persistent challenge and demand filled him with doubt and inner conflict. He knew of course that Kelly was right, that opportunity and money and change and everything that made life exciting now were tied up with the railroads and that here in the north was the center of activity for the whole country. He could even admit to himself that in the long run he would have to move. Didn't he always have to move? It seemed true that for him the wisdom of life lay in moving at the right time and that always he moved into a new kind of life. But he also felt or hoped that the right time had not yet come. Because just now he wanted, more than anything else, to get home. Now he was a rooted man, as he had never been before, and pulling up roots is a painful business. Just now he wanted to get away from the noisy challenge of change, he wanted to get back to familiar and beloved things.

It was a great relief to be mounted and on his way.

His route followed the well-cultivated upper valley as far as Socorro, crossed a barren upland near the river to the hot springs of Las Palomas, then over the Jornada to Fort Selden and down his familiar valley to Don Pedro. By this time he knew every mile of the road, had accustomed places to stop and relays of horses waiting for him. He took his annual trip north in early fall when the weather was cool and the rains had filled the water holes. It was over three hundred miles from Santa Fe to Don Pedro and he could make it in four days with luck. For he had become a first-class horseman, a long rider who could stand eighty miles a day in the saddle, and like all good horsemen he despised the stage coach.

He still dreaded the wide empty waste of the desert, but he loved to ride the valley roads where people lived and traveled, especially the road from Bernalillo south where he had peddled his wares in the old days. Here he had walked his way back to health, here he had learned to dance and swim—here he had learned to live.

The valley now was at its beautiful best with the scarlet of drying chili festooning the houses, the cottonwood bosques along the river turning yellow and the grapes purple in the vineyards. He rode through towns where he had slept and eaten and talked, spots beside the river where he had stopped to bathe and rest. Places brought whole days back to mind. He remembered what he had done and even what he had said, but often with a kind of uncomprehending surprise as he might have watched another man and wondered how he felt and why he acted as he did. When a way and a phase of life is over, the man who lived it dies and must be reborn.

He still had friends along this road, and on other trips he had stopped to visit, but this time he was in a hurry. Stopping meant long talk and urgent invitations to meals and could add days to his journey. So he rode hard, husbanding the strength of his mount, eating up the long miles with his eye on the road ahead. He knew he was running away from the noise and dust of the track-end town, the derisive, challenging voice of Joe Kelly—from a new life he didn't like—but primarily he was a settled man running for home, one who dragged a long tether whenever he left it. Especially when he struck the arid stretch of the Jornada, where he had nothing to look at but inhuman wilderness, his mind was filled with images of home. He longed for the sanctuary of his office behind the store, for his cool thick-walled house, for the strong young arms of Magdalena. It seemed to him now he had never wanted her more than he did in this womanless wilderness. He rode toward her, nursing his desire, as though she had been the only woman in the world.

He had been gone barely a month but it seemed like a year. He was haunted by a kind of senseless anxiety that is common in home-bound travelers. He wondered what had happened while he was gone. His imagination vaguely pictured disasters and changes. He knew that in all probability nothing had changed, that all the routines and habits of his life were there waiting for him, that he would fall back into his easy ways like a wheel into a rut of its own making. But yet anxiety rode beside him, punishing his horse, having almost the force of premonition.

4.It was dark when he dismounted in his own corral, tossed his bridle rein to a stable boy and walked stiffly to the house, feeling his weariness suddenly, now that his long struggle with the road was over. Avandera greeted him in the long front room.

"I thought you might come today," she said. "I have meat on the fire, and there is hot water."

"Many thanks," he said. "Where is Magdalena?"

"She told me she was going to her uncle's house for supper."

This was not surprising since no one could be sure when he would return and he could send no message. He nodded and went to his bathroom, grateful for hot water and soap. When he had swallowed a slug of brandy and sat down before a dish of steaming lamb stewed with beans and red chili, he felt a great deal better.

Avandera stood across the room from him, her back against the wall, her sinewy arms folded across her flat breast, her face impassive and unrevealing. She was a tall, lean old woman, her dark skin and high cheek bones showing her Navajo blood. No one knew how old she was. Her hair was almost white but she was erect, quick-moving and energetic. In his bachelor days, when she was the only one in the house besides himself, she had often stood against the wall, as she did now, and they had sometimes carried on long conversations. They were never idle conversations. Avandera never stood there long unless she had something to say that she thought he ought to know. All the news and gossip of the village seemed to come to her ears, and much from farther away, from Mesilla, and even El Paso. Leo had the impression that all the peons who worked in the great houses were somehow in touch with each other and knew a great deal more about their lords and mistresses than they were supposed to know. Avandera knew also from her numerous relations what went on among the humble. Some of her news was mere scandal and tattle, but some of it was information useful to him in his business and some was in effect a plea for help to the needy. Avandera was always worth hearing.

In the early days when he was just beginning to invade the society of the Ricos, she had lectured him, sometimes severely, about how he should behave. Like many old servants she was a walking compendium of the traditions, etiquette, morals and immoralities of the society she served. When he blundered she sometimes scolded him like a strict mother. She might thus step briefly out of her proper place in the feudal hierarchy, but she never forgot it. He could always silence her or dismiss her with a wave of the hand.

Most of this easy talk had come to an end when he was married. Avandera never stayed in the dining room and never spoke when Magdalena was present. As mistress of the house she had been superseded and she knew it. Magdalena had asked him to let her go. She wanted to choose her own servants, mostly from among those she had known on her uncle's estate since childhood. Leo had refused, with the uncomfortable feeling which so often afflicts a man caught between two women. He found it hard to cross Magdalena, but impossible to show Avandera the door. Besides, he trusted her supervision of the storeroom and the kitchen and not all house servants could be trusted.

Avandera showed no resentment of her altered status—in fact, she never showed any emotion of any kind before her betters—but he knew very well that she did not approve of his unconventional marriage. She did not approve of any departure from tradition, religious or social, unless it was managed with strict secrecy. He felt sure also that like many others she considered it peculiar and unfortunate that after two years of marriage Magdalena had borne him no child. The girl should have been firmly anchored at home with a baby at her breast and another on the way, instead of running about with almost as much freedom as she had known when a child. The only safe way to manage a wife was to keep her big. This was accepted social doctrine and Avandera doubtless approved it. Leo had done what he could to save his wife from pregnancy. Because of her youth it had seemed right to wait a few years. Perhaps it would have been better . . .

He checked his reflections, looked up at Avandera expectantly, with a feeling of rising anxiety. He knew she was going to tell him something soon, something she thought he ought to hear. Why didn't she speak? And why did he fear what she was going to say? He felt a need to crack the rigid impassivity of that ancient and inscrutable face, to get the conversation moving again.

"Has Magdalena been well?" he asked. "And all her family?" It was customary to inquire about everyone's health when you returned from a journey.

"Yes, they are all well," Avandera replied.

"I must go to the Vierras after supper," Leo remarked.

There was a short silence before Avendera spoke again. When she did it was in the spirit of advice and warning that had moved her so often years before.

"I think you had better not," she said shortly.

"Why not?" Leo demanded.

"Your wife might not be there."

Again she relapsed into silence. Neither her voice nor her face revealed her feeling, yet Leo felt an acute tension of suspense, felt sure she was about to strike.

"There is no telling where that girl may be!" she burst out suddenly. "She runs about the town day and night. Is that any way to manage your wife, a young wife and pretty? She can see anyone, any time. What can you expect?"

What could he expect? Leo laid down his fork and leaned back in his chair, feeling suddenly unable to eat. He knew well enough what Avandera meant. She could mean only one thing —that Magdalena was seeing some man, that even now she was probably gone to meet him. He knew how hard it would be for Avandera to tell him such a thing. He knew she had spoken only because if he went to the Vierra house and asked for Magdalena and she wasn't there, it would be a painfully embarrassing situation for everyone. He ought not question Avandera—he knew that, too. And he didn't want to question her. But who could this man be? He thought first of Adolfo— and then remembered how Magdalena had always laughed at him. No, he couldn't imagine her keeping a tryst with Adolfo. And then there was the lieutenant. An affair with the lieutenant was even harder to imagine. That young man was too inhibited and too completely owned by the Army, and also too much the soul of honor, as he understood honor—and Magdalena had always treated him as a bashful boy. . . . He looked up at Avandera who was still standing there. She wouldn't be standing there unless she had something more to say. He couldn't question her but his look was a question. Avandera answered it with a single blurted sentence.

"Can you believe it? A Texan!" Then she turned and fled to the kitchen. She had done what she considered her duty. She left him to his thoughts.

"Un Tejano!" the word in her mouth rang with hostility. She had been a girl when the Alamo fell and had always hated Texans, as younger Mexicans did not. She was doubtless shocked by Magdalena's easy freedom but she was fiercely resentful that Magadalena should use it to see this hated alien.

Her words could mean only one thing, of course—that

Magdalena had been seeing Robert Coppinger in secret, or
at least that village gossip had carried such a tale. At first
it struck him as an incredible tale. He had thought of Coppinger as one admirer who had removed himself from the
scene. He had still been away from Don Pedro when Leo
left. True, he had planned to return, but only to collect his
horses and settle his affairs. So he had returned while Leo was
away. . . . Now he began remembering things, painfully. In
particular he remembered those two dancing together that
night in El Paso and their long talk on the dance floor and
how they had clasped hands and turned away from each
other. Perhaps they had agreed to part, had thought of that
moment as a final one. And then Coppinger had returned and
here in Don Pedro no one could escape anyone else, and it
was also true that no one had any control over Magdalena.
. . . Now it didn't seem incredible at all, when he thought of
this big magnetic man who had some curious power in his
hand and voice, this wandering, unloved, untamed man, who
had something ruthless and dangerous about him but certainly nothing ridiculous. No, there would be nothing ridiculous about it if these two came together. . . .

He heard footsteps out toward the kitchen, knew that
Avandera would be coming back to clear the table, rose and
fled to the other room. He didn't want to see the old woman
again, didn't want to question her. He knew enough.

What he needed now was something to relieve his pain
and relax his nerves so he could think. He knew he must
think. Only thought can conquer feeling. When a man faces
trouble he must think. He went back to the dining room
briefly, listening to be sure no one was there, got a bottle of
brandy out of a cupboard and a big silver mug and a silver
pitcher of water. He carried them back into the sala, very
deliberate and careful in all his movements, poured himself
a stiff drink, sat down in a corner, put brandy and water on

the floor beside him, drank deeply but slowly, feeling the
alcohol pour through his blood, into his fingers and toes, feeling a numbing relief throughout his body that seemed to set
free his mind.

He knew what he was doing. In time of trouble he had
done it before. He could drink and think. He could so achieve
a measure of detachment from his own destiny and contemplate it. He could lecture himself. So now he told himself that
what had happened was only what he should have expected,
what in fact he had expected, for he had been much aware
of rivals ever since his marriage. And was it not the custom
of the country that almost every married woman should take
a lover, soon or late, and usually not too late? He was a Mexican gentleman now and had to accept his fate as such. And
what would a proper Mexican gentleman do when he suspected his wife of infidelity? He might warn his rival or even
shoot him, if he felt equal to such drastic measures, but although a gentleman was always ready to fight in defense of
honor and chastity, such measures were rare. It was more
customary simply to ignore the matter and go about one's
own business. After all, adultery was just as old an institution
as marriage and just as necessary, and many of the very best
and even greatest of men had endured cuckoldry with dignity.
Leo poured himself another bumper of brandy and water and
took another deep drink. He was not at all drunk, but it
seemed to him now that his mind was floating free, that his
reflections were carrying him away from the pain that stabbed
at his heart and gripped his throat. A man had to think. So, as
a Mexican gentleman, what should he do? There was one
good thing about an unfaithful wife—she released the energies
for other adventures. If now he was going to live up to his role
as a Mexican gentleman, he would turn his attention to other
women and preferably to the young and the virginal. He knew
how easy it would be. Avandera would find him girls if he gave

her the word. She had often hinted in his bachelor days that he was neglecting opportunities which had almost the character of duties. Few of the village girls would dare to refuse and most of them would be proud to bear the weight and the offspring of El Patrón, the great man of their world. He might appropriately deflower three or four selected virgins a year, like a bull in September, working on the new crop of heifers. He might do much to raise the average intelligence of the local population, and he might adorn the faces of its young with a nose that would rival the celebrated Vierra nose.

He poured himself another drink and checked the tenor of his thought, aware that he had been thinking nonsense simply to get away from the painful fact. He knew he was not a typical Mexican gentleman and that he was not going to collect a harem of shapely peons. He knew even better that Magdalena was not a typical Mexican woman who would have a series of affairs, discreet and surreptitious. Nor was Coppinger a Mexican gallant who understood all the rules and conventions of intrigue, the proprieties of sin as they had been cultivated in this country for centuries. . . . Thinking of Coppinger and of how long they had been friends he tasted the bitterness of betrayal. A stir of violence flooded him with hot blood, clenched his hands and tightened his guts. It seemed like an alien thing invading his body, this sudden anger such as he had not known for years, not since boyhood fights on the streets of New York. Briefly it clouded his brain, impairing the clarity, the detachment he now so much needed. But it didn't last. The luxuries of rage and blame, the awful self-assurance of the self-righteous—these had always been denied him and they were denied him now. He was too much a fatalist to be a good hater, and now he couldn't afford to be confused by hatred. He had to think. And it was not Coppinger but Magdalena he had to think about. What could he say to her? What could he do? There was one very decisive, positive, imminently proper, highly dignified thing he could do—a thing every right-thinking Mexican gentleman would approve. He could pack up his wife along with his other chattels and take her away from here. He knew he would probably be leaving Don Pedro before long, anyway. Most assuredly he could take his wife with him. He had a perfect right to do so. He could even tell himself, with a good deal of plausibility, that it was his duty to do so. He could take her north to Santa Fe, east to St. Louis, even all the way back to New York. For a moment his imagination played with the idea. Magdalena would be equal to any society, she would adorn any society. He pictured himself presenting her to people.

"Gentlemen, my wife!" There would be a flutter among the women, a stir among the men.

My wife! Marriage was ownership and nowhere was it more complete and uncompromising than here in New Mexico. He had just as good a right to take his wife away with him as he had to take his saddle horse. She belonged to him. But did she? That was the question that now began to undermine all his imaginative structures of hope and desire. Doubt is at once the wisdom and the weakness of the reflective man. Did she belong to him or did she now inevitably belong to someone else? And if she did belong to someone else, what could it be but mutual misery to drag her away? He knew very well that Magdalena did not regard herself as a chattel. He knew she felt very strongly that her body and her life were her own. And who had taught her to feel that way? Who had planted in her mind the idea of freedom and given her the taste of it, the sense of her destiny as a thing to be explored and discovered as she had explored the river and the bosques in her truant days? He knew very well he was more the author of Magdalena's character and feeling than anyone else. He knew that if now she had followed instinct and impulse where they

led, she was only living up to the tradition he had taught
her. What he had to accept now was the fact that Magdalena
perhaps no longer needed him. In a backward-looking flash of
insight he understood that his whole life had been built more
and more upon the fact that she had needed him. He remembered how she had crept into his life as a child, sitting there
in his office, hardly noticed at first, gradually claiming more
and more of his attention. She had needed a refuge from home,
she had needed someone to set her free. With her curiously
sure instinct about what she needed she had seized upon
him as an instrument of her destiny. He remembered the day
he had first found her in his arms, felt the thrust of her breast
and the shock of her kiss just before she went away. He had
learned to do without her and then she had come back, more
demanding than ever. He didn't want to remember any more,
but he knew that when she had come to his house that night
he had set her free again, and he knew it was as much her
doing as his. He had been full of doubt but Magdalena always
knew exactly what she wanted and needed, not because she
was wise, but because she trusted completely in her own
feelings, never made the mistake of trying to think. It is often
a mistake to think and also painful, but a man has to think
and conquer his feeling by thought. So his part in her destiny
had been to set her free. This fact struck him now with painful
force. Must he set her free again, and if so, how?

One thing was sure: his mood of final decision had evapo-
rated. He had felt much better while it lasted. Anything is
easier than to bear uncertainty. He had learned that again
and again. It was his conviction that most men acted most of
the time merely to relieve their feelings. That was not his way.
He was a man of patience. "Vamos a ver." It was a good old
Mexican saying he had made his own. We are going to see. He
would have to wait and see. He might have to wait a long
time. Maybe after all this was not a serious attachment.

Maybe Coppinger would vanish. He had not renounced his idea of taking Magdalena away with him, but he saw, as he had seen so often before, that the quick decisive gesture was not for him.

Sitting there thinking of Magdalena and of all the years he had known her, he had yet forgotten her, forgotten that she would be coming home—until he heard the front door open and close. Then she came quickly into the room and he had a revealing glimpse of her before she saw him. It was a painful glimpse which told him much, answered many questions. She looked very beautiful, as do all beloved women in the moment of their love, with her face flushed and her hair rumpled and falling about her ears and her lips parted. She had her shawl drawn tightly about her body, showing the curve of her breasts, as though she were cherishing some remembered warmth.

She saw him as he rose and they stood for a long silent moment, looking at each other with the painful wordless understanding that comes of long intimacy. Her face went blank with surprise, and then her lips began to tremble and he could see tears shining in her eyes.

"I didn't know, I didn't know you were here!" She blurted the words with difficulty, struggling with sobs.

"I am sorry," he said. He didn't know what else to say. He meant to apologize for surprising her. It was an intolerable moment, for neither of them could move toward the other nor think of anything to say. She covered her face with her hands for a moment and then turned and fled and he heard the door of the bedroom close behind her. He sat down again, sat for a long time, thinking nothing. Then he followed her very quietly and stood for a moment at the door. He could hear her crying softly. He could not bring himself to enter. He wondered whether he ever would again. He returned to the

sala and picked up his bottle and glass and went to his office.
He kept a cot in a corner of the storeroom and long ago he had
often slept there in busy times. Now he wanted only solitude
and oblivion.

1.During the days that followed Leo worked with a restless energy such as he had not known since the year he opened the store. He was learning that pain is a powerful stimulus and that work is the best of all anodynes. So he spent long hours behind the counter and in the saddle, and at night he sat late in his office working over his books.

He had been a bookkeeper first and always and like his father he was a meticulous bookkeeper, who made his figures with great care in a fine small hand, taking pleasure in their perfect form and clarity. He worked just as his father had done, sitting on a high stool before a sloping desk which held the great ledger. To put things in order is always a relief to a troubled man, and symbols are the only things that can be put in perfect order. Life is confusion and contradiction, a sum that never comes out right, a book that never balances, but figures can be made to march in perfect order to a perfect end.

Often it was past midnight when he fell asleep on the cot in his office, for he seldom went home now and Magdalena spent most of her evenings with the Vierras. For some days after his return from the north he and Magdalena had met for the evening meal, just as usual—except that nothing now was the same. They tried to talk about trivial things but the talk always died on their lips. They sat there in a frozen silence neither of them could break. It seemed as though an impalpable, invisible barrier had come between them and that it grew steadily and pushed them further and further apart. Once their destinies had flowed inevitably together. Now it seemed as though they were pulling painfully apart, as though they had turned in different directions and there was no turning back. He could see compassion in her eyes, he knew she was sorry for him—and that was all he knew. It struck him suddenly they had become strangers, that perhaps they had always been strangers, at least since she had become a woman. Certainly she had become a mystery to him and he suspected that perhaps she now understood him even less. If only something could happen to break this painful calm, if only they could quarrel and argue and even curse each other! A quarrel might either bring them back together or fling them finally apart. But they had never quarreled. There had never been any antagonism between them. And they couldn't start quarreling now. Neither of them had any anger for the other. What had come between them seemed an almost impersonal thing, an accident of destiny neither could help. He was relieved when she began staying away. He had not yet given her up for lost but he knew these silent meetings were worse than none. Something had to happen—he didn't know what —something to end the suspense and reveal the underlying necessities of a situation that couldn't possibly last.

So he went back to a solitary life, such as he had lived in the year or so after he first opened the store. Sometimes,

before he locked the door at night, he would go out and walk
for half an hour about the sleeping village, reduced now to a
dark and silent huddle of earthen blocks beneath the arch of
the desert sky with its great bright stars which seemed so
much larger and brighter in this dry land than anywhere else.
The night sky was the only immensity he had ever liked, and
he liked it precisely because it did not seem either immense
or formless. It seemed a perfect bowl, bending intimately
above him, with every star in place and every star moving in
its appointed round, so that he could tell the time by the
position of the little dipper. It gave him a feeling of timeless
peace and dignity that shamed his aches and confusions.

He always left the front door unlocked and a light in
the store while he worked, and now and then he had a customer, usually some man coming home late from the high
ranges, craving coffee or sugar. These interruptions he always
welcomed. There was no one he could tell about his trouble,
but he could offer a man a drink and a cigarette, talk about
weather and people, get back for a moment to the trivial
and soothing routine that makes life livable.

Several times Aurelio was a welcome but slightly surprising visitor. Over the years Aurelio had become an increasingly
important part of Leo's establishment. The man was abso-
lutely reliable in a society where reliability was a rather rare
virtue, and he had also proved himself a good man of business,
who could take charge of the store whenever Leo was away.
Aurelio had to have his periodic escapes into the mountains
but he would always come back exactly when he promised.
So he had become almost a partner, but since Leo's marriage
their social relations had inevitably declined. They could no
longer sit down on the floor and share their beans as they had
done when they were rebuilding the store. In fact, they never
ate together except once in a while out on the range. Aurelio
would not have come to dinner as a guest of Magdalena and

Leo understood that. Now they belonged to different classes and Aurelio, like all Mexicans, had a lively sense of class.

Aurelio, of course, knew all about Leo's trouble, as did almost everyone in Don Pedro, and he evidently wanted to show his sympathy. He did so by dropping in late at night when he saw a light burning and felt sure no one else was there. They would drink a brandy together and smoke and talk awhile. Aurelio knew when to keep his mouth shut and how to talk about indifferent things. Only once did he mention Coppinger—a man he had never liked, chiefly because Coppinger was from Texas.

"That Texan!" he remarked. "When he left here last summer I thought we were rid of him. He told everyone he was going to start a ranch in the north. But then he came back while you were gone."

He seemed to feel that Leo ought to know this. Leo made no comment and both of them were silent for a long moment.

"I guess he couldn't stay away," Aurelio remarked at last. He was himself a man of much experience with women, and he had the Mexican feeling that passion is and should be overwhelming. Leo did not question him and nothing more was ever said about Coppinger. Leo had not seen the man since his return and he began to hope that perhaps Coppinger had truly carried out his plan and departed.

He got his answer to that question a few nights later when he heard the door open and close and then a step, coming down the length of the silent store to the door of his office. It was a step he was sure he recognized, for there was no other step quite like it in the town—the long slow stride, the rap of pointed heels, the soft jingle of spurs—the step of the tall horseman. So he was not surprised to see Coppinger standing in the doorway, grave and embarrassed.

"Come in, Bob," he said. "Sit down."

Coppinger sat down, stretched out his long legs, fished out

his little bag of tobacco, his packet of brown papers, rolled a cigarette skillfully, deliberately. As usual he seemed relaxed but Leo noticed that his face, always lean and hollow in the cheeks, now was positively haggard. It struck him suddenly that this man too was going through an ordeal, that in some sense they were fellow victims.

Coppinger licked his cigarette and rolled it, twisting the end skillfully, lit it and took a deep puff, exhaled a cloud of blue smoke, then for the first time, raised his eyes. The expression in them was chilling, repellent—a look of veiled hostility without a trace of the quizzical, good-humored twinkle Leo had so often seen there. This man had been his friend, but friendship now was dead and another spirit had taken its place. Those who hate you most are the ones who believe they have wronged you.

Leo knew that he faced an antagonist, but he had no sense of danger. He had learned long since that the source of this man's integrity was his pride. No doubt in some depth of his being Coppinger wished him dead, or at least forever out of the way, but a Coppinger would never lift a hand against a man who had befriended him. He now took one more deep puff on his cigarette, ground it out on his boot heel, dug into the pocket of his trousers and came up with a huge handful of money, the mixed money of that border country—Mexican pesos, American dollars, silver coins and gold and a few bank notes—a wad of uncounted wealth. It was plain from the way he handled it that he cared nothing for money as such, had never learned to think in terms of money.

"I made a little killing the other day," he explained. "Sold a couple of colts in El Paso. I want to pay what I owe you."

Leo understood now. The man wanted to be clear of all obligation—at least all financial obligation. He nodded and turned to his desk.

"I'll tote it up for you," he said.

It took him nearly fifteen minutes to make out an itemized bill in his slow, careful hand. He was himself surprised at the amount, which was over six hundred dollars. While he was working, Coppinger had sorted and counted his money and lit another cigarette. Now he took the bill and stared at it a long time, frowning, his face flushed with embarrassment.

"I haven't got that much," he said.

"Of course you don't have to pay it all now," Leo said. "In a business like this few ever pay in full. I've got the whole county on my books."

"I want to pay it," Coppinger said. "I may be pulling out of here—for keeps."

He laid his money on the desk.

"I'll pay that on account," he said. "And I'll get the rest— somehow!" He jerked out the last word like a short, hard blow.

"All right," Leo said. He counted the money, made out a receipt and handed it over. Coppinger folded it carefully and stowed it away in the pocket where the money had been. He got to his feet slowly, never looking Leo in the eye, mumbled a good night and strode for the door, walking fast, for him, obviously eager to escape.

Leo watched his retreating back with a feeling of pain and also of suspense. What, he wondered, would Coppinger do next? For he knew Coppinger was bound to do something. He was a man for whom action was an organic necessity.

1.About a week after Coppinger's visit, Leo mounted his horse and struck out for the salt lake which lay a few miles south and east of Don Pedro and just across the Texas line. He had not visited the place in years but he was bound for it now because he had just heard what Coppinger had done. He had heard only rumors and gossip from customers in his store, but all agreed that Coppinger had bought the quarter section of land that surrounded the lake from the State of Texas, and had duly filed his claim to it. Beyond that there was no agreement as to just what had happened and no one seemed to know whether he had tried to take possession of the lake or not. Leo felt he had to find out, for he knew this might mean trouble, and not for Coppinger alone.

He knew that Coppinger must have a backer—perhaps some monied newcomer to El Paso who thought the lake might be a good investment in the long run. But that Coppinger alone should try to claim the lake and defend it and sell salt to all comers—that seemed a little preposterous. He would face endless trouble and resentment and he would have to haul drinking water and live there lone as a wolf. For the salt lake was a peculiarly desolate and uninhabitable place.

Leo pulled up his horse at the summit of a slight roll in the land about a mile away. From that distance the lake looked like a great round blue eye, rimmed with white, staring at the sun. Beyond the edge of the glaring salt the earth was bare in the dry season for a space of fifty yards. Beyond that the rolling dull green of the greasewood plain reached to the horizon, angular with barren desert mountains. All over the Southwest there are old lake beds like this one, left behind by the retreating ice cap of millions of years ago. Most of them are dry except for a brief period when heavy rains fall. Some hold pools of permanent water, heavily impregnated with alkali and gypsum. This was one of the few that laid upon the earth every year, as it shrank in the summer sun, a gift of salt pure enough for human use.

Most of the time this was a lifeless spot, for there was no fresh water within miles. A few buzzards always patrolled it, circling on rigid wings, and usually a raven or two were there in the same hope that something would die of thirst or exhaustion in quest of salt. But periodically bands of antelope came from ranges clear across the Rio Grande, and deer at night came down from the mountains, daring the dangers of the treeless flats to lick the salt with eager tongues. Mexicans had been coming here for over two hundred years and the Indians probably for thousands. If you looked closely you could discover many traces of human presence—the scars of old camp fires, fragments of wagon wheels and pack saddles, perhaps an ancient rusting gun barrel and often an obsidian arrow head.

When he surveyed the situation from his hilltop, Leo knew

that Coppinger had truly taken possession. Close to the lake, at the edge of the greasewood, stood a little white A-shaped tent such as sheepherders use. A light spring wagon stood nearby and he could see a water barrel on the ground beside it. Three horses were grazing between him and the lake, and one of these he could recognize as a big gray that Coppinger often rode. He could recognize also the tall figure working near the lake, but it took him quite a while to understand what Coppinger was doing. He could see a few widely spaced posts and the gleam of sunlight on metal. Then he noticed the great wooden spool lying on the ground and knew he was looking at something he had seen only once or twice before on his trips north. Coppinger was building a barbed wire fence.

Barbed wire was then a new thing in the West, spreading slowly across the plains, making it possible to fence great areas more cheaply and effectively than land had ever been fenced before. In a country where wood and stone were scarce, barbed wire would enable men to claim the earth, to shut out man and beast—to set the seal of ownership upon a wilderness that could never have been fenced without it. Barbed wire was cruel stuff because horses and cattle, meeting it for the first time, would try to force their way through. Feeling the prick of steel they would often tear themselves to death in a terrified struggle. Herds of antelope had struck barbed wire fences at full speed and rebounded, leaving their dead and maimed on the ground. But any beast that survived its first encounter with barbed wire would never go near it again.

Leo sat his horse for twenty minutes, puzzled, disturbed and undecided, watching Coppinger spin his deadly web. There was something supremely ruthless in this violation of an ancient and customary right and something heroic, too, about this lone man, staking his claim to the face of the earth, pitting himself against all comers. Leo wondered what

plan or hope of success Coppinger could have. Perhaps someone had promised to buy him out if he could make good his
claim, but that seemed doubtful, too. No one else would want
to take over the job of dealing with the Mexicans.

He strongly suspected that Coppinger was making a desperate gesture because he was in a desperate mood—that he
had been moved by a passionate need to put his fortune to
the test, to bring an intolerable situation to a climax. And
there might be a kind of crazy and dangerous logic in that,
because Coppinger had created a situation that was big with
dangerous possibilities. What would happen if a pack train
of Mexicans arrived at the lake and found it fenced and
guarded by a single man with a rifle? Leo knew how patient
the humble Mexicans were in bearing the afflictions they
had borne for generations, and also how quick they were to
resent any kind of change, any infringement of their ancient
rights and privileges. And many of the Mexicans who came
for salt lived across the river. If anything happened they
could easily escape into Mexico.

Did Coppinger know all this? Had he taken all chances
into consideration? Did he truly believe he could sit there
with a gun in his lap and defy all comers? The man had
enormous self-confidence, complete physical courage and a
streak of recklessness. These were not, perhaps, the most de-
sirable qualities for dealing with a situation of this kind. It
would seem that Coppinger had perhaps not calculated very
carefully the possible odds against him—that is, in case anything violent did happen.

Sitting his horse there on the hilltop, watching the busy
Coppinger, who obviously had not spotted him, Leo knew
he might be looking at a doomed man. He could imagine a
troop of Mexicans riding up to the fence. They would not
have many arms but there would be guns among them. He
could imagine a demand, a shouted defiance, a burst of fire.

Even better, he could imagine a shot in the dark or at the crack of dawn. Coppinger might be doomed—the man who had been his friend and had become his enemy and the problem of his life. He had hoped Coppinger would disappear. Now he might truly vanish off the face of the earth.

Leo sat his horse for another ten minutes, looking at Coppinger but hardly seeing him. He was trying to see this whole situation clearly in his own mind. He might be wrong but he believed it was a situation that contained the making of serious trouble. It looked as though Coppinger had deliberately courted trouble, tried to create it. His danger was of his own making. It was none of Leo's business. Or was it? If there was trouble, it would not be merely Coppinger's trouble. It would surely involve others, no telling who or how many. Didn't it necessarily involve him, Leo Mendes? Since he saw the situation and understood its possibilities, wasn't it his responsibility? Here his pride was involved. He had come to feel that everything that happened here in the valley was part of his business. So what could he do? Could he go back and sit down in his office and just wait? No, he couldn't do that. The very waiting would be intolerable. Neither could he decide anything right now. He would have to consider and inquire and consult. Certainly he would have to talk it over with Aurelio Beltrán and then probably with the Padre.

Just how great and immediate was the danger of violence? Maybe he was exaggerating it. He had heard more than once that there had been other plans to take over the salt lake, not long after the American conquest, and that men had been warned away and had found it wise to heed the warning. Aurelio would know all about that—he turned his horse back toward the village—Aurelio could tell him just about what would happen.

2. Aurelio looked worried when he came to Leo's office. He of course had heard about Coppinger's project. The whole village was talking about it.

"Someone will kill him," he said gravely in response to Leo's query. "If he tries to stay and sell the salt. There are men across the river who would kill anyone for ten dollars. You know that. They can shoot him at dawn any morning. And some of those smugglers know how to shoot."

"Won't they give him warning?" Leo asked. He was hoping that Coppinger might see how hopeless his situation was.

"Perhaps they will give him warning in their own way," Aurelio said. "Perhaps they will shoot into his campfire at night. That has long been their way of warning. Perhaps they will cut his fences in the dark and stampede his horses. But it would be much simpler to shoot him and run for the river."

He paused, shaking his head, looking deeply distressed.

"The worst of it is, the people here in the valley will be suspected. None of us would do it but we will get the blame. When a Mexican is killed, nothing much is done, but the murder of a gringo is bad business. The sheriff will come and perhaps the United States Marshal and maybe even the soldiers, for Coppinger has friends at the post. It will be bad! Why did that fool have to do it?"

Leo didn't try to answer the question. After Aurelio had left him he sat thinking a long time. When a man faces supreme emergency he has to take stock of all his values and beliefs. He has to be very candid with himself. To him violence had always seemed the essence of all evil. He had dreaded violence, he had feared it—perhaps he had been a timid man. But he had also repudiated violence as a way of life. He had declined ever to carry or use a weapon, even when his own safety seemed to require it. So now here, in all probability, was violence in the making. If blood was shed and he had done nothing to prevent it, was not he then the author of violence?

For weeks he had felt that something had to happen, something that would bring an intolerable situation to a climax. It seemed that this necessary thing now had happened. Perhaps this situation could answer all the questions that had been troubling him. How vital and how binding was the relation between Magdalena and Coppinger? If this man was her destiny, even though it might seem a hard and hazardous destiny, then she had a right to him. This situation could put her feeling to the test. It could also put Coppinger to the test. He had no conviction of magnanimity about this. If these two wanted and needed each other he was not renouncing anything that truly belonged to him. He was only accepting the inevitable.

It was now a question of how to proceed, and about this he knew he must consult his friend, his best friend, the one to whom he had turned in every emergency.

But this time Padre Orlando came to him. He came late that afternoon and for the first time in all the years Leo had known him the Padre was angry and excited.

"You know what Coppinger has done?" he demanded.

"Yes," Leo agreed. "I rode out to the lake. He is already building a fence."

"That means trouble!" the Padre exclaimed. "It may mean murder."

"That is what Beltrán says," Leo said. "I talked to him this afternoon."

"I feel that I must take a horse and go out there and warn him," the Padre said. "But I doubt that it will do any good. If he were one of my people it would be different."

"He will not listen to any warning," Leo said. "I can assure you of that."

The Padre sat looking at Leo for a moment, evidently puzzled.

"You seem strangely calm," he remarked.

"I have made up my mind," Leo said. "I cannot sit here and see a man murdered any more than I could take a gun and shoot him myself. And this may mean trouble for many others."

"Yes, but what is your plan?" the Padre demanded.

"If I should leave here," Leo asked, "would Magdalena be free to marry again?"

"Yes, since she was not married in the Church," the Padre agreed. "She can get a civil divorce. But what are you proposing? Are you going to leave her to this godless man?"

"You know that Coppinger is in love with her," Leo said.

"I have heard the gossip," the Padre agreed. "I have been sorry for you. This man is nothing but a disturber, a transgressor. I wish he had never come here."

"So do I." Leo spoke with a wry smile. "But Coppinger is not a bad man. He is one who will keep his word."

"You propose to give her up and go away?" The Padre sounded incredulous.

"Not unless it is necessary," Leo said. "That is for you to decide. I am asking you to take a heavy responsibility, but there is no one else who can help me now."

"But what do you want me to do?" the Padre demanded.

"I want you to see Magdalena first and then both of them together," Leo said. "That is, if she will send for him and if he will come."

"You want to find out how she feels?"

"Yes, how both of them feel," Leo said. "I have thought of all possible alternatives. I have thought of taking her away with me. But if she is wholly in love with this man, what could be more futile?"

The Padre sat gravely silent for a long moment and it was a moment of acute suspense for Leo. He knew that he could do nothing without the help of this man. He was greatly relieved when his friend finally spoke.

"I can't refuse you," the Padre assented.

"I knew you wouldn't," Leo said. "And I know you can tell, if anyone can, whether they belong together, whether I have truly lost her."

"I will certainly see Magdalena," the Padre promised. "I am sure I can learn just how she feels about this man. But as for him—"

"He will have to agree to abandon the lake and take down his fences and go away for a while," Leo said firmly. "I am sure you can learn just how much she means to him."

The Padre rose, nodding gravely.

"I will send you a message, then," he said. "I think there is no time to lose if we are going to prevent trouble."

After the priest had gone Leo sat very still for a long time, puffing his pipe. Destinies now, he knew, were in the making, but he felt no suspense, only resignation. He felt sure he had read his own destiny in Magdalena's eyes, in Coppinger's desperate gesture. Curiously, now his mind turned away from them and went back across the years to Dolores, the witch, who had always felt so sure what was going to happen. "You are a man of many lives." The words had always stayed with him, had veritably haunted him. After a while he got up and went to the locked closet in the corner of his office and got out the hardwood staff he had long carried on the road and the money belt he had worn. He had kept them there all these years, without any conscious intention, as though he might at any time pick up his staff and buckle on his belt and take the road again. He stood holding them in his hand, look-

ing at them. He knew he would never again walk the road
behind a burro with all his wealth strapped about his middle,
but these relics of his past seemed to be symbols of his destiny.
He knew that once more there would be the pain and struggle
of uprooting—and then perhaps the discovery of a new world,
of a new self. He dreaded what lay before him here, but he
did not taste despair.

1.♦Most of that night and the next day Leo
spent working furiously among his papers and personal be-
longings, amazed at how he had accumulated stuff and also
at how little of it seemed to have any value now. Most of it
he wanted only to be rid of. He burned papers in the fireplace
and tossed clothing into a corner to be given away. Only a
few things he packed so they could go north by wagon. For
he had no doubt he was going. He had the same feeling of all
the forces of his destiny conspiring to direct him that he had
known in all the other crises of his life. He might have to come
back once to settle his affairs, but that could be months
later. Meanwhile he could leave the store in charge of Beltrán.
So he worked like a rodent, digging up the roots of the life
he was leaving, covered with sweat and dust, getting out of
this act of destruction a necessary relief. He paused only at
intervals to read an old letter or to look at a book, deciding

whether to keep it or throw it away. One book he felt sure he would keep, for it was the only one he had brought with him from New York and kept all these years, though he had seldom looked at it. It was an English translation of bits from the Talmud which had belonged to his father and had his father's name written on the fly leaf in a small light script, beautiful and clear, in ink that had faded to a faint rust color. He riffled through the pages, reading parts his father had marked—the aphorisms and epigrams which embody the lasting wisdom of an ancient culture.

"He who destroys one person has dealt a blow at the universe and he who makes life livable for one person has sustained the whole world."

He stared at these words for a long time, reading them over and over. They were truly like a voice out of the past—not his personal past but the cultural past of his people—speaking words that were somehow relevant to the moment. He read them with no feeling of self-righteousness or of personal pride. He knew that he was doing the only thing he could do, that he had no conceivable alternative. But yet this sentence, written in an ancient world, carried on the blood stream of his people across oceans and continents, gave him comfort and assurance, seemed to lend the hard necessities of fate a meaning and a dignity that were part of his heritage.

---

2. Late in the afternoon a boy came bringing him a note from the Padre, telling him Coppinger had promised to come at eight that evening. Leo sat down, feeling suddenly tired. So now everything was arranged. It remained only for him to see Magdalena and tell her what he had done. That was all—and it seemed almost too difficult to face. This leaving a life and a woman was like cutting off a leg and

all the pain seemed to be concentrated in that last moment, in what would probably be the last time he would ever see her. How could he tell her? What could he say? He sat trying wearily to compose speeches and knew only that he was not equal to the task.

It seemed to him Magdalena was the one person on earth he feared because she was the only one who could greatly hurt him. Something cowardly in him wanted to evade that last meeting, get on a horse and go now. But he knew he must see her once more, knew he would regret it the rest of his life if he didn't.

But was it necessary to have a final scene full of tears, pure agony for both of them? It came to him as an inspiration that perhaps it was not necessary, that perhaps their last evening together could be good, or at least not wholly painful. His instinct was all for finding the easy way, for smoothing the bumps. He felt a little better already.

Magdalena had gone to her aunt's house, as she had almost every afternoon for weeks past. He sent a message to her by Avandera, asking her to come to his office at six. He added that this was important because he was called north by urgent business and must see her before he left. He also told Avandera to prepare a very special dinner with chicken and rice, and he got out a bottle of an imported white wine which he had long saved for some special occasion. Then he shaved and bathed and dressed himself in what had long been his festive costume—a suit of soft brown corduroy, a bright blue silken shirt and tan boots highly polished. He looked at himself in the mirror and suddenly remembered another time he had dressed himself with care and stared at his own image, the first time he went to the Vierra house with the Padre years ago. The man he looked at now was older and heavier, with white streaking his dark hair. Nor could he make a face at himself and laugh as he had then. It was a grave man he saw now, for whom life had suddenly become an ordeal.

When Magdalena came to his office he told her simply that the Padre had asked for her to call on him at eight, that he had something important to say to her. Magdalena seemed bewildered, but she asked no questions. He wondered how much she knew about Coppinger's venture. She looked grave and somehow older than she ever had before, and she spoke very softly.

"And why did you send for me?" she asked.

"Because I may not see you for a long time," he told her. "Will you dine with me this evening?"

"Of course."

"And will you put on your red dress, the one you wore the last time we had a dance here, and your yellow shawl with the blue flowers, and put your hair up high with a comb?"

She smiled at him a little sadly.

"I will do anything you wish," she said.

At dinner they were almost gay over their wine and he did all of the talking, aware that he had to keep the conversation going and wholly under his control. It would never do to let any question rise between them, to let any feeling break through the surface of their talk. He had to create a mood and sustain it until she left. So he told her all about his last trip north and about the great changes that were taking place there. He implied that this was what had made it necessary for him to leave so soon again.

He knew that a railroad was something she could barely imagine; much less could she understand what a transforming force it was. So he told her how it would bring many strange people, thousands of them, and would cause whole new towns to be built, wooden towns, gringo towns, the like of which she had never seen. He explained how it would now be possible to travel in a few days to the great cities of the East.

He tried to make her understand that she would live in a new world, one wholly different from that of her elders.

Talking somehow gave him emotional relief. He found himself full of words, almost eloquent. And he knew that he had captured her attention—that was his triumph. He could tell by the look in her eyes that she was trying to imagine this new world in the making, and also that it interested her greatly, that she welcomed the idea of change. In particular she seemed to be stirred by the notion that now she might be suddenly transported to great strange cities, the like of which she had never seen.

"I wonder if I will ever go there," she said.

"I am sure you will," he told her, and hurried on with his talk. He felt like a man walking a tightrope. It would be so easy to lose the precarious emotional balance he was holding between them.

He looked at his watch.

"It is almost time for you to go," he said. "When you leave the Padre I wish you would go to your aunt's because I will be gone a long time and I would rather have you stay there."

She nodded assent as they rose and went into the hallway and stood for a moment, facing each other, neither of them able to speak. He took her by both arms and kissed her lightly, and knew at once that this had been a mistake because his hands trembled a little and he knew she felt the tremor. He released her and held her cloak, hoping she would not say anything, but she turned toward him again and looked him in the eyes.

"I have loved you for a long time," she said. "I would always love you, no matter who . . . no matter what . . ."

She was floundering and he tried to help.

"I understand," he said.

"I have loved you," she went on resolutely, determined to

have her say. "But I have never known you, never understood you, never less than now."

He knew this was true. A stranger he had come and a stranger he would go.

"I am grateful to you for loving me," he said. "It has made another man of me."

He opened the door for her and she smiled at him over her shoulder as she left. He stood watching her as she hurried away. He could see her almost all the way across the plaza, and then she was lost in the dark.

————————————————————

1.He went to the Padre's house late that night, riding his best horse, all prepared for travel, with a blanket rolled in a light tarpaulin behind the cantle of his saddle, food in his saddlebags and a small sack of corn for his mount.

He did not have to ask the Padre any questions. His question was in his eyes as they shook hands.

"You were right," the Padre said gravely. "They are wholly in love with each other, bound together by some necessity that is stronger than either of them. I am sure they will struggle and suffer, but that may be what both of them need. I think it would be no use for anyone to try to come between them."

"You gave them your blessing, then?"

The Padre nodded.

"What else could I do? He agreed to everything I asked. He will take down his fences and go away for a while. He is

246

perfectly willing to become a Catholic. I know it will mean little to him at first but perhaps it will come to mean much. And I felt as I sat looking at them that this will be a marriage in the Catholic sense of the word—a devotion and a discipline. They do not merely desire each other. They seem to have accepted each other completely, as though each had found something that answered to his deepest need."

"Did he say anything of his plans?" Leo asked.

"He wants to take her back to his own country," the Padre said. "He wants to show her to his family. He is proud of her. And I was surprised to learn that he is not merely the vagrant cowboy I had supposed. His father has wide lands in Texas and many cattle. In fact, they are people much like her own in everything but race—cattle people who own the earth and have the habit of command."

The Padre paused thoughtfully.

"This is hard for you, Leo," he said. "But I feel sure Magdalena needs this man. She has always remained a child in her relation to you. Now she will have to grow up. And so will he. I believe he has been just a youth bent on adventure, not bad but wild. Now he has found a discipline and I am sure he knows it."

"You have told me all I want to know," Leo said. "Let us talk no more about it."

"You are right," the Padre agreed. "And let us not talk about your going either. You know how much I will miss you. Whom will I talk with now? You have been that best kind of a friend, one to whom I could say anything, and the only such friend I have had in many years. I have only one question to ask. Can I help you here with your affairs?"

Leo shook his head.

"I can sell the store in Santa Fe," he said. "I own nothing but the goods on the shelves. I never wanted to own land— I don't know why. Maybe I always remained a peddler at heart. It seems as if this has been only a longer stop in my travels."

"You know you have my sympathy," the Padre said, "for what you suffer now. But I must admit you have also a little of my envy. Believe me, it is not the worst fate in the world to lose what you love and set out in search of new experience. The worst fate is to know that your adventures have come to an end. And I am sure that yours have not."

Leo nodded his grave agreement.

"This going away is pure hell," he said. "But it is not a new experience for me. Twice before the same thing has happened to me. I painfully pulled up roots and moved, and each time I found something new, I even became something new."

"It is true," the Padre said. "You are not the man who came here ten years ago. What lies before you now I cannot guess."

"Neither can I," Leo said. "But the railroads are making a new world in the north and I have a place in it waiting for me. When I went to Las Vegas a few weeks ago, I wanted only to leave it, to get back home, back to what I loved. Now I am eager to go north. I have work to do there and I long for new work."

"Are you determined to ride tonight?" the Padre asked. "I wish you would wait until morning."

"I thank you," Leo said. "But I can neither rest nor sleep."

"Well, at least you can eat and drink," the Padre assured him. "I have cold birds and crab-apple jelly and wine and coffee, and if you have a stiff brandy first I am sure your appetite will not fail you."

He led the way into the dining room and for an hour they ate and talked and sipped their wine, just as they had done so often before—as though they might meet again next day.

When Leo rose and offered his hand he saw a distress in the Padre's eyes which answered to his own.

"You must come back some day for a visit," the Padre said quietly. "I cannot accept this as the end."

"That I promise," Leo told him.

"And don't wait too long. I will not be here forever. Now God speed you."

---

2. His horse's hooves beat loudly across the sleeping plaza and out of the town. When he struck the valley road he let out his restless mount in a fast gallop, then briefly in a dead run, getting relief out of speed, out of flight, as though he could outrun all the pains of parting, as though distance might bring some of the mercies that come with time. He knew it was foolish to waste the strength of his horse and soon he settled down to the easy jog, which is the standard gait of long riders all over the West.

In two hours he had left the valley and followed the long lonely road across the Jornada. It was a sprawling road of many wheel tracks, one that had been traveled for hundreds of years but had never been graded or worked, so that coaches and wagons took the best routes they could find in the circumstances of load and weather, going around mudholes and patches of sand, weaving a crazy pattern of ruts. But no one could lose his way, even on the darkest night, for all along the road grew hedges of mesquite brush, sometimes seven or eight feet high, towering above the scant greasewood of the mesa. Teams and pack animals for generations had been eating the mesquite beans in the valley and planting and fertilizing them along the road, so that the whole route was marked by a long dark welt of thorny brush across the barren land.

It was a cool night of late October with a brilliant show of stars and a rustle of wind. He felt strong at first and thought perhaps he would ride all night, stopping only to eat and feed his horse, hoping to reach the river at the Hot Springs by dawn. But his weariness caught up with him suddenly as if it had been chasing him all night. All the tension of pain and trouble seemed to leave his body, so that he rolled in his saddle like a drunk and almost dropped the bridle rein. He knew now he had to stop and began looking for water, knowing the fall rains had made puddles that would last a few weeks. In a shallow arroyo he saw the welcome gleam of starlight in a little pool, and it was none too soon. He was barely able to unsaddle his horse and let it drink and feed it with a nose bag. Then he wrapped himself in his blanket with his saddle under his head. Briefly he remembered back to the first time he had crossed this waste that was called the journey of death, and for him that had been a journey of desire. He remembered how anxious he had been on that trip of long ago, and how fearful, thinking of bandits and wild Indians, painfully conscious of the money in his belt, longing for the sight and sound of human life. Now as then he felt cut off from everything, suspended between a life he had left and one unknown. But otherwise he was not the same man at all. He was one who had outlived his fears, and for the first time in his life he was glad of wilderness, of space and solitude. After the agony of human contact, the ordeal of love and friendship, the prickly tangle of pain and confusion in which he had lived for weeks, this unpeopled quiet seemed a welcome refuge, and so did the weariness that promised oblivion. Then the whispering voice of the wind was hushed, the cold blaze of the stars went out, and he knew the mercy of dreamless sleep.